Beyond th

Copyright ℂ

The right of Jeffrey Brett to be identified as the author of this has been asserted by him in accordance with the Copyright, Designs and Patents Act 1988.

This book is a work of fiction, references to names and characters, places and incidents are products of the author's imagination. Any resemblance to actual events, places or persons, living or dead is purely coincidental.

For more information, please contact:

magic79.jb@outlook.com

Beyond the First Page

Introduction

The psychic astrologer with an ever increasing loyal following and reputation to equal their inflated ego may well predict a person's destiny from the alignment of the planets and stars including the forecast of a writer of books, stating that on any particular day they should look favourably to the future and forget the dark shadows of the past, for fiction can so easily control the emotions of the reader.

For one such writer, Mortimer Valdis, the past and the stars held no surprises any longer and his predictions only ever came true if and when he intervened in the fate of others. The voices inside his head helped, but whatever the day, whatever the alignment everything came down to certain events that had already taken place.

Chapter One

With automatic ease the reception doors came together drowning out the noise of the traffic outside much to the relief of the reception as the visitor, a regular averted his eye from a woman walking by to the young girl sitting behind the desk.

She prompted a response looking up at the clock on the wall, knowing that he was late. The man sighed, gestured that the traffic was heavier than normal and scuffed the back of his heels on the coconut matting in case they were dirty.

'I swear that traffic will be the death of me!' he implied as he sung down the heavy bag from his shoulder. With accurate dexterity it landed beside the reception chair and the receptionist's long smooth legs. His eyes travelled all the way up to the hem of her skirt as he feigned a pulled muscle in his shoulder.

'One day Eddie Albright, your thoughts will get you in trouble!'

The grin across his face grew as he leaned on the counter top. 'If you could read them Julie, they would land us both in trouble!'

The postal worker acknowledged an older female who rushed on by heading for the stairwell door. Tapping the counter top the receptionist made him focus back on her. 'I'm still here!' she announced.

'I was only being polite to my customers,' he cheekily replied 'and besides you know that I've only got eyes for you Jules!'

'Is that today's delivery?' she asked.

'It was everything when I loaded the van,' he loosened the knot tying the neck of the bag, making it easier for her to extract the contents. 'Hamptons is always one of the heaviest on my round, you must have a lot of interested writers going by the weight.'

Eddie was close enough to capture the waft of her perfume, a light musk, but memorable. Julie had used the bottle when her sister had gone to use the bathroom.

'Do you like it Eddie, I wore it especially for you!'

Seductively he sniffed the air once again. 'Devine, like you Jules.' He ran his fingers through his hair pushing the locks into shape. 'It's windy out there!'

'Would you ever write?' she asked, probing to detect his level of education.

'Naff off. I'd sooner be in the pub or dancing the night away, rather than be stuck in front of some computer exercising my brain!'

Julie felt her expectations of him sink. She recognised that she was young, but her mum had told her that if a man was really interested, he would be educated, intelligent and courteous. She wasn't that naïve not to know what else Eddie wanted to exercise.

'My mum has warned me about blokes like you!'

He laughed. 'She sounds like a wise woman. I'd like to meet her someday.'

Julie took several of the letters from the top of the pile. She had heard that very few submissions ever got a second viewing on the second floor, where the senior editor, marketing department and directors had offices. The only time she had walked the carpeted corridor was for her interview.

'So how much do they make, if they make it in the big league?'

'Thousands, depending upon how many books you sell. Ten to fifty thousand sold is about the average for a best seller.'

Eddie whistled through his teeth. Writing was that much of a mugs game. Reaching down he collected the empty bag from the day before and headed for the doors. 'I had best dash, errands to run and the like.' At the automatic doors he looked back. *'Same time tomorrow sexy!'*

Julie felt the flutter in her chest. Eddie was a charmer, probably said the same thing to all the receptionists that he met every day, but all the same she liked the flattery. It made her stomach buzz. At school she had developed faster than most sprouting breasts and long legs, but the boy's had been immature and although they wanted to touch, none had ever called her sexy.

She watched as he walked over to his van, pull open the driver's door and toss the empty bag onto the passenger seat. He turned, instinctively knowing that she would be watching and wiggled his hips, as though dancing. Gesturing with his hands he suggested that they should embrace a dance together. Julie smiled her agreement.

Heading off into the traffic the red van was soon swallowed up by much larger vehicles. She craned her head above the reception desk until he was no longer visible. Was Eddie like the boys at school or was he genuine, she wasn't sure. Reaching down for her magazine she opened at the page where she read her horoscope *'With the alignment of Venus in Jupiter, romance is starred to arrive soon, but beware of anyone with the star sign Sagittarius.'* Julie closed the magazine and dropped it back into her bag, wondering under what sign Eddie had been born.

Switching the telephone console over to answerphone she dragged the heavy mailbag over to the lift, taking the short ascent to the floor above where she would sort the mail with the office junior.

'We've done it!' Julie whispered into the ear of the girl sitting behind the desk.

Andrea who was not much older than the receptionist, looked startled. *'What downstairs, in the cloakroom?'*

'No stupid,' Julie chided 'we're gonna have a drink and go dancing!'

'Oh is that all. I thought you hit first base the way you explained yourself.' She looked up to see that nobody in the room had been disturbed. Somebody in the room coughed and the conversation between them ceased instantly. Andrea pulled open the neck of the post bag.

'Christ, you'd never believe that there could be so much coming in each day!'

Together they lifted the bag up onto the desk and tipped out the contents. Julie leaned forward. *'It stops this lot from getting bored!'*

Every so often a finger tapped the keys of a keyboard punctuating the silence as eyes scanned down through the pages of another electronic submission.

'All you ever see are the tops of people's head's,' Julie indicated by patting her scalp. *'I wouldn't be a literary agent if they paid me!'*

Removing the physical submissions from the envelopes they sorted them into different categories, most times getting the genre right. Julie watched as eyes glued to the screens, read down the page, scrolling to the next, before sitting back and pressing another key.

'And they all went to university to do this all day?' she whispered.

'Get a good story and they can make the author and Hamptons a lucrative amount of money.'

'Oh yeah and how often does that happen?'

'Not as much as they would like. They reject a lot so I believe.'

Julie raised her eyes up into her head. 'Upstairs made it sound so interesting when I had my interview. If it wasn't for Eddie coming in every day, I'd go mad on reception.' Julie noted that there were two empty desks, where they had been occupied the week before. She asked why.

'Times are competitive. Some of those in the room say that the industry hasn't caught up since the last recession. Upstairs, had to let a couple of assistants go end of last week.' Andrea looked at the four piles of submissions on her desk. 'Maybe there's a winner amongst this lot, who knows.'

Back down on reception Julie had a list of the big named authors, the regular contributors who despite any hardships felt continued to sell despite dipping sales and the advance of eBooks.

'I've not seen any of the well-known authors visit, do they ever come in?'

Andrea placed her finger over her lips. 'Clients with the most pulling power tend to meet outside, lunching with one of the directors away from the office. Jim in marketing told me it was so that they can both be seen in public. Occasionally Sandra, head of marketing gets invited along as well. Publicity sets trends that helps sell books.'

Julie picked up a heavy looking envelope. *'There's a lot of people, wannabe writers out there!'*

'There's a lot of stories floating around this room,' Andrea replied, it was then that she remembered 'what ever happened to the one that you submitted, did you ever get a response?'

Julie shook her head. 'No. It took me ages to write as well. I got an email to say that they liked the concept of the story, that it had promise, but that it wasn't quite what they were looking for at that particular time and I was wished well for the future.' Julie made sure that nobody was eavesdropping. 'Truth be known I think that whoever looked at it, realised who the author was and they weren't prepared to let a lowly receptionist make it big!'

'That sucks!' whispered Andrea *'I wonder who looked at it?'*

Julie frowned 'Don't worry, I ain't giving up yet. I'll try with another agency.'

Andrea gestured that they should go out back where the floor had a kitchenette and they wouldn't be overheard. She switched on the kettle as many the room liked to start the day with a caffeine injection.

'My brother is at college studying art and he say's things are pretty much the same there. Just like writing, somebody can paint a damn good picture, but in the great mix of the professional art cauldron, unless your face fits or you know the right, who is a name themselves, you don't stand a chance. David reckons if you reinvented the ark, it would be over-looked. My opinion for what it's worth is that agents and critics address the balance, keeping the status quo on and even keel.'

'Meaning what?'

'So much has to get rejected so that the market doesn't get over flooded. Too many overnight success stories would smother the top of the tree and send the celebrities into panic mode. Competition can be a dangerous contest.'

It made sense. Some of the names that Julie had grown up with, pop stars, film celebrities had been absent for a while only to suddenly re-emerge from the bushel and back into the limelight. Marketing knew when and where to pull the strings on behalf of the known names and the public would believe anything that was thrust in front of them.

'So ghost writers work away tirelessly without ever being recognised?'

'More or less. The room outside is one powerful arena. Trust me!'

As the kettle boiled the words *'well-written, providing the basis for a good story, shows potential'* stung even more. Somewhere deep inside the rejection hurt Julie. She empathised with the writers who never took their writing any further.

'I'd best get back otherwise somebody from human resources will be calling down and wondering where I've been all this time.' The two girls arranged to meet for lunch as Andrea wanted to know more about Eddie.

Sitting behind the reception desk Julie failed to notice the man who was watching from the far side of the street. What she did find was a single sheet of paper that had been left on the desk during her absence. The message had been typed.

'Confucius once said that a wise man who writes, thinks and works alone, but the thoughts that become his words are the soul of many. Like the tree the soul can wither and die, or grow strong and age beyond obscurity.'

Julie read it again. It didn't make sense the second time so ignoring the implication behind the message she slipped it into her desk drawer. At that point the man watching left and walked away.

Chapter Two

Charles Trent, senior editor for the Hampton Group entered the room ashen faced, clearly shaken by what he had just heard. When he coughed standing by the door, fingers lifted from various keyboards to look his way. Although each recognised Charles and they saw him often they detected that his visit was neither professional nor social.

'I have just had some very grave news, which I wish to impart upon you all,' he paused to gather together his words, coughing once again 'I alone find this rather upsetting, as will many here. A few minutes ago I came off the telephone having spoken with the police and for those of us that remember Vivienne D'Corscy I am sad to say that she was found dead last night in her apartment.'

Most felt the air sucked from their lungs as they grasped the reality of the news and somewhere a person started to cry as the silence made heavy the news.

'Are there any other details Charles?' asked Richard Quince, one of Hamptons longest serving authorities on adult fiction and sport.

Charles Trent looked up, the rim of his eyes red where he had suffered the pain. He avoided looking at the desk where Vivienne had once sat happily reading, exploring and recording suggestions about the authors work. When she had been alive.

'As you would understand the police can only release scant details and as the investigation is still in its infancy we will expect to be told more later in the day. I know they are treating it as murder!'

Death however sudden, however raw can be accepted by most, but murder put a different slant on Charles Trent's news. For those closely and professionally acquainted with Vivienne, the one quality that shone through which they admired was that she had never possessed a cruel or aggressive thought ever. Murder seemed unacceptably cruel.

'I would expect a suspect a protracted investigation.' Added Charles as the sound of crying ebbed.

'I hope that it was quick,' remarked Quince, nearest Trent. 'What I mean is that I hoped she didn't suffer and that death was instantaneous.' Others around agreed. Nobody liked to think that she died a lingering torment.

The men in the room wanted to support Quince, but the females were already forming opinions against their gender. It was expected. Most perpetrators of crime were men. Although none wanted to imagine the worst, almost every woman pictured in her mind assault before death. Since the beginning of time men had been hurting and raping women, leaving them for dead. Intuitively the room split with the men gathering to discuss the facts with Charles and the females huddling together for comfort.

Andrea arrived during the silence with the coffees. The only death that she had been associated with had concerned her elderly grandmother. D'Corscy's demise was the second, she wasn't sure what to think as life and death walked a very fine line. In the huddle, one of the women asked.

'Was Vivienne... well you know... was she sexually abused?'

'The police didn't say Anne, it's probably too early to say and speculation will only cause more pain.' Somebody put a supportive hand on his shoulder. Tapping the return key on the keyboard Stephanie Garland saved the work on her screen. 'No doubt an autopsy will help prove either way.'

Charles felt a sudden shudder bolt through his shoulder blade, remembering when Vivienne had rubbed ointment in to help with his attacks of arthritis. Knowing that his task was done he to return to his office, although as senior editor he felt duty bound to stay and give support. Somebody in the room asked about sending flowers.

'The directors wanted to get the feeling of the office before I placed an order?'

Trent asked Andrea to take an extra-long lunch to get a card, so every employee could write their condolences. An hour later, tears running dry he managed to close the door of his office feeling the pain stab at his chest. Moments later he rushed to the men's washroom to be alone.

Charles Trent sat solemnly at his desk for the rest of the day reading the words on his screen, but paying no attention to what of them said. However he tried he could erase the memory of Vivienne from his thoughts. Having given her the opportunity to join Hamptons, their friendship had cemented a lasting bond. Having wept for her loss in the men's bathroom, Charles felt his heart would break in half at any given moment.

When the rest of the office had left returning home the senior editor was glad of the solitude. Opening he wallet he removed a crumpled photograph from the inner section. The woman who smiled back at him was young and attractively beautiful with her slightly tanned olive skin, soft brown eyes and the figure to grace an ice-skater. Charles Trent kissed the image before putting it back in the wallet. Now all that he had left were the dreams.

Chapter Three

The first uniformed officers to respond to the elderly woman's call for help arrived to find the block of private apartments all quiet, not that they had expected anything different at Waterfall Heights. This part of the neighbourhood was rarely visited by the police or authorities. Knocking at the door of the occupant from the where the problem was originating they had decided to go back down and speak with the informant.

'Well look for yourself,' insisted Elsie Bracknell, as she pointed to the splash marks centre of her living room carpet 'I might be getting on in years young man, but my eyesight is as good as when I was your age!'

James Templeton didn't need to touch nor inspect the liquid staining the fabric of the carpet. He looked up and saw the deep red line where it had created a thin veil between the plasterboards. Instinctively he recognised blood when he saw it. Standing beside him Karen Walsh was going white.

'I suppose we have to go upstairs?' she asked. Templeton nodded.

'I can go. You stay here with the informant and get some details.' Walsh smiled.

'Thanks James.'

James Templeton thought about calling for back-up, but as a double-crew he had his partner's feelings and reputation to consider. He rang the door-bell at the flat, then knocked several times even looking and calling out through the letter-box, but when he received no reply, he steadied himself before shouldering open the front door.

The moment that he stepped inside the hall he sensed something was wrong. The presence of death came flooding down the hallway as though inviting him inside. Standing between the framework of the entrance to the lounge, he was glad that Karen had stayed downstairs. Fighting back the bile in his throat he radioed through to control for additional patrols to attend as soon as possible, to include supervisory, scenes of crime and a divisional detective.

Standing on the spacious landing of the second floor James Templeton threw open the landing window wanting to dispel the smell that had seeped into the cavities of his nose and throat, burning the memory of the dead woman into his soul. Hearing a noise from behind he turned quickly in time to prevent a neighbour from going in.

'Is the young lady alright?'

'Unfortunately, she's had an accident and died. Now if you'd please go back inside your flat, somebody will call soon and want to speak with you.'

The middle aged neighbour, an eccentric, possibly an actress by the way she was dressed reluctantly went back inside leaving her front door slightly ajar, whether to hear the arrival of more police or for simplicity Templeton didn't know. What he did he reasoned that there was always somebody around when you least wanted them. In the distance sirens were coming his way and fast.

In the shadows across the road from the curving drive of the Victorian mansion block a darkened figure stood deep in the shadows shielded from sight, he watched as the officer on the top floor sucked in great gulps of night air smiling to himself. It was something else that he could add to his story. When the sirens were only a few streets away he left feeling that his work was done.

'That's inhuman,' remarked a colleague who had arrived as backup to Templeton and Walsh 'who the hell would do such a thing!'

Lying centre of the carpeted room Vivienne D'Corscy was almost naked, bar her underwear. It was difficult to tell if she had once been beautiful, happy or otherwise, just as it would be impossible to know her thoughts as her life was taken from her. The heavily blood stained cavities above her nose gazed vacantly towards the ceiling where her eyes had been savagely removed from her face, along with her tongue and the fingers of both hands. To anyone daring to look, the ferocity by which she had been slain instantly pointed to a ritual killing, but perhaps the only ones to know the real reason were the victim and the assassin.

An unnatural rash on the skin beneath her nostrils and either side of the mouth suggested that she had been gagged with some sort of adhesive tape, unceremoniously pulled away when she was required to talk, sometime before her killer had removed her tongue. On the carpet strands of blue nylon twine had been left behind where her hands had been tied together, without doubt to aid the removal of her fingers. A kitchen knife, long and sharp stood upright having been thrust into the boards beside where she lay, not that the reminder was necessary, more as a warning to the police.

On the floor below Karen Walsh shared a cup of tea with Elsie Bracknell, she avoided telling the truth suggesting that the resident above had suffered a nasty fall.

'That's a lot of blood for just a fall,' remarked the elderly lady as she sipped her tea 'I've seen less in a car accident victim. I was a nurse you know!'

Walsh smiled back vainly proposing that it might be wise to spend the night elsewhere, so that arrangements could be made to deal with the ceiling and carpet. Elsie nodded looking up at her ceiling where the lampshade still had red streaks appearing every so often.

'My sister lives around the corner, she has a spare bed.

*****

Daniel Spence, detective chief inspector from the nearest divisional criminal investigation office stood in the doorway of the lounge taking in a panoramic mental sketch of the room and the victim. It was his habit to picture everything in his mind before jumping to conclusions. What he looked for most was anything that looked out of place. Most obvious was that missing from the woman.

Treading carefully into the kitchen Spence checked the waste disposal unit and sink where the grisly remains of blood, cartilage and bone had discoloured the stainless steel panels. It was a hunch that the killer would not have taken her body parts home. Madmen only kept trophies when the kill had not been executed as they had wished.

Aware that somebody was standing behind Spence turned.

'That's stomach churning!'

The older detective nodded. 'We've a long night ahead Tom. Has anybody informed April?'

Thomas Hawkes checked his watch. 'She'll be here soon. She was on another call when control told her about the events here.'

'Good, we will need her expertise.'

Chapter Four

Together they formed a plan and what rooms they would take individually, doubling back on one another, not checking, but making sure. Spence never left a crime scene without turning over every stone. When they met in the hallway, they compared finds.

'It's probably too messy to be a professional job, but there are signs that the killer came with an obvious intention. '

Spence agreed with his young protégé. Hawkes had not been with him long, but already he was proving to be a damn good detective. He especially admired the way he thought outside of the box.

'What signs?' he asked.

'Domestics tend to be here, there and all over the place, sometimes starting in the bedroom, the lounge or the kitchen leaving trace evidence wherever they touched, fought or died. This place is almost spotlessly clean and the victim doesn't appear to have gone any further than the lounge. The murderer had already planned this execution and where it was going to happen!'

'Any other deductions?'

'Only the obvious. Probably a single occupant as there are no signs of any men's clothes or toiletries. Was a young woman from the texture of the skin, foreign ancestry from the colour, possibly Greek, Italian or Spanish and from the number of bookcases around I'd assay that she either liked reading or was somehow connected.'

Spence was impressed. In his eighteen years as a detective and transferring into London on promotion he had encountered most crimes, violent, sexual and deadly, with one or two broaching upon satanic methods to terrorise their victims. This didn't look domestic, but more an attack with deep feeling, a motive for revenge.

'Did you find anything with her name?'

'Miss Vivienne D'Corscy,' the voice coming from behind belonged to April Geddings, head of forensic investigation, SOCO. 'I checked the communal mailbox in the lobby. The Victorians didn't like having a noisy letterbox disturb their sleep, so the postman would leave any correspondence in the box allocated to each apartment.' She smiled at Thomas Hawkes nodding her respect at Spence.

'She was young!' the DCI added.

'Late twenties, not more than thirty three on the outside. Susan Weekes will be able to give us a more accurate age, if we don't find any documents here to help.'

'The constable outside said that he applied brute force to open the front door, so it was locked before he and his colleague arrived.'

April Geddings looked up from where she was kneeling beside the dead body.

'She knew her caller then, a friend, relative or a stranger. Whoever, they made a mess of a beautiful young soul.'

'How can you tell?' Spence asked.

'Her hair, it's not been hacked, but professionally cut and looked after. What's left of her features, they're sharp with good bone structure. This woman looked after herself, kept herself fit and ate healthily. The touch of her skin tells you that.'

'If this place is as clean as it looks, I doubt you or your team will find any prints!'

April went about her business, dusting, advising and working alongside two other white suited investigators. After an hour she called Spence and Hawkes into the hall. She pointed to the plaster wall adjacent to the doorframe. Both detectives bent over to look closely.

'Whoever came calling, dragged her backwards I would guess. She's left a piece of her fingernail in the plaster where she tried to grab the doorframe and hold back from being hauled into the lounge.' April dug out the fragment dropping it into a clear evidence bag.'

Hawkes scratched the stubble on his cheek. 'So her attacker took her by surprise, secured the front door before dragging her down the hall and into the lounge before silencing her using duct-tape. The rest we know.'

'It's about right,' Spence interjected 'but I'd rule out the theory of a stranger. This is a second floor flat and middle of the block. Killers don't just stand outside and pick a number at random.'

April looked around. 'It's a nice flat. Nothing garish, a mix of modern and old. She has a lot of books.'

'Yes… Hawkes has already noticed.'

April pointed to the wardrobe in the bedroom. 'Some of the clothes have Italian designer labels. Expensive stuff, but not what you'd get over here. They've come direct from the fashion house.'

'And you'd know that how?' asked Spence, his look of surprise not lost of the lead forensic examiner.

'Because I'm a woman Spence and women know these things. Specifics like that are an important component in a girl's arsenal. They're on par with the mystery that confounds you men as to what we keep inside our handbags!' She was the only one to notice the wry smile from Thomas Hawkes.

With each passing second they were rebuilding Vivienne D'Corscy's life. On the fridge door they each scrutinised the mix of colour and black and white photographs. Hawkes pointed to a Polaroid snapshot where the victim was sitting on the marble surround of the Trevi fountain. She much younger, carefree in her youth and naturally beautiful.

Inside her bedside chest of drawers they found a bible and set of rosary beads. The inscription inside the front cover was in Italian, it read *Dio camminera sempre accanto a te ovunque tu vada e in qualunque cosa tu faccia*. April translated as *god will always walk beside you wherever you go and in whatever you do*.

April smiled at them both. 'My mother made me do Latin at school. I hated it at the time, but it's come in handy more than once.' She closed the cover of the bible carefully replacing it inside the drawer before pushing it shut. 'God must have been busy this evening elsewhere!'

Hawkes picked up a couple of paperbacks kicked under the bed, within reach of an outstretched arm, but hidden from view to keep the bedroom tidy. 'She liked mystery and horror by the looks of it!'

'That's interesting.' Spence as them to follow him back into the lounge where he went back over to a bookcase. He pointed at a single book spine. 'I noticed that when I was looking around earlier that this one has been pulled out beyond most of the others. It's either been looked at or read recently.'

With her examination gloves protecting against contaminating evidence April removed the book in question. *Retribution of the Angst by Mortimer Valdis.*

'Strange title?' Spence mentioned as he studied the cover that April was showing him.

Hawkes pointed to another spine where the book was equally as apt. *When a Stranger Comes Calling by Rosalind MacTavish*. 'She certainly went in for the thrilling and sensual stuff.'

'You read a lot then Tom?' Spence asked.

'A bit... when I can. When I was younger I liked the classics, writers like Arthur Conan Doyle, Tolkien, C. S. Lewis and Stevenson. Anything that stretched my imagination. I guess that's why I became a policeman.'

24

Spence grinned and shook his head. 'I joined because nobody else would have me and my extent of reading stretched no further than *the famous five* and later on Blackstones Police Manual.'

April shook her head. Spence wondered if it was in disgust or remorse at his lack of interest.

'You know many writers, actors and agents suffer from a delusional reality problem. They cannot differentiate between fiction and non-fiction.'

'You mean like a prostitute wanting to get beyond the trick hoping that there's more to lying on her back.'

'It's an example Spence, but I could have thought of others!

'I mentioned it because the profession is as old as Adam and Eve and yet we still waste our time hauling them in.'

'As I mentioned, a reality problem.'

Going door to door they conducted enquiries, but the time was getting late and many residents were reluctant to answer the door or help. The lady opposite who had tried to see into the flat having spoken with James Templeton had gone to bed unable to fight sleep any longer. She wore a hairnet and a mask to protect her eyes from the early rays of the morning light, placing buds of cotton wool in her ears to shelter herself from the trauma's experienced by the outside world. Not hearing either knock Annabelle Du Renard slept soundly until late into the middle of next morning.

'Did she say anything?' Spence asked Templeton.

'Only that she heard the front door of number seventeen click shut sometime around seven. She said that there was nothing unusual about that as the girl, who was a literary agent in the city often worked late at the office. She didn't know which agency employed the victim.'

On the floor below they were told a similar story by Elsie Bracknell who stated that the doorbell from the flat above had reverberated down her wall around seven and that later during the commercial break either side of her favourite evening watching of the long running soap she heard a moan, but took no notice knowing that the occupant was a young girl and that when she had been her age, she had moaned every so often when her Albert had come calling.

Neither occupant mentioned anything about seeing anybody leave the apartment block. Standing on the landing outside of number seventeen the two detectives felt that the air outside had changed, become colder and less inviting. There was a stillness about the place as the souls of the departed were watching and waiting ready to observe their next move.

'I suppose she could have been followed home from work by an unknown admirer, a druggie or piss-head.'

Spence shook his head, not convinced.

'No. Somebody who knew her did this Tom. She still has on her underwear and unless it's been replaced after an assault, which I doubt, my guess is that the killer didn't come looking for sex. This is a very violent assault, one that I would categorise as a revenge killing.'

April appeared at the front door holding up a small batch of papers. Amongst which was an address book, a copy of a literary degree and another for art. There were payslips from the Hampton Group Literary Agency where she had been employed as an editorial assistant, a gym membership card, a library card and an annual membership subscription to the London theatre group association.

'There's enough to be getting on with,' Spence acknowledged as he flicked through the address book. 'We can forget the library, I hardly think she was killed because some books were overdue.' He stopped at an address that looked interesting. 'If I'm not wrong, I would say that she hailed from a village near Naples.' He showed the address to April and Hawkes.

'She certainly would have met a lot of people, men especially going to places like the gym and the theatre. Any one of them could have followed her home.' April watched their expression as they each gauged the size of the problem.

'Any men, youths in the photographs, they we're all in Italy by the looks of it and the place here is clear of anything masculine. I don't think it's a discontented boyfriend.'

Spence looked at April. 'Was she gay?'

April shook her head. 'No. I'd put that theory to one side for the moment. Something about this young woman girl tells me that she was straight. D'Corscy was another citizen living an ordinary life until she met with an untimely and violent end. London's full of mysterious and abrupt endings.'

Sitting himself at her writing desk Spence had put on a pair of latex gloves. He mused over the book that had been protruding from the bookshelf. He passed it over to Hawkes.

'Have you ever heard of the author, only you're the literary expert here?'

'No. I could work backwards from the publisher and so forth, maybe somebody has a record somewhere of the author.'

They were interrupted by Karen Walsh who asked if Elsie Bracknell could go to her sisters. Spence was happy to agree, he wouldn't have wanted to stay in a place where somebody's life blood had been dripping through to the living room. Spence wanted to have the flat left open so that he could take one last look.

'It would seem that the shutters have gone down and the rats are deserting the sinking ship. Not that I blame them!' April suddenly acknowledged another person who had been watching and listening from the doorway.

'I cannot say that I am surprised Miss Geddings!'

Home office pathologist, Susan Weekes was smartly dressed as she approached and stood before the bare feet of the corpse. With a grim smile she recognised the two detectives.

'I'm glad that I had my evening meal before coming here tonight Inspector. Has anything unusual been established yet?'

To an outsider unconnected with criminal acts the question would have seemed extremely impertinent and disrespectful, but those present had expected her to ask.

'Only that I've a hunch this was done as a revenge attack. Possibly a warning to others!'

'That's a strong statement to make, even for a killer!'

'We've our fair share of weirdo's lurking around the corners of London Mrs Weekes.'

Susan Weekes opened her bag of tricks and knelt down beside the body of Vivienne D'Corscy. Assisted by April she took samples of blood, temperature and tissue, anything that would help the investigation and her autopsy. It was important to gather as much information as possible before the deceased was moved from the crime scene. Standing by and watching Spence was unable to prevent his stomach from growling.

'I don't suppose this call has helped with your nutrition diet?'

Spence held his stomach feeling the pains of hunger tighten his belt.

'As a detective we get used to not eating!'

Weekes glance across at April who was making notes. She raised her eyebrows.

'We might be sometime Inspector, if you would both like to cut away for some food.'

Without deliberating over the invite Spence asked if either of the women wanted anything as he dragged Hawkes out of the room. Both said that they were fine. The idea of consuming something hot was beginning to gnaw at his insides. Taking a ten pound note from his wallet Spence asked Hawkes to find an all-night kebab house.

'And make sure that those grease pocked bastards don't put all that spicy shit over my meat,' he insisted 'only it plays havoc with my intestines and heartburn.' Spence told Hawkes to get something for himself and add a couple of strong coffee's to the order. 'If it comes to anything more than a tenner, flash your warrant card in their face and tell them that I will be around later to check on their hygiene certificate.'

He watched as Hawkes descended the stairs and briefed the crews waiting outside. If anybody knew the best kebab shop in town, it was surely going to be one of them. Spence smiled to himself, the young detective had promise and would go far. He just needed to make sure that he understood the basic rules and have Hawkes believe that the law ran the streets, not the other way around.

Taking himself back inside he went to the kitchen where a member of the forensic team was dealing with the mess in and around the sink and waste disposal unit.

'Anything worth salvaging?' he asked.

The masked figure nodded and pointed. 'One or two bits perhaps, might be more inside. We've called out an emergency plumber to help us with the mechanics. I don't fancy losing my fingers if those macerator blades suddenly kick in!' Spence sensed a presence behind, turned and saw April standing there.

'Depends on how much the killer whizzed the unit. We'll either be lucky or shit-out Spence.' She motioned her towards the living room. 'Susan Weekes has done what needs doing here. The rest she can do back at her lab. Most of the flat has been photographed, we just need to collect a couple more samples to ensure that I'm satisfied and then we'll leave you in peace. The van will collect the body.'

Spence muttered *'thanks'* as he leaned against the kitchen base units. 'Was it regular duct-tape that he used?'

'That would be my guess and the knife was from the kitchen set.' She looked at him, placing her hand on his forearm. 'Are you okay Spence, you look all-in?'

'Long day again April. All that I really want is a bite to eat, a cup of coffee, hit the shower then my pillow. Sometimes this job can be hell.'

'Anything I can do to help?'

Daniel Spence looked deep into April's eyes. He had never been so close before. They were amber green, soft and full of mystery.

'If I wasn't so tired, I could suggest any number of things to help, but maybe another time!'

April smiled as her hand slipped from his forearm.

'When Weekes has left there's something that I want to show you!'

They waited until the coroner had packed up her bag and pocked her head around the kitchen door. 'I've done as much as I can here. I'll schedule the autopsy for two this afternoon!' With that she bade them goodnight and was gone.

April knelt down once again and this time gently rolled Vivienne D'Corscy to one side so that her buttocks and spine were on show. Spence noticed the long red cuts, marks on both.

'Putting aside the fact that D'Corscy met an obvious woman hater, she recognised the face of her caller. I've looked for the obvious signs of struggle, defensive fight, scratches and normal bruising, but there are virtually none, except these cuts.' She pointed to each. 'Ignoring the obvious bits that are missing, these incisions were made with a very sharp instrument and made deliberately.'

Carefully letting down the body as though it was made of china, she continued.

'Those lines run symmetrically Spence. She was tortured!'

'Knowing why would help.'

'That I cannot help with, but maybe as the investigation progresses something will explain why.'

Leaving her mask over her face with only her eyes on show April pushed back a loose strand that had fallen from beneath the hood. She had known Daniel Spence from the time that he had arrived in London admiring him from afar, considering him to be calm and thoughtful, not given to outbursts or inflammatory views on sex, racism or politics. She knew that he was liked by both senior management and those below his rank. It was only recently that she had transferred division and worked alongside him becoming more familiar with his odd little mannerisms, habits and methods. Some thought he was unorthodox in his approach to crime, but Spence got results. She ignored the loose strand when it fell back down.

'I checked the linen on the bed before I came and found you and Hawkes. Although nothing showed on the ultraviolet I've taken some samples just in case. Both Weekes and I believe that she wasn't interfered with Spence, which I find surprising as she was virtually stripped naked. I think making her remove her clothes was a control thing where the freak wanted to show that he could dominate her every action. She must have been petrified to have taken her clothes off.'

'And the cuts,' he asked 'what about them?'

'Acts of strength, the male dominance over the weaker female. With every cut that he inflicted he grew more confident, gained more satisfaction.'

April spread her many instamatic images across the floor for Spence to see. Like a good many others he had heard about her tempestuous marriage, the break-ups, the reunions and the vicious assaults. Fortunately, there had been no children. The last that he had heard was that the relationship had ended acrimoniously.

'Satisfaction...' he pondered 'I would say that the bastard got more than satisfaction from what he did here.'

It was one of the few times that April had seen Spence so vehement in his opinion. Respectful that the dead woman was still in the room he whispered. 'And the eyes, fingers and tongue, do you think that they were removed before or after she drowned in her own blood?'

April Geddings liked him all the more in that moment for his passion and his reverence.

'Before. The skin discolouration clearly signifies that it has darkened due to the time that the injuries were inflicted. Other injuries although probably administered at the same time, are less prominent.'

'Then I sincerely hope that this is an isolated incident.' He meant it as well.

'The database will tell us if there's been any similar murders here or abroad.'

Rolling the body once again April pointed to where the retaining clasps held the bra together.

'They're misaligned Spence. No woman goes around all day like that, it's uncomfortable.'

'The killer?'

She nodded. 'More control. My theory is that he undone them, mismatching when he tried to clasp the hasps together. Just undoing the back straps would have put the fear of the devil through the centre of her heart. This bastard knew what he was doing.'

'You think it's a man!'

'Women fight Spence. They bite, scratch and claw hair and skin, but none however much aggrieved would do this, not to their own kind.'

Standing in the doorway Thomas Hawkes put down two doner kebabs and coffees. He handed another to April taking two more through to the other members of her team working elsewhere. Returning he smiled. 'As you said guv'nor, sometimes our warrant card can be a bonus!'

Chapter Five

Jack Chilvray incessantly balled his hands over and over, vigorously rubbing in additional quantities of anti-bacterial soap, creating a generous lather. Minutes later he rinsed away the soapy solution and inspected each hand. Tutting with annoyance, he repeated the process until satisfied that any trace of the woman's blood was gone.

Stepping under the warm water of the shower he let the refreshing droplets wash clean the scent of her perfume and her death. Washing had become a ritual that he had long committed himself too before sitting at his desk to write up the experience. It was as though each assault was sanctioned by the cleansing approving of what he had done for the sake of art.

Throwing the soiled clothing into the washing machine he turned on the cycle having already disposed of the gloves that he had worn in a stranger's waste bin several streets away. Next day they would end up miles away on a public utilities waste site, where neither trace nor ownership would ever be known. His final act was to add diluted bleach to both the shower tray and the sink before slipping into freshly laundered jeans and a tee-shirt.

Taking the weight from his legs he lent against the kitchen worktop. The walk home from her flat had been further than he had anticipated and there had been a good many security camera's to avoid. Keeping his head low the brim of his hat had served its purpose. Cameras annoyed him, they were everywhere, on petrol-pump forecourts, street corners and looking down at you from a high lamp-post. Intrusive eyes that recorded every sight and in some cases sound.

Reaching up he lifted down a half used bottle of whiskey from the overhead shelf quickly unscrewing the cap and pouring a generous measure into a glass tumbler. Jack needed a drink, always relishing the first of the evening. As the alcohol stung the back of his palate, warming his gullet on the way down to his stomach he thought about the visit to Waterfall Heights.

Had he meant to hurt her, kill her, he wasn't sure. He had planned the visit, but had left the rest to chance and how she reacted when she recognised him. The conundrum, the enigma had been her fault, her surprise at seeing him standing on her doorstep. He had clamped his hand over her mouth when she had tried to scream and from thereon in fate had intervened. The voices inside his head had controlled what happened next.

Jack swallowed another mouthful hardly tasting the rich gold liquid as it disappeared. On the far side of the kitchen sat the *tigers claw* which he had used to scratch her soft skin, lightly tanned and oh so European. He couldn't tell why he had taken along the claw, other than to terrorise. It had worked. He would need to clean it before he tenderised any steak. Again he blamed her for not co-operating. Had she said the right things, meant them, she might still be alive.

Initially upon opening the door to her flat Vivienne D'Corscy had been startled to see a man standing on the landing, but when he had introduced himself to her the name had not only triggered a memory, but a look of surprise. When she had tried to close the door suggesting that the caller contact Hamptons Chilvray had become agitated and aggressive feeling that another rejection was coming his way. Clamping her mouth, he had gently shut the door with his free hand then pulled her down the hallway and into the lounge where he had taped her mouth and tied her wrists.

Jack wanted the memory to be stored inside his head, but not relieve every moment, knowing that he could get it all down on record later, but for now holding onto the neck of the bottle all he wanted was to forget the evening. Like an unperturbed toddler it kept coming back and back, the blood, the expressions before he removed her eyes and finally her tongue. Lying beside the tiger's claw was his copy of the manuscript that he had sent to Hamptons.

He had waved under her nose, demanding that she explain why it had not been good enough. It had made him more angry that to get it published it had cost him, having paid a publisher to print the book. Jack had made her lay there and listen whilst he read the first chapter turning the pages until he was satisfied that she understood the reason for his visit. When she had not answered his questions, he had at first slapped her face, then returned from the kitchen brandishing a carving knife.

He had surprised and confused her when he had cut her bonds before ordering her to strip down to her underwear, but knowing that it was useless to resist she had complied. Lying beside her he had replaced the plastic ties then toyed the tip of the blade up and down her body, over her breasts and up her neck. At one point he had pushed her sideways

38

and undone the clasps of her brassiere, then for some reason secured it again. Jack wondered why he had done that. She was vulnerable, defenceless to his attack and completely at his mercy.

Ignoring the manuscript he walked across the tiled floor to the lounge where the laptop lid was inviting him to sit at the desk. He taped the return key and fired up the screen. Swaying diagonally the liquid crystal motif changed colour from red, yellow, green to blue before disappearing in a shower of ethereal light. Jack read the last paragraph that he had been working on before leaving the house, he added a full stop, dropped an insert onto the page then headed up the next chapter. He stared back at the screen, if only she had read beyond the first page.

Taking his tumbler and the bottle outside he pushed shut the French doors to prevent an invasion of moths where they had gathered around the borrowed light above the doors. He descended down a short flight of steps onto a grass lawn below following the beam of iridescent light that cut a path across to the tall oak tree where he sat himself down. Someway off an owl hooted, calling a mate.

Beneath the branches Jack poured another measure into the tumbler. He was still annoyed with himself at the ferocity of the attack, although it did add a different dimension to his book. The voices were arguing amongst themselves, some saying that it had to happen, others not so sure, stating that she should have lived, been a warning.

When a pigeon sitting in the branches overhead flapped its wings, stretching its limbs Jack smiled. *'Bollocks, she got what she deserved. Doesn't anybody that fucks around with me!'*

He toasted the moon and the stars above the rooftops refilling his glass. The whiskey tasted good at last having slowed the rate that he was consuming the fifteen year old malt.

He looked at the moon through the cut glass crystal turning the tumbler one way then the other eyeing the distortion as a child would a kaleidoscope.

'There are some who think that I'm mad and not worthy, but I'll show them!'

Jack thought about the neighbours, had they seen him arrive or leave. He had heard the sound of the television from the floor below, but what had the old girl that lived there heard. She had been a resident for some time, would know each and every one of the other occupants, knowing about their habits, the times that they went and returned home. Old people filled their days with useless information, but intelligence that they could tell the police. Jack hadn't included the neighbours in his plan. It was a mistake.

Finishing off the bottle he thought about the parts that he had removed. No longer would she be able to read another manuscript, turn over the page without fingers nor type any future rejection letters, but most of all Vivienne D'Corscy would never speak to another living soul. As the whiskey took effect, changing his mood so did the breeze blowing through the branches overhead. The pigeon flew away to somewhere more sheltered as Jack accepted that what he had done had been necessary. Writers had to make a stand against negative judgement and certain individuals.

Despite being unwilling to accept that he had written an intriguing and accurately researched piece of fiction Jack Chilvray raised his glass once more to the heavens above and toasted her bravery. The young woman had recognised her failings and acknowledged her fate.

Staggering back over to the steps ascending up to the small veranda he chuckled to himself. By now the police would have found the bloody mess in the waste disposal, they could make what they like of whatever was left. He had thought about dumping her dead body in the lobby of Hampton's office, but London was a city that never slept.

Sitting back at the desk where the screen had once again gone to sleep Jack Chilvray did the same. That night his dreams were a mix of past and present and somewhere Mortimer Valdis appeared momentarily before walking away with a huge grin on his face. Using a pseudonym had been a stroke of genius, but anonymity was important for what he had left to plan.

As Jack slept soundly occasionally twitching as another memory flashed through the cells of his brain, on the desk top lay a single sheet of paper, it was hand written and recorded a name.

Mortimer had been an apt choice, derived from old English to signify *'the departed'* and Valdis from ancient Norse meaning *'the dead, the slain'*.

Somewhere in the void of time, maybe another dimension Vivienne D'Corscy wished that she had done more research and made the connection as well.

Chapter Six

Spence and Hawkes stepped outside of the old mansion block and peered back up at the façade where the ravages of time and the weather had not been kind. Creeping between the chimney pots and cranes in the distance the first rays of an incandescent sunrise had begun to flood the sky with light signifying that each had missed another night's sleep.

'One day the lunatics of this world will graciously show is a little more consideration.' Spence stretched his hands and arms above his shoulders, yawning. I don't know about you, but I'm just about all in.'

Thomas Hawkes followed the façade to the left and right of the flat that they had just vacated.

'I doubt they ever think beyond the last breath, that their victim takes!'

A face momentarily appeared at a curtained window then disappeared. It had seemed uninterested in their presence as if murder and the police happened to be the norm in Notting Hill. Spence shook his head.

'We've a lot to be getting on with Tom, but first I think we need to get our heads down for a few hours. I'll leave the team some tasks to perform that should keep them busy most of the morning. Remember we have a post-mortem at two!'

They parted company with Spence going back to the office to call Hampton's and brief his team coming on duty for the day shift. In his pocket he had a business card for Charles Trent which he had found in her bedside drawer. He thought it might prove useful.

*****

The few hours spent in bed were restless and charged with flashing, disturbing images of the dead woman. Normally Spence could attend a crime scene and later dispatch the memory for another time, but today his subconscious refused to let him relax. He woke with a start observing from behind a crowd as he was lowered into the ground, the grave diggers standing nearby ready to fill in the cavity.

Annoyingly he dragged himself from his bed and hit the showering keeping the temperature tepid rather than hot hoping that the cool water would invigorate his tired limbs. There was something about Waterfall Heights that didn't seem right. What annoyed him most was that he didn't know what. In most cases victims left behind a clue, something that could be worked on to help build a picture of their life before they departed this dimension. Vivienne D'Corscy had instead hidden her secrets well.

Towelling himself dry he thought about the conversation with Charles Trent. It had obviously come as a shock, but Trent could add nothing to the investigation or the reason as to why she should have been so savagely murdered. Just after eleven thirty he walked back to the office happy to be amongst pedestrians and other people. He was surprised to see April Geddings hunched over her laboratory desk.

'I don't suppose your excuse for not sleeping is any better than mine!'

She looked up from the lens of the microscope and smiled, pleased to see him.

Nothing adds up Spence. I've been to countless crimes, homes, industrial and commercial premises, but none has been as meticulous as the one we visited last night. Take out the blood on the carpet and in the sink, plus the corpse and we have nothing, as though nothing had happened.'

'I couldn't sleep neither.' He peered into the microscope. 'Find anything?'

'I was just checking hair and fibre samples, but they match the deceased, nobody else. Is it the perfect crime?'

'There's never been one. Something always crops up, sooner or later!'

'Did you call the Senior Editor?'

'Yeah… he sees himself as a friend rather than a colleague. Couldn't give me much, but I think a visit will extract more.'

'Did he mention friends or family?'

'Only family and that she hails from a small village a couple of kilometres outside of Naples. Are you coming this afternoon?'

April looked along the line of bags that had been laid out systematically along the bench, numbered and identified from the room that the evidence was found. Despite her frustration, they each had to be checked.

'Why not. Susan will maybe brighten my afternoon. I doubt that there's anything amongst this lot to help.'

'Did the plumber extract anything usual?' She pointed to the counter top behind. Spence walked over to where a bloody bag sat all alone.

'I see better down my local butcher's!'

April scoffed. 'It was a butcher that produced what's in the bag.'

Spence turned the bag one way then the other, it was a grisly mess, but there were bits that could identify from which part of the body they had come. On the second spin he saw something glint under the ultraviolet light.

'There's something shiny in here, metallic.'

April left what she was doing and came over. He handed her the bag.

'It's a ring.' She pulled a magnifying glass from the bench drawer. On the inside is what looks like the beginning of an inscription.' Spence came in close to see the first two letters. 'Maybe D'Corscy did leave us something.'

He looked at the wall clock and gauged how long they would be at the coroner's office wanting what was in the bag to be thoroughly checked rather than rushed.

'Perhaps we can go through the contents later, after the post-mortem?'

April nodded. 'I'll make it my first priority.' She too noticed the time. 'I suppose you want me to drive to Weekes Chamber of Horrors?'

He smiled coming away from the lens of the magnifying glass.

*****

In the car April was keen to take advantage of her time alone with Spence.

45

'I've noticed that you've been burning the midnight candle a lot lately.'

He looked her way as she weaved her way through the traffic on the one way system.

'Crime seems to be on the increase April and upstairs want results.'

She pulled up at the traffic lights that had changed from amber to red.

'It wasn't a criticism, just an observation. You need to rest Spence, recharge the batteries once in a while.'

He smirked. 'Suggest a nice retreat away from it all and I'll give it consideration.' As if to emphasise the point his mobile rang. He spoke for no longer than a minute before dropping it back inside his jacket pocket.

'It was Ben Stebbings. They've been around the area collecting data from the various CCTV. Hawkes and I can scan through it later.'

'I retrieved a little black book from the bedroom last night and although her place looked as though it didn't receive too many visitors, she certainly has a few entries.'

'Did any jump out at you?'

'As you'd expect a good many were Italian, so it's hard to say.'

He shook his head despondently. 'Women.'

April shot her head left. *'And what's that supposed to mean?'*

Spence held up his palms indicating a truce.

'Only that women keep all their secrets, names, events and dates in a little black book.' He tapped the side of his head. 'Where men keep it up here.'

April laughed. 'Yes and most of what you lot are told, you forget.' She pulled up at a parking bay allocated to the coroner's office.

Spence looked up at the façade of the building where the London grime had taken its toll and turned the stone a dirty sand colour.

'In the cold light of day, I wonder if Vivienne D'Corscy is about to tell us anything different.'

*****

In a fresh laundered suit Thomas Hawkes was already inside the Coroners building when they walked in. On first impression it looked as though he had suffered as they had from the lack of sleep.

'D'Corscy get to you as well Tom?' Spence asked.

He shook his head. 'I think I went beyond it in the end. I'm interested to see if she was pregnant. It might only be a thought, but would indicate if any friends were close.'

April smiled. 'Proving not all Roman Catholics are true virgins!'

'Who is...?' Spence pushed aside the door so that they could proceed down the walkway to the autopsy room.

Hearing their footsteps echo along the old tiled passage April thought about her marriage and how fortunate it had been that she had not found herself pregnant. Bringing a child into the world with Barry Moyne as the father would have been disastrous.

Before entering the large clinical chamber they each sniffed a pinch of coffee granules from the dish beside the door, hoping that the neutralising effect of the granules would help defuse the overpowering presence of the formaldehyde.

Standing alongside the exposed cadaver Susan Weekes was already busy going through her routine as she examined Vivienne D'Corscy with the naked eye. She looked up, acknowledged their presence, but didn't interrupt her flow of concentration. With the help of her assist they rolled the body to one side so that she could measure the length of depth of the cuts on her back. When it was done she looked over at April.

'We bagged up her underwear. You'll see that there is a small piece of black man-made fibre caught under the brassiere clasp. I would assume from the glove of the assailant. It might help with your investigation.'

Spence looked, spinning the bag back and forth.

'Leather?' April muttered. Spence nodded.

After that they watched and observed as the coroner went through the ritual of cutting, lifting, separating, examining and weighing before putting Vivienne D'Corscy back together again. When it was over, she noticed that Thomas Hawkes was standing beside the next table.

'Something fascinate you detective?' she asked.

Hawkes looked up from the cadaver and directly at Weekes.

'Yes. A couple of things. Was she pregnant?'

'No, but she has been, although some time back.' April looked at Spence, but he was focused on Hawkes and Weekes.

'And the way her fingers were extracted, were they neat cuts or rough as though hacked?'

Weekes held up what was left of a hand. 'Swift cuts, almost surgical as though the person doing the slicing knew what they were doing.'

Hawkes thanked her and said that he had no further questions. They watched as the assistant a female carefully added suture to the torso opening.

'Why the fingers Tom?' Spence asked as April spoke with Susan Weekes.

'Our murderer had training. None of his actions were hurried or frenzied. The attack, cutting and removal was all calculated as if he had done it before!'

Spence scratched the underside of his chin. Hawkes was right. Everything pointed to the torture and the execution as having been planned. His thoughts were interrupted by the coroner who was ready to wrap it all up.

'Have you any leads chief inspector?'

'None yet.'

Susan Weekes removed her gloves and dropped them into a biological waste box.

'What the perpetrator did to this poor woman was truly barbaric. Men performed such atrocities in the dark days of the medieval era, not here and now in the twenty first century.'

Spence agreed. 'I believe that he was making some sort of statement.'

'This is one hell of a statement.'

Susan Weekes raised her eyebrows at April and said that if she needed any help, she was at the end of the phone. She smiled at Hawkes and told him that it was good that he took an interest, but she looked inexpressively at Spence.

'I hope that you catch this monster chief inspector and soon only I've a feeling that Miss D'Corscy is not the first nor the last victim that we will see.

Chapter Seven

Standing anxiously at the side Spence and Hawkes watched April as she painstakingly sifted through the human remains that had extracted from the waste disposal system. Spence was keen to get to the end of the examination knowing that for every second that they wasted Mortimer Valdis could be planning his next attack.

'Other than what's left of the ring, the macerator unit did its job!'

Thomas Hawkes put on a pair of gloves so that he could examine the ring closely. On either side the gold was badly scratched, on the inside mount there was just visible the words *'dare a casa'*.

'Languages were never my strong point, but I'd hazard a guess at Latin!' He showed Spence who suggested giving it back to April. She turned the ring several times until the answer came to her.

'I did Latin, but it was a long time back Tom. If I'm not mistaken I think it should say *ricordare a casa,* it means *remember home.'*

She gave it back to Hawkes who replaced the ring in the evidence bag.

'It's obvious that somebody in the D'Corscy family wanted Vivienne to remember her roots. Has her family been contacted?' she asked. Both detective shook their heads.

'I wanted to get the outcome of the post-mortem before I went visiting the Italian Embassy. Natural causes is easy to explain, but murder of one of their nationals complicates the explanation!'

'I'd be happy to come along, if you think it might help?' Spence looked at Hawkes, who looked at April. 'Sometimes a female presence can diffuse the tension.'

'I would agree with that guv'nor.'

Spence grinned, felling that he was in a corner. 'I'm sure you two conspire against me sometimes. We need to be there at a quarter to five, can you sort this lot in the time allowed?'

'I will if Tom gives me a hand with some of this stuff. Some of needs a second pair of eyes!'

Spence thought the experience would prove valuable so he was happy to release Hawkes for the rest of the afternoon. Going back to the office he pushed aside the paperwork mounting on his desk knowing that he had to go upstairs and brief the senior management on the circumstances at Waterfall Heights, informing them of his visit later that afternoon to the embassy.

When they had both finished sifting through the rest of the artefacts taken from the flat Spence sent Hawkes back to the neighbouring roads to see if anybody had remembered seeing anything suspicious whilst April drove to Mayfair.

The closer to four thirty the denser the traffic seemed as she cut in and out trying to avoid lights and busy junctions. Travelling here and there each day in the busy city she was accustomed to the rude gestures and arrogant driving from the other road users. Out of the corner of her vision she saw Spence watching. She chuckled.

'It's all part and parcel of modern day driving Spence. A girl has to be tough to survive road rage these days.'

'Things change so damn quick, that's half of the problem.'

She couldn't help, but laugh. 'You've been living by yourself for too long chief inspector. You need to get out more. If we get time after the embassy, do you want to stop off and grab something to eat, only I could do with eating today?'

'I was going to suggest the same, only you beat me too it!'

April returned a hand gesture from a white van going in the opposite direction that had adversely cut across her path causing her to brake sharply. It was all over, done and dusted by the time that she placed both hands back on the wheel.

Without the blink of an eyelid she asked 'How did the meeting go with upstairs?'

'Alright, you know that lot, all brass and cold hearts, they never give much away. Mostly they're covering their backs, keeping everything political and saving face, their own mainly. I would be the scapegoat if this investigation went south.' He changed direction. 'Did you find anything of interest after I left the lab?'

'Nothing really that throws any light on the investigation,' she glanced his way before looking ahead at the junction where she needed to turn left 'I'm sorry Spence. I was however grateful for Tom's help.'

'I didn't think that you would.' He took a few moments allowing his thoughts to come together. 'He's shaping up into a damn fine detective April, I'm lucky to have him around!'

'He's so much like you Spence, a dogmatic bugger who doesn't believe in giving up until he's turned every stone. Tom will go far as long as upstairs don't get in his way.'

'I know. They see an opportunity to put a feather in their cap and they take it, regardless of the individual. Some things don't change, despite the politics.'

He wanted to ask about her home circumstances and delve deeper, but it didn't seem appropriate to go probing into a ladies private life. As April took the left turn Spence was all the same curious.

'I could have delivered this agony message by myself. What are you looking for there?' he asked.

Taking a final left she flicked off the indicator seeing a convenient spot to park.

'I'm sure Spence, only when I heard that you were paying a visit I wanted to tag along. Vivienne D'Corscy was Italian so for now that's the only connection with the embassy, but I had a hunch, a professional intuition that there was more and the answer would be found inside.' She engaged the handbrake, put the gear lever in neutral and switched off the engine. 'When Tom asked about the inscription on the ring, it got me thinking that rings are normally given to daughters by loving fathers. There's a connection that needs unravelling.' She was about to open the door when she stopped herself, not yet finished with the explanation. 'Something else Spence, about the flat. There was a second when I was inside when I sensed a *déjà vu* moment. I'm not given to fantasy, but it was strong, as though I'd been there before, only I cannot remember when.'

'You didn't you mention to me at the time?' he looked puzzled.

'It's not something that you suddenly convey to a lead investigator. *'Oh by the way Spence, I feel that there's something about this crime scene that seems oddly strange. I can't quite tell you what, but it's something that I feel.'*

'I see your point.'

'I'm your lead forensic examiner Spence and that's how I want it to remain.' She gazed directly into his eyes so that he couldn't avoid the emphasis. 'Occasionally, on a private and a professional basis I met up with Lucy Beningfield. I like Lucy and she's helped, especially after my failed marriage, but I wouldn't want to make it a permanent arrangement.'

Spence knew of Beningfield, a specialist in the medical team who dealt with officer's welfare issues, where her role involved helping with psychological struggles. He didn't blame April for seeking help, Barry Moyne was well known and being married to a serving detective from the West End Division could only have complicated her sessions with Lucy.

'I'm always around if you wanted a drink after work, a chat or even a coffee.'

April smiled. 'That's what Lucy offered, only your offer is more attractive!'

Spence indicated with a flick of his head that their arrival had been noticed. Standing under the covered door to the rear entrance was a smartly dressed embassy official.

'They don't miss much,' April said as she pushed open the door.

The waiting official waiting smiled enthusiastically greeting April first and then Spence.

'The ambassador is grateful that you use the rear entrance. There are always annoying photographers out front, asking awkward questions that would be better addressed through the correct channels. If they were to find out that you were the police, there would be more.'

Abiding by protocol Spence showed his warrant and introduced April, giving special emphasis to her position, knowing that the weight of forensic science would cause a ripple of attention in their visit. Inside the embassy was as April had imagined, grand and lavishly decorated with fine furniture and portraits of previous ambassadors. They were shown into a large office and asked to wait.

'Is our embassy anything as grand?' April asked as she took a seat admiring an expensive looking Italian flower vase.

'I very much doubt it. We're too stiff upper lip and all that nonsense in this country!'

Watching Spence take the seat opposite April could contain her thoughts no longer. Completely out of the blue, she asked. 'Have you ever been married Spence. I know that you're not now, but I was just wondering?'

He grinned back, she was like no other woman that he knew. April was not only attractive and discernibly intelligent, but she was also forthright. Spence liked that in people, believing that you should say and think what you feel, rather than disguise any true sentiments.

'I came very close once, but the lady in question had the good sense to catch the earliest ferry back to Ireland, never to be seen or heard of again.'

'I'm sorry Spence... I didn't mean to pry, I was just curious.' April felt ashamed for having snooped.

He smiled once again to show that there was no harm done. 'Well you asked and now you know. The last I heard, she was dancing her way around the ward of a mental home somewhere just south of limerick suffering from a severe psychological imbalance, bordering between bipolar and schizophrenia.'

April felt her jaw drop. *'The relationship was that good, eh?'*

In the corner of the room a small security camera was recording them sitting talking.

'If her mother was here now, she would definitely say that I was to blame, but the truth is that none of it was my doing. When her father died she took it hard, real hard turning to drink and dabbling at first in medicinal drugs then finally the hard stuff. The mix doesn't go together well and the brain will object somewhere down the line. Siobhan unfortunately created her own downfall.'

'That's rough though, losing somebody that close. It can leave you vulnerable and needing help!'

He was about to ask to whom she was referring to when the door to the office opened and in walked a kitchen maid with a tray of fresh coffee and baked biscuits. She made sure that they needed nothing else before leaving as quietly as she had arrived. April volunteered to do the honours. As she poured she noticed the look of apprehension masking his expression.

'I'm not talking about my ex-husband, but my grandparents. I lost both relatively close to one another and it was a wrench, an emotional hard slap of reality. With Barry I could understand your ex-partners need to drink. Living with Barry would drive any woman to alcohol, only drink never resolves problems.' She passed across the biscuits watching his face soften. 'Did your partner drink whilst you were together?'

'Only when we went to the pub or so I thought. I was a young DC at the time and hardly ever at home so who knows. My work commitments was one of the reasons that we split.'

'And there's been nobody else since?' April was bringing his private life bang up to date.

'Nobody else, in a way I'm married to the Met, although I am serious thinking about getting a divorce in a year or two and taking myself off to the south of France or Italy maybe, somewhere warm!'

'And do what precisely?'

'Invest part of my pension on a boat and navigate the bays around the coastline.'

'Sounds idyllic.' He was tempted to say join him, but the office door suddenly swung open and another official, obviously more senior than the one that had met them at the back door walked in.

'I am sorry to have kept you both waiting. We had expected the ambassador back by now, but official business in Whitehall has detained him longer than he thought it would. He has however empowered me to assist you and offer any assistance necessary in this regrettable matter.'

Franco Bianchi took the chair behind the desk and poured himself a coffee. It was then that Spence noticed that there was four cups on the tray. Not waiting for a cue he briefly outlined the demise of Vivienne D'Corscy loosely touching on the fact that the victim had been attacked which had resulted in her death and that a copy of the post-mortem would be sent across to the embassy. At his side April nodded in support.

'It is a sad affair, most unfortunate.' Bianchi made comment. 'How can we help Chief Inspector?'

'Did you know Miss D'Corscy?' Spence asked.

'Why yes, the young lady come to the embassy a few times to see an employee of ours, Roberto Cortelli, he works in our translation department. According to Roberto they met at a book launch where Miss D'Corscy was inclined to use Roberto's expertise. He is fluent in several languages and so can be very helpful professionally or socially.'

April remembered seeing the name Cortelli on Hawkes list of contacts that he had pulled from the little black book.

'Is it possible to talk to Mr Cortelli?'

Bianchi replaced the cup on the saucer as he shook his head. 'Not today I am afraid, Roberto is presently on holiday in Rome. He will of course be most upset to hear of this tragic news.'

'And why would that be Mr Bianchi?' April couldn't stop herself from asking. Spence looked at April, which was noticed by Bianchi.

'As friends, Roberto and Miss D'Corscy were close.'

'When exactly did Roberto leave for Rome?' Spence asked, sensing that if he didn't April would.

Franco Bianchi wondered where the questions would lead.

'He left the country ten days ago. Did you know chief inspector that the D'Corscy family are well known throughout the Naples region. They own a vast amount of land given over to producing wine.'

'No. I didn't know that. We would like to speak with Mr Cortelli when he returns, as I believe that he could prove valuable with our investigation.'

Bianchi nodded. He understood protocol and how such matters were conducted. In the detectives shoes he would do the same.

'Have you ever heard of an Edoardo De Luca?' Spence asked. Once again Bianchi nodded his head.

'Most Italians have. De Luca is a respected Venetian artist, is Edoardo on your list of suspects?'

'No. It's just that Miss D'Corscy had a number of his prints dotted about her flat, we are just ticking boxes and reducing our number of enquiries.'

Bianchi seemed somewhat intrigued by April.

'In my ignorance Miss Geddings I would not have thought such a beautiful woman to be connected with such horrible circumstances. Is forensic science that engaging, only where I come from women with such beauty rarely see such horror, let alone investigate such crime. My Maria, my wife, unless the children were in danger would be aghast at some of the things that you must see.'

'And you Mr Bianchi, would you be appalled like your wife?' Spence lowered his head as he smiled.

Bianchi politely coughed and cleared his throat. 'I am a simple man with simple needs. The evil that exists in some quarters of our world revolts me. I abhor violence.'

April crunched down on her biscotti biscuit, making both men smile and look her way.

'I am sure that Miss D'Corscy was no different to any of us Mr Bianchi. Her life however was cut short and violently. If Roberto Cortelli had not left the country, would you believe him capable of carrying out such an atrocity?' Hawkes had been right, bringing April along would add something extra to the visit.

'No. That I very much doubt. Roberto likes the theatre, dining out and pleasing women in general, but no murdering them. I think you will see this for yourselves when he returns.'

April saw Spence nod her way, an indication that he was happy for her to continue with the questions.

'You asked how I could be involved with such extreme scenes of violence. I like what I do and I do it well because I feel that I make a difference. Women see things differently, they feel things personally, where men can detach themselves without emotion. Some may see our sentiments as a weakness, but I see them as an advantage. At her flat I formed a bond with Miss D'Corsy, perhaps even a pact.'

Bianchi was definitely intrigued now. 'A pact… how?' he asked.

'That together we will unravel this mystery and not only find her killer, but the circumstances leading up to her death, including any outside influences.'

Bianchi smiled, although Spence sensed that he was rattled. 'Then we will offer any assistance that we are able to extend through our official channels.'

The embassy official suddenly got up and out of his chair indicating that the meeting was almost concluded.

'I am sorry to bring our meeting to an abrupt end, but I have another engagement that will be pressing in a few minutes. I speak for the ambassador and assure you that appropriate measures will be taken to inform the D'Corsy family of poor Vivienne's demise. It is better to come from the embassy than to have the Carabinieri drive up to the door in a marked car.' Bianchi turned to shake Spence's hand. 'This man that you seek, he is a monster… yes, no?'

'Without doubt, it has to be a man chief inspector. I would not expect a woman unless provoked to do such things.'

Spence gave Bianchi his contact card and left instruction asking that Roberto Cortelli call the station upon his return. From behind the curtain Bianchi watched them get back into the car. When he called out the ambassador walked in from the next room.

'When is Roberto due back? The ambassador asked.

'The day after tomorrow. Don't worry ambassador I will speak with him before the police do.'

The ambassador picked up the office phone and spoke with his secretary requesting that she put the call through to the office in Naples. Ernesto D'Corscy was an old friend of his and the news would be hard felt.

*****

Approaching the junction Spence guided April through the back streets to a pub that he knew where the food was good and reasonably priced. They found a corner to sit where they wouldn't be overheard or disturbed. Loosening his tie and top button Spence sat back and relaxed.

'You pressed Bianchi hard at one point!'

'I meant too. I felt that he knows more than he's letting on.'

'How?'

'Pure feminine intuition Spence. Neither of us mentioned how exactly she had died, but he seemed to know.'

'You think he was involved?'

'Not necessarily. Bianchi is no fool, but he would employ a fool to do his dirty work.'

Spence agreed. 'That was my impression.'

April was fast becoming as cynical as Spence.

'You think the brass upstairs had called Bianchi before we had arrived?'

'Nothing would surprise me, although what they would gain by doing so beats me.' He paused to remove his tie. 'Bianchi got his information somehow and I doubt it would be from Susan Weekes. Sometimes I have trouble getting information from her!'

April smiled. 'Maybe it's the way that you ask.'

Spence ignored the insulation. 'Did you get the impression that somebody was listening in?'

'Yes. In the adjacent office, yes, I did. A couple of times I thought that I heard somebody sigh or wheeze as though they had a cold.'

The waitress arrived with their food then left quickly realising that she had interrupted their conversation. April picked up her fork, but wasn't finished.

'There was something about Bianchi that I didn't trust Spence. He was polite on top surface, but under that façade there was another side to his character and despite his insistence that he would be appalled by violence, I felt that he would actually revel in acts of aggression.'

Spence wondered what she thought of him as he forked in his first mouthful. 'And…?' sensing that there was more.

'Cortelli has allegedly been out of the country for ten days and the bed linen at her flat could have been laundered the night before or changed during his absence. The coroner found no signs of recent sexual activity. If Cortelli was as good and close a friend as Bianchi had made him out to be, then Roberto had not come calling lately. We went through that place thoroughly Spence and we found virtually nothing.'

He continued to eat as April waited for a reply.

'Bianchi was adamant that the killer would be a man. A positive statement for somebody that doesn't know much!'

April started to eat and talk. 'Bianchi was right on that score. It would take a seriously pissed off female or a deranged amazon to torture another of the same gender, brutalising the victim as the killer did with Vivienne D'Corscy.'

They both appreciated the hot food as it filled their stomachs and the conversation naturally died away for several minutes as they ate. When Spence was finished he felt re-energised and more alive.

'Do you have any contact with Barry?' he asked, believing that now had the right to ask.

April looked up from her plate amused. She shook her head.

'None. The house was divided, even down to the cutlery and towels. I wanted a fresh start with no entanglement from the past. I gave my half over to charity. What I have in my little flat belongs to me and is untainted by Barry Moyne.' She finished eating and put together her knife and fork. 'I do however keep tabs on his career, purely so that I can avoid our paths ever crossing.' April placed her hand on his forearm. 'We're not doing any wrong here Spence.'

He looked amused. *'I didn't think we were!'*

'You know what I mean.'

'Where did you pick up your Latin?'

'My grandmother on my mother's side was born in Florence. *Ricordare a casa* was a phrase that she would use whenever my sister and I went wandering when we were at university. Sadly she's no longer with us and it was her home that became my salvation when times got rough with Barry.'

'Sometimes being alone can have its advantage.'

'Sometimes... only not all the time!' She liked his company and the easy way in which she could tell him things, private things that she had not discussed before.

Chapter Seven

Having woke with a start, tasting the residue of whiskey on the inside of his mouth Jack Chilvray sat thoughtfully at his writing desk staring at the blank screen absently tapping the edge of the keyboard before his fingers started to dance their way back and forth across the keys typing out the words putting together sentences and paragraphs.

Soon, the more his head cleared the easier everything became. Shortly he had the basis of another chapter forming one page after another. Convinced that what he was writing would please the voices in his head he forged ahead eager to check through it and make sure that the chapter had exactly the right detail.

The shadow which had seemed much darker than usual suddenly emerged from the corner of the building in the shape of a man as the young woman entered the lobby of the apartment block unaware that she was being watched. She was beautiful and appeared innocent, unaware of the danger that was to tread malevolently across the path of her destiny. Cautiously the watcher scanned each of the windows above where the light from the room beyond would signify that the occupant was at home.

Standing inside the lobby door he waited tentatively expecting the telling creak of an unoiled hinge, giving away his being there, but fortunately the lobby remained silent. Two floors higher he heard another door shut the latch engaging as the occupant was welcomed home. The man smiled to himself, so far so good. Believing it prudent, he patiently waited a couple of minutes before knocking, letting her believe that she was safe.

When the woman did answer the doorbell her face was a mask of both doubt and apprehension. At first she didn't recognise her caller, but when the memory did materialise her expression changed along with her belief that her home was her castle, somewhere she thought she would always be safe.

Her unease was the trigger that switched on his control as he grew in both stature and confidence. Within seconds his friendly approach had turned ugly, angry as she made a futile attempt to shut the door in his face stating he had made a mistake. When the voices had said 'now, do it now' he had laughed, swiftly grabbed her hair and pushed her back inside, closing the door with his free hand. If anybody had made a mistake it was her.

It was accurate, had been thrilling and even now the recall excited him. Sipping more whiskey he felt compelled to write on. When it was done he pressed save and added a spell check just to be sure. Jack Chilvray sat back in the chair with his hands behind his head. Fiction was good, although only up to a point serving an obligation to the reader, but nothing could ever replace the excitement and exhilaration of the real thing.

Sitting out in the garden had helped put everything into perspective and Jack had come to the conclusion that he wasn't to blame, if anything the system had made him do it. Perhaps if Hamptons had taken his submission seriously, none of this would have been necessary and Mortimer Valdis would not even exist. Tapping the symbol in the page section of the screen he added a break, his imagination picturing the office where he had once stood, wondering who had possession of his manuscript, which incidentally had not been returned.

*****

Having spent the afternoon and early evening knocking on doors, with the occasional occupant impolitely telling him where to go Thomas Hawkes had decided that around a quarter to eight he was going to gain nothing new so he returned to the station. His enquiries had proved insignificant, but that was life and policing was a game of patience with little reward.

Hawkes was a realist not blaming people for not wanting to get involved. What they didn't see couldn't complicate their lives. Residents went to work, came home, shut the door and got on with whatever entertained them without their ever being involved with other people's problems.

At an all-night petrol station the only image that had been retrieved from the security recorder had been of a man walking past the forecourt around the time that the killer would have been going home. Maybe the evening had not been a complete waste of time.

'Give it to the tech boys Tom and see if they can enhance the image. Anything will help!' they watched as April took the ring from a vat of cleaning fluid where it had been soaking all afternoon. Fingerprints would have been impossible because of the other matter glued to the yellow metal.

'How did it go at the embassy?' Hawkes asked.

Spence appraised him regarding Bianchi and Cortelli, stating that April was suspicious of the embassy official. April looked up, her eyes telling Hawkes that she didn't like the smarmy Italian.

'You think they're involved?'

'I'm not sure. We will need to talk to Cortelli, but he has a concrete alibi for the murder. I've checked with customs and he did leave the country when Bianchi said he did.'

Picking up the hardback written by Mortimer Valdis, Spence loosely flicked through the pages, picking upon a specific phrase or word, but not collecting anything meaningful. He gave it to Hawkes.

'Here, bedtime reading. You're the bibliophile amongst us.'

April grinned at Thomas Hawkes then focused on Spence. 'Tom might occupy his time away from the station with better interests than just reading!'

The sentiment was lost on Spence who lived, breathed and slept with work.

'He shouldn't have told us that he liked reading.'

Hawkes turned to the page where the publisher's details were recorded. 'Mortimer Valdis, it's a strange name, unusual. I don't suppose that there are many listed that are similar. I'll call the publisher as well and make time to pay them a visit.'

Spence looked at April. 'You see, give a dog a bone and they'll start gnawing away.

'*Retribution of the Angst*' Thomas Hawkes was thinking aloud. 'I read quite a few books whilst I was at university, but this one is different to most of the fiction that I've read.'

'How's that?' April asked.

'Fiction generally follows a familiar pattern depending upon the style and depth of the writer's imagination. Valdis goes deep, very deep, not just shocking his reader, but as though sending a warning.' He read a passage to emphasis his point.

'As the stranger came close, he saw the look of terror in the young woman's eyes, sensing the purchase of pleasure in her torment, knowing that he was responsible. Society was always banging the drum about how safe it was to walk alone nowadays, but it wasn't society that was locked deep underground where the rats called the disused vent shaft home. Soon her cries for help, her pleas for mercy would be lost in the passing wind and another unfortunate soul would vanish forever, her body never being found, as though she had never existed. In time even the memory of loved ones would fade. Life was inescapably cruel.'

April pushed what she was looking at away from where she was sat.

'Did you know that between nineteen seventy four and nineteen ninety four a writer named Johann 'Jack' Unterweger murdered a total of twenty one women. His trail of terror took him across Europe and Los Angeles, eighteen of those women were prostitutes. Whilst in custody Unterweger hung himself in his cell using his shoelaces and belt. Some of the modus operandi adopted by Unterweger to terrorise and murder his victims was by using the same implements.'

'Meaning what?' asked Spence.

'Meaning killers chose a method by which they kill. Authors latch onto a killers mind and they adopt a certain practice, a technique which they can use in their book to give emphasis to the story, something that will keep the reader engaged. Hollywood uses the same approach when they make their movies. Sometimes the darker, the more gruesome the better the film or the scene.'

'So Mortimer Valdis isn't just writing fiction, but something that he's been involved with!'

Both April and Hawkes nodded, agreeing.

'That small segment of fabric that Susan Weekes pointed out at the post-mortem. It's man-made and almost certainly from a pair of gloves. I don't think we'd find them even if we found the killer.' She stretched, inducing fresh oxygen into tired limbs. 'I'm done here. There's nothing else to be found from the bag retrieved from the waste disposal. I'll take it back to Susan in the morning.'

'Why?'

April licked additional moisture across the dryness of her lips, where the air in the room had gone stale.

'Because I believe in a body going out of this world with everything that it came in with, whatever the condition. It's my belief that we go elsewhere, wherever that is and do it all over again, only I hope better next time around.' Her explanation was directed at Spence who had asked the question. 'But, besides whatever I believe, it's dignified.'

Spence apologised, his question had been perhaps insensitive. 'I'll come with you if you like. There's one or two things that I'd like to ask Weekes without having to stare at a corpse when I'm doing it!' He looked up at the clock, it was gone midnight and time had simply slipped away without any of them realising it.

An hour later sitting in his lounge at home all alone, wearing just a dressing gown with a coffee in one hand and a photograph album in the other Spence flicked open the front cover and stared at the image that looked back. The expression on the woman's face was blank as though nothing was registering at the time the photograph had been taken. He looked hard at Siobhan's eyes, hoping to see a flicker of life beyond her stony stare, but there was nothing, nothing but, the lost look of a woman struggling with life. Spence left the album open at the page as he sat back and drank his coffee. Somewhere out there a killer was planning his next move. Maybe, Siobhan had seen the darkness coming. Maybe, he thought she was in a much better place than him, safe and where Mortimer Valdis could not get to her.

Chapter Eight

Around one thirty, maybe a few minutes later Spence rolled over in the bed and grabbed his mobile which had activated beside his head. Somebody had sent him a text message. Rubbing his eyes to readjust to the dark, he punched in his password to unlock the screen. *'Meant to say earlier thanks for the meal. I enjoyed the food and the company. Maybe, we can do it again sometime. AG.'*

Spence thought about sending a reply, rationally thinking through the various connotations that might arise if he did. Women could so easily pick up on the least likely vibe and twist the meaning with which a message had been sent. Having thought it through, he sent back a simple response *'Me also.'*

April Geddings lay in her bed, tucked up warm and safe thinking about Daniel Spence. She liked him, really liked him. His temperament suited her nature, but she especially liked the way that you were never certain as to what he would do or say next. When she read the text *'me also,'* it was one of not knowing moments. What exactly did it mean, that he enjoyed the meal and her company or that he did want another meal out with her?

April let the breath in her lungs escape loudly as she shook her head into the indention of the pillow. What was it about men that made them so bloody dark and mysterious? Outside, somewhere close a dustbin lid was disturbed. She leapt from her bed and went to the window, but there were too many shadows to define shapes and building lines. She went back to bed thinking about Spence again.

From the shadows in the recess of the fence beside the garages a figure moved and a cat looked up from where it was sat watching. Within seconds the mysterious figure was gone and so was the cat. Inside her bedroom April sent one last text. *'Sleep well Spence.'*

When sleep finally arrived it took Daniel Spence to a place that he found himself in often, pulling at tugging at his unconscious state it would not let him rest as the sensory activity moving through his brain flashed up different images, some living, some dead. They were not exactly nightmares, but black unexplained episodes that he could not remember being involved with. One such event kept returning and so did a face, but it was never around long enough to recognise. When the scream woke him, he wasn't sure if it had been in his sleep or from outside.

Reaching up for his mobile he read the time, five minutes to five. Moving his finger across the facia of the mobile he opened the text field. 'Sleep well Spence.' He laughed momentarily, it had been some time since he had slept for a full eight hours, undisturbed or uninterrupted.

When the dawn rays broke through the gap between the curtains he took himself off to the bathroom to shave and shower adding cologne. When Ted turned the key in the lock of the café Spence was stood beside him.

'Don't you ever sleep?' he asked.

'Not as much as I would like.'

Spence helped Ted get ready the coffee machine, fry the sausages and butter the bread rolls in readiness for the early morning rush which normally kicked in around seven. Spence liked the monotony of helping his friend, giving his mind time to ease into the day. When Ted insisted that he take a table Spence opted for the one in the corner where it was far enough from the window not to be noticed.

Chewing on the bacon that he had cooked, he looked up to see a familiar figure arrive and head his way. Hawkes sat without being invited.

'How did you know that I would be here?' Spence signalled to Ted to bring another coffee.

'One of the most important things when you join a new division is to know where your guv'nor takes his breakfast.'

Spence pushed across the table top the sugar bowl, but Hawkes tapped his stomach, indicating that he had to watch the calories.

'Do you want breakfast?'

'Have we got time?' Hawkes replied.

Spence ordered another bacon sandwich and told Ted to mark up the book accordingly.

'A book?' Thomas Hawkes queried.

'I'm like the royals until I get the chance to get to a cash machine I'm penniless. I don't carry money, unless it becomes essential. Ted and I have this arrangement whereby anything that I have here goes in a special book kept under the counter. At the end of the month I pay my dues, adding ten percent. We call it the *divvy fund*. Every six months Ted counts up what's in the tin and that coming Friday night we either go to the dogs or a casino uptown. That ten percent can soon mount up, trust me!'

'Sounds good and an ideal arrangement.'

Spence smiled as he chewed. 'It is and it's not complicated Tom. Women complicate your life, but there are times when you need them!'

Hawkes was going to ask if that meant April Geddings, but he didn't want to spoil his breakfast and especially as it had gone into the book too.

'Have you known Ted long?' he asked.

'Since we sat next to one another at school. We were always visiting the headmaster's office in them days for doing what we shouldn't have been doing. Ted's alright though, straight as a dye and he never beats about the bush. If it needs saying Ted will tell you. If the world was a straight as Ted we wouldn't be in the shit that we are.'

Hawkes looked across to the counter where Ted was getting ready four coffees for a group of young women. He winked at the detective and said something to the women that made them laugh. Spence shook his head in admiration.

'We're chalk and cheese, always have been. Ted could charm his way out of any tight spot whereas I always got my arse slapped with a cane or gym slipper.'

Hawkes finished off his sandwich and washed it down with the coffee, which was strong just how he liked it. He admired his chief inspector, never before believing that he would like the dogs or the roulette wheel. He watched Spence as he scanned the faces in the café, never letting an opportunity pass him by. Like barbers, corner cafes were hives of information where all sorts would meet to discuss personal problems, business and crime.

Replacing his mug on the table checked his watch. 'You were up and about early this morning?'

'I had trouble sleeping and I've things to do today. Before I pay Pritchard Davis, the publisher of *Retribution of the Angst* a visit, I want to drop in on Hamptons in Holborn. When I called yesterday afternoon to say that I might be calling in, I was put through to the director's office. The person that I spoke with seemed wary as though there was some hidden secret that couldn't be discussed in public. I thought I would start by delving into their archives and see what lies beneath the tiles on the roof. Ruffling a few feathers might help jog a few memories.'

'Including that of Mortimer Valdis?'

'Yes, especially him!'

Spence dug out an obstinate shard of bacon from between his teeth with the tip of his tongue. 'If it's okay with you Tom I'll tag along as well?'

'Sure, two pairs of eyes and ears are better than one, but what about April. I thought you said that you would accompany her when she goes to see Susan Weekes.'

Spence asked for another coffee guessing that he would need the additional caffeine to get him through the day, without asking he ordered another for Hawkes.

'April can cope.' It was all he said. When Ted had delivered the coffee and gone back to the counter Spence continued. 'I know we've not worked together long Tom, but I think that I know you and you're fishing for something at Hampton's?'

'D'Corscy was an ex-employee and by now the reaction to her death should have sunk in. Having the police pop in this morning will unsettle things, it's when I expect somebody to talk. Very often guilt and death tend to bring things to the fore!'

'You think there's a dark secret lurking in the woodwork?'

'More like sitting at a desk.'

'Then we had best go test your theory!'

They said their goodbyes to Ted as he marked up the book then replaced it under the counter. The six months was almost up and they had enough saved to pay a visit to either Romford or a Soho nightclub.

When Julie saw the two men walk in through the reception doors she knew immediately by the way that they dressed and their manner that they were the police. Producing identification she put a call through to the senior editor's office. Charles Trent came down to reception via the lift, where he proffered his hand in greeting, suggesting that they conduct their enquiries in his office where it was less intrusive. Immediately that the lift door closed Julie buzzed Andrea on the floor above and told her about their visitors. Surprisingly the lift stopped on the first floor and Hawkes stepped out, much to Andrea's surprise, although no more than that of Charles himself.

'He feels claustrophobic in offices and much prefers big open spaces!' exclaimed Spence, knowing that Hawkes wanted to look around.

'Andrea will make him welcome,' Charles responded as he pressed the controls to take the lift up another floor.

Spence smiled back at the senior editor. He was charming, possibly too friendly, but it was too early to decide whether his affability was guilt or nerves making his tongue and brain work faster than usual. Closing the door of the office Charles offered the chief inspector refreshments, but Spence declined the bacon and coffee still laying nicely in his stomach.

'Did you know Vivienne D'Corscy well?' he asked, hitting on the subject immediately.

Charles was slightly suspicious having expected a more subtle approach.

'Professionally we did our jobs to the best of our ability, outside of work we saw one another occasionally.' The expression across his face changed. 'I feel her loss more than most around here.'

'And why's that?'

'I felt responsible for Vivienne. It was me who offered her the position of assistant, then put her forward for promotion. I saw myself as a sort of father figure.'

'Do you adopt the same approach with anyone else working here?'

'No.' The response was empathic.

'Outside of work, what did you do, where did you go?'

'We both liked the theatre, attending art exhibitions and if there was a book launch we would go together. Everything was above board chief inspector of that I assure you.'

'Are you married?' Spence asked focusing directly on his eyes, looking for a reaction.

'Once, although we've not seen one another for a good many years. In fact come to think of it, I cannot categorically say that I know of Dorothy's whereabouts.'

'Is she a missing person?'

The loose skin under his chin wobbled as he shook his head. 'No. We parted on consensual terms.'

'Divorced?'

'No, although I cannot see how this is relevant to poor Vivienne's enquiry?'

'Just building a picture Mr Trent. Did Vivienne know Mrs Trent?'

'No.' Charles was becoming a little agitated and frustrated at how the questions were aimed at his private life.

'So legally you are still married?'

He sighed, his only previous contact with any police to report an attempt break in at the office some eighteen months previously. 'I suppose in the eyes of the law we are, although I would never want her back!' Spence nodded, momentarily thinking about Siobhan.

'The outings, to the theatre and book launches, did they involve anyone else besides Miss D'Corscy?'

'Initially it was just the two of us, but later a young man joined us sometimes.' There was a slight irritation in his voice when he mentioned the other man.

'Do you recall his name?'

'Roberto. That was how he introduced himself, never giving his surname. He worked for the Italian embassy as an interpreter, making a big deal of the fact that he was fluent in several languages. To tell the truth chief inspector I found his company annoying and intrusive.'

Spence detected a slight grimace when he said intrusive.

'How?'

'He was always trying to find a way to get rid of me, have Vivienne all to himself.'

'At the book launches that you attended, did you ever see anybody approach Miss D'Corscy who you thought looked or acted in a suspicious or aggressive manner?

Charles Trent didn't think about the answer, his reply was instant. 'No, although I consider the question as an all-encompassing conundrum. There are literally dozens of people at a book launch, more if the author is well known or successful. Our role is to mingle, promote and market the product. Vivienne could have talked with any number of people that didn't come to my attention.'

'Including her killer!'

For several seconds that followed the room was silent as the gravity of what Spence had said, sunk in.

'I suppose so.' Charles replied.

'Did this friend, Roberto attend any of the launches?'

'One, maybe two. I cannot remember, he didn't interest me so if he did I would have ignored and avoided him!'

It was plainly obvious that Roberto Cortelli was more than just a nuisance. Charles Trent had seen the Italian as a threat.

'In confidence did Miss D'Corscy ever mention a stalker, an over-zealous writer or infatuated admirer to you?'

'Not that I recall.'

Spence noticed the dark lines under both of the senior editor's eyes.

'Do you have a liver complaint Mr Trent?'

Charles dubiously stared back. 'A very strange question to be asking chief inspector?'

'Merely an observation, only I've seen colleagues with similar dark patches under the eyes and above the cheekbone.'

'If you are insinuating that I drink, I do only to be sociable, but never to excess. If you must know I have slept very badly since poor Vivienne death. It weighs heavily on my mind night and day. I was very fond of the young woman.'

'Did you ever sleep with her?'

Charles glared back at Spence, the anger blazing from his stare.

'That's an impertinent thing to suggest. No, never!'

Spence raised his palms in truce.

'We have to ask all manner of questions in an investigation Mr Trent, offensive or not. Did anybody else in the office?'

Charles Trent shook his head. 'No, Vivienne lived alone and she liked her private moments.'

Trent had skirted the question, but Spence was ready with his next.

'Was she intimate with Roberto?'

'You would have to ask him that!'

Spence would and soon.

'This Italian, what can you tell me about him?'

Charles Trent calmed once again. 'Not much, he's about Vivienne's age. Stands a little higher than myself. Athletic build and tanned of course. From what she did tell me, he flits between here and Italy quite a bit. I got the impression that she had tried to cool the relationship with him.'

'Why did she leave Hampton's Mr Trent?'

'Young people, agents and the like they come and go. Society nowadays does not see loyalty to a firm as a priority. Live and love for today Mr Spence, tomorrow will take care of itself. More successful agencies offer better chances of promotion and interest, if I were a younger man, no doubt I'd be just as tempted. Vivienne had promise and lots of it and she was well known throughout the literary circuit. We promoted her on one occasion, simply to ensure that she stayed at Hampton's, but in time the lure of what lies beyond our doors was sure to tempt her elsewhere. In times of austerity this can turn into a very cut-throat business.' Charles Trent immediately recognised his inept choice of words and so quickly made amend. 'I meant competitive chief inspector.'

'What was the name of the agency that she joined when she left here?'

Once again his jowls wobbled, coming to life.

'That was what was so strange. She left Hampton's intending to join the employ of Havers, Reed and Norton, but I found out about a week after she left that she had accompanied Roberto on one of his trips back to Italy. Several times during a month later I telephoned and visited her flat, but received no reply. I knocked at the door of the neighbour opposite, an actress I believe, but she hadn't seen anything of Vivienne neither.'

'Have you ever heard of the name Mortimer Valdis?'

Spence noticed the look flash across the senior eyes at the mention of the name. Charles Trent tapped a key on his keyboard firing up a page on his screen. He pointed to the entry.

'One Mortimer Valdis. His only submission to the agency, a manuscript entitled *Death Belies the Innocent*. It was reviewed by Vivienne in the January of the previous year, several months before she left us. She rejected it.' Charles read down the notes placed at the side of the entry. 'Unfortunately, due a computer glitch our server encountered problems and many comments and some records were lost during that period. The rejection advice to Valdis being one of them!'

Spence looked confused. *'Not Retribution of the Angst?'*

'Charles rechecked. 'No, there's only the one submission.'

'Would you have recorded any personal details on Mortimer Valdis, an address or telephone number, maybe an email etcetera?'

Charles went up and down twice checking, scrolling through the entry, but hit a dead end.

'What do you know about a publisher who goes by the name of Pritchard Davis?'

'Only that poor Pritchard is dead. That dreaded cancer attacked his prostate end of last summer. He was a real gentleman in the profession. Never refused business and executed every assignment passed his way with the utmost professionalism. Thankfully the end was quick and the poor man didn't suffer. Together with Jean, his wife, they ran a family publishing business over Stratford way. Jean sold up soon after the demise of her husband. Understandably she lost all heart for London and books. The last I heard was that she had moved back down to Cornwall to live with a sister. Why do you ask?'

'Because the book written by Valdis was published by Pritchard Davis.'

Charles nodded in agreement. 'That would seem feasible. Pritchard Davis was a vanity publisher. They take on a book and get paid by the writer to produce the publication of the book. We on the other hand front the cost and take our costs from the profit made by the sales.'

A light inside Spence's head suddenly switched itself on. If there was a monetary transaction, there had to be bank records, unless the agreement was paid for in cash, which was highly unlikely.

'And once a manuscript is rejected, what happens to it then?'

'Physical submissions are stamped and recorded on the computer. They are then returned in a pre-paid envelope to the writer along with a rejection letter. If however, we think that the manuscript was worth keeping for perhaps a future review, it could go down to the storeroom in the basement of the building. Not many do, but some are considered worth keeping.'

'Do any writers refuse to accept you rejection?'

'Occasionally one may want to know more, but our policy is never to get involved in lengthy explanations. It can get messy and achieve little.'

Spence stood up an indicating that he was done. Charles also rose from his chair pleased that the inquisition was at last over. Once again he offered his hand, but he had no intention of seeing the policeman back to the lift or down to reception.

'If you take the stairs chief inspector they will take you down to the floor below where you can collect your colleague.'

The moment that Spence had disappeared from sight Charles pushed shut his office door and went immediately across to the window. Some of the detectives questions had been offensive, seemed very personal and Charles didn't like being attacked in that way. He watched the two detectives leave the building and walk back across the busy junction to the pavement opposite, soon they were both lost amongst the traffic and pedestrians. He hoped that it was the last time that he would see either. Taking the photograph of Vivienne from his wallet he stared at it for some time.

'I am so sorry Vivienne. I should have been there for you.'

Chapter Nine

An hour later the senior editor called Stephanie Garland up his office, stating that he would explain when she got there. Apprehensively, Stephanie took the seat the other side of his desk.

'Is something wrong Charles?' she asked.

Trent smiled, but it was thin and not loaded with pleasure. 'I am not sure Stephanie. I have just gone through the painful process of being cross-examined by the police.'

'Oh that. I had a young detective sit at my desk until he was collected by the one that you saw.'

Charles turned questioner. 'Did he ask much?'

'Mainly about how our system works, what the agency specialises in and if we have any troublesome clients.'

Charles spiralled his fingers together as he pondered.

'You were assigned a vast majority of Vivienne D'Corscy's workload. Do you recall a book that she had previously rejected written by an unknown, named Mortimer Valdis?'

'That's difficult Charles, I would have to check the records only we read a lot in a month and we reject just as many.'

'Can you please check and soon, only I'm interested to know why it was rejected.' Stephanie stood ready to leave and go back downstairs. 'And if you do find that we kept the manuscript, can you run me off a copy. I would like have the chance to peruse through the content.'

When he had the office to himself Charles took a small book from inside his jacket pocket, an address book where he kept his list of contacts, amongst the handwritten entries were the details of Roberto Cortelli. He dialled the number for his flat and waited for the call to be answered. When it was the man at the other end held the receiver in his hand wanting to know who was calling, but Charles said nothing, instead he just listened to the infuriating voice of the Italian as he grew more frustrated by the call. Smiling Charles replaced the receiver back on the cradle and ended the call. He would keep annoying the obnoxious interpreter until it drove him crazy, then when the moment was right, he would disguise his voice and inform Cortelli that the police were coming for him.

Stephanie Garland had left the office of the senior editor unsure if she had just been used as a sounding board, to explain why the police had been snooping around, or whether Charles Trent was onto something regarding Mortimer Valdis. As the agent for horror and crime, her mind was walking through the possibilities of a story evolving within. First checking the screen then taking herself down to the basement she returned with a dust covered copy of the manuscript. She photocopied *Death Belies the Innocent* taking a copy back up to Charles Trent. Before she made the ascent to the floor above, she slipped the second photocopy into her shoulder bag, intending to take it home where she could read it in peace. Finding his office vacant she left the manuscript on his desk, grateful that he was no around.

That evening Stephanie sat down on her settee stretching out her legs, armed with a coffee and a packet of chocolate biscuits. After reading the first chapter she sat with the coffee mug nestled between both hands staring at the clouds that were gathering outside her window. Night was approaching fast, the time when ghouls and ghosts came to life, when evil and murders walked the streets, keeping to the shadows, avoiding the stares of those that seemed unafraid. Soon though, there would be one whose courage was not nearly as strong, a victim although they didn't know it. Applying stealth, speed and cunning the hunter would lay in wait, waiting to pounce.

On the coffee table within reach of her arm, she looked at the contact card given to her by Thomas Hawkes earlier that day. She considered calling him, but thought it too soon to talk. Instead she sipped her coffee trying to forget what she had just read. Mortimer Valdis was graphic in his detail, not just recording what his imagination wanted him to write, but describing every enth element of the story as though he had been present when the victim realised their fate. It had scared her.

Picking up her mobile she recorded Hawkes number in her listing. It was there now, just in case. Stephanie liked the young detective, liked his looks and liked the way that his voice made her think of white wine, strawberries and cream and sex. Lying back on the settee with his card in her hand she started to unbutton her jeans.

Chapter Ten

Jack Chilvray tapped into the dialler the four digit code which would prevent his call from being recognised then waited patiently for somebody to answer, moments later Julie Carter picked up. *'Good morning Hamptons!'*

'That's a nice welcoming voice for a brisk morning.' Chilvray implied, hearing the sound of police sirens some distance off from where he was calling.

Julie smiled, it was nice to receive a friendly call, rather than from some of the ones that ranted and raved. The man sounded educated and polite. 'How can I help you Sir!' she replied.

'To begin with I was extremely distressed to hear about the sad demise of one of your agents, a Miss Vivienne D'Corscy and from what I understand a promising young lady who was not far away from lighting up the literary world.' Chilvray let his breathe exhale so that Julie could hear it and have her believe that he had been wounded personally. 'Such a waste, however and not to sound uncaringly indifferent I was wondering who had taken over her desk?'

Julie was only too happy to oblige. 'Stephanie Garland. Would you like to put me through?' she asked.

Jack Chilvray thanked the receptionist, patiently waiting for somebody to answer, but as often the case his call went straight to voicemail. He listened to the recorded message on her phone speaking after the metallic beep.

'It was a real shame that we didn't get the chance to talk today only I would have welcomed the opportunity to have discussed my previous submission. My last book cost me dearly, but that is all water under the bridge now and sadly as Pritchard Davis is no longer with us, irrelevant. Perhaps we can meet up sometime and discuss future proposals. Maybe when you hear what I have to say, you might reconsider giving my book a second review. I think that the circumstances of the late Miss D'Corscy's demise could possibly help change stony hearts.'

Jack sat back in his chair gently bouncing the end of the pencil between his upper and lower dentures. He liked leaving little posers about, liked the game that he played. He looked at the blank sheet where he had been doodling. The image was good, not quite professional enough to add to his latest book, but graphical all the same. Making a slight adjust here and there, he nodded to himself. Jack wondered how many stores had taken his published book, how many readers had been policemen and women, not realising that what they had read were the confessions of a killer. It amused him to think that they were so naive. Tapping the pencil once again up and down, he looked at the image on the screen of his laptop. Stephanie Garland's image did her justice. She was different to Vivienne D'Corscy, but Jack liked that. Too much similarity made for a boring world.

Changing screen, but keeping her image as a corner inset he added ideas to the beginning of the next chapter. They were only rough notes, nothing more nor intricate, but it was important to keep alive the story and as important was to please the voices inside his head. On the opposite top left hand corner of the screen Jack had open another inset picture. It was much darker than that of Stephanie Garland, much less inviting and hauntingly abhorrent. When a big brown rat came up close and peered into the camera lens, its pinkish nose was close enough to leave a thin veil of moisture on the glass. Chilvray tapped the screen with the pencil end, not that the rat would have noticed, but he liked playing with the creature. Suddenly the ideas started to flow, more fluid and without inhibition.

*****

The dental appointment that morning had overrun longer than Stephanie had meant it to last. Stepping out across the reception to the stairwell beyond the desk she smiled and said hello to Julie.

'You've just missed a call Steph. He sounded rather dishy!'

'Did he give his details?'

'No. I put him through to your extension as he was insistent that he wanted to talk to the agent that had succeeded Vivienne D'Corscy. I'm sorry Steph, I didn't realise that you was out of the office.'

Stephanie Garland played the message twice not quite trusting what she had heard. She had thought about involving Charles Trent, but decided to keep the message to herself rather than advertise it around the room. Instead she took a recording on her mobile.

Lying beside the bed where she had not managed sleep until the early hours of the morning her copy of the manuscript *Death Belies the*

Innocent lay open at the page where it had been marked with an asterisk. In the margin were several notes made by Stephanie Garland, indicators that certain words, actions suggested that particulars events as written were not merely fiction. At the top of the page she had written four words of her own *'who is Mortimer Valdis?'* It was a question many others would ask.

When Andrea dropped the morning's mail into her tray Stephanie looked up caught off her guard, her thoughts momentarily interrupted. Fleetingly she appeared agitated that she had been disturbed, but her expression mellowed realising that her visitor was only the office junior.

'I am sorry Steph, I didn't mean to startle you!'

'It's alright Andrea, I thought that you were Charles. Is he in?'

'Yes, but he's in a meeting with Justin Bannerton. I was told that neither was to be disturbed.'

'That suits me fine.'

Andrea smiled then passed onto other desks where she idly chatted with the owners. To her the morning routine was just another day, neither exacting to brain or energy levels.

Scrolling through her list of contacts Stephanie called Hawkes.

'Can you meet me this morning?' she asked 'it could be important, only I'd rather not say why, not here!'

Twenty minutes later Hawkes walked in through the door of a coffee bar that she had suggested around the corner from Hamptons. He ordered then sat at the table opposite.

'Your call had an urgency attached, is everything okay?' he asked as the waitress brought across his coffee.

'Me, I'm fine, but I think that you need to hear this.' She handed him her mobile and told him to play record.

'He's articulate... you don't think that it's a crank call?'

Stephanie emphatically shook her head from side to side. 'No. He knows me Tom. The caller specifically asked for the successor to Vivienne D'Corscy and he made reference to Pritchard Davis, knowing that he's also dead.'

Hawkes tested the coffee to see if it was suitably tepid enough to drink.

'Details of the investigation that only the killer would know!' he agreed. He sipped his coffee. 'I think he was testing the water, only had you been in the office, he would have got a reaction from you. You had no prior connection with the original manuscript, so there's not a lot to worry about.' He took another mouthful, it was good coffee. 'At least now we know that the killer is a man.'

'And what do I do now?' she asked, her vulnerability showing in her eyes and the tone in her voice.

'As far as this Mortimer Valdis knows you might not be in work today, especially as the call went to voicemail. I'll speak with my detective inspector and get his advice. For now though I suggest you go about your day as though there was nothing out of the ordinary.'

Sitting in the chair opposite she wasn't entirely convinced that it was just another ordinary day.

'I didn't get much sleep last night Tom. I was awake till goodness knows what time reading through a copy of his submitted manuscript that I photocopied yesterday. It made for scary reading. One of my literary likes is horror and crime, but this wasn't just fiction. What he did to his victim's was graphic. Through his description I could picture the pain and the torment that they must have felt. When I did fall asleep it was with the light on.' She focused her eyes on his, letting him see how it had affected her. 'I'm not easily scared Tom, I read some real shit sometimes, heavy, dark horror, some good, some real crap, but Valdis goes deeper than anything that I've ever seen. I suppose reading it now makes me involved!'

'So where's the manuscript now?'

She remembered. 'I left it beside the bed, although I wish that I hadn't.'

In a show of unexpected support Hawkes let his hand rest on hers. 'You know watching a bad movie can have the same psychological effect. You need to put things in perspective Stephanie!'

She liked his hand on hers. 'Steph... call me Steph. I know that Tom, but Jack Nicolson doesn't exactly call the next day at work when you've watched *The Shining* the night before. Perspective is one thing, but a reality check is another!'

Hawkes realised that he had been wrong to suggest that she just forget everything. It was clear that the call from Valdis and her reading his manuscript had unhinged her day.

'Can you get me a copy?' he asked.

'You can have mine, I don't want it in my place.' She was wary of everybody that entered the coffee bar or who walked by. Hawkes changes places sitting beside her.

'You know Tom... the essence of it all when you write a book is too enthral the readers, make them believe that they are part of the story, a character, something that they can relate with and enjoy. With horror the writer wants to keep his reader perched on the edge of their seat, unable to resist putting the book down and turning over to the next page. Mortimer Valdis tortures and executes for fun. He enjoys what he does. He enjoys scaring people!'

'Does anybody else know about the call?'

'Only Julie on reception, but she's so wrapped up in loves blanket with her postie boyfriend that I doubt she would recognise the implications of his calling.' She shook her head. 'No. Julie's harmless. I gave Charles Trent a photocopy yesterday, he specifically asked for it.'

'Any ideas why?'

'Not really. I got the impression that he wanted to check on the reason as to why it was rejected, although I felt an underlying tension in the air as though he felt responsible,' she hesitated 'guilty!'

'About what?'

'About why Vivienne D'Corscy had died.'

'If you had been the first to review the manuscript, what would have been your initial thoughts?'

'I would have rejected it like Vivienne D'Corscy did. There's something terribly evil about Mortimer Valdis and what he writes, what he does. If indeed it does turn out to be a work of fiction, then he has a dark warped imagination. You will see for yourself when you read it, that there are several references to rape. As a literary agent I have a long established duty to both readers and the firm that employs me. Hamptons has a good reputation in the city, hard fought and won.'

*****

When Charles Trent sat back at his desk, he read the email that had been posted from Andrea explaining that Stephanie Garland had gone home feeling unwell due a dental anaesthetic. Taking his copy of the manuscript from his desk drawer he started to read again where he had left off before attending a meeting with the marketing director.

So far what he had read didn't interest him. Mortimer Valdis was just another unknown amateur grasping a dream that they could be a professional writer. In the commercial jungle where surprises were around every corner there were no guarantees of survival in a very competitive speciality.

Charles Trent spent another ten minutes flicking through various pages trying to get a feel for what the author was trying to express in words, but horror and crime didn't interest him. Give him a historical account of the theatre or an autobiography and that would grab his attention. Charles saw crime and horror as things that happened, only not in his world, not unless they were being portrayed in a play, an opera or on canvas. Dropping the manuscript back into the drawer it was palpable why Vivienne D'Corsy had not recommended the book go before the selection committee.

Just after five that afternoon he stepped out onto the pavement and stood back for a moment against the front façade of the building allowing the warmth of the early evening sunshine to invigorate his face. It felt good and particularly welcoming having been cooped up in a stuffy office for eight hours. Later after supper, he might take a stroll around Shaftesbury Avenue checking out the billboards of the theatres. Of course he would invite Vivienne along. Wherever she was, he believed that she was still with him.

Blending in with the normal rush-hour crowd the senior editor opted to stand close to the white safety line expectantly awaiting the sudden onward rush of unventilated air that would indicate that the train was due any moment. Then, when the first carriage rounded the bend of the tunnel commuters of all ages, creeds and nationalities shuffled, picked up bags and held onto children as they prepared themselves in readiness to board the nearest carriage and secure a seat.

Rattling down the track the teeth-cutting squeal of metal on metal echoed loudly around the concave cavity throwing up a cloud of dust and abandoned newspapers from the concrete pit below. Craning forward

Charles judged which carriage he would choose to board. He was about to right himself when from behind he felt a solid fist jab him hard in the back. He instantly lost his balance propelling his bulky torso over and down onto the tracks.

The train driver saw the man fall, but with fifty feet of platform left and the train under pressure, he knew that it wouldn't stop in time. Letting go of the dead man's handle he willed the brakes to hold fast, but the screams and faces of those standing nearest the falling man had already marked his fate.

None saw Jack Chilvray slip back as others moved forward to look. With the deed executed, the stranger in black gradually made his way down the platform to the exit. It would be sometime before the train was rolled back along the track and what was left of Charles Trent gathered together and placed in a black body bag.

In the street above where the flow of pedestrians and traffic continued to go about their journeys home Chilvray made sure that the brim of his hat was kept low and over his eyes to avoid the familiarity of the ever present security cameras that shrouded every street corner and walkway. All about sirens were growing louder in intensity as ambulance, fire and police rushed to the tube station. Walking home in the warm sunshine Chilvray allowed himself a smile, his plan had worked perfectly. Later over a glass of wine he would add the demise of Charles Trent to the book.

Chapter Eleven

An hour into the task of reading certain chapters they decided to take a break and evaluate their findings. On each copy highlighter pens had marked or ringed specific words or sentences, names and places.

'There are definite correlations to the Emile Johnson case!'

'The unexplained death from Soho, sometime about two years back?' asked Hawkes.

Spence showed him the page. 'The very same.'

Having heard the recording that Stephanie Garland had sent to his mobile Spence was under no disillusion that Mortimer Valdis was responsible for Vivienne D'Corscy's death.

'That's interesting because what I've read so far points to the Benjamin Wilkes murder over at Epping Forrest sometime last year. Valdis keeps himself busy.'

Spence looked up from the manuscript where he highlighted another event.

'Yes, serial killing is all the rage. Besides the meeting with Garland did you manage to track down the business account for Pritchard Davis?'

Hawkes nodded. 'Odd though, because having contacted nearly every bank in the inner circle, none have a registered account with either the late husband, his wife or the business.'

'An off-shore account?' Spence asked.

'No I don't think so. Asking around at nearby businesses who knew Davis and his wife they said that were an eccentric pair, traditionalists. It's likely that they would only have traded with an English banking corporation.'

'Maybe we should broaden our horizons Tom and dig deeper. Look at foreign possibilities and delve into their background, use a research genealogist if needs be, I'll lose the cost in some other budget. Traditionalists hand down family run businesses, not trusting outsiders. They've stashed their money somewhere and Valdis helped balance the books. It has to be somewhere.'

He went back to the manuscript.

'Johnson and Wilkes, coincidence or conjecture. Whatever the case, there was a distinct lack of evidence by all account.'

'Like we have with the D'Corscy.' Hawkes added.

'Exactly.' Spence checked the time on his watch. 'Not that I want to take anything upstairs, but I think I should at least brief them with what facts we do know.'

He was about to leave when April knocked and walked in. She noticed what they had been working on.

'How the mystery going?'

'Slow,' replied Hawkes. She handed him an envelope.

'The blow-ups from the petrol filling station. The image is still a little grainy in places, but it's acceptable.' She pointed to the face. 'We can at least get a profile going, shape of nose and chin. It's a start.'

Spence explained that he was going upstairs when his phone rang on the desk. A minute later he replaced the receiver. 'That was control, they've just had word from Central that Charles Trent is lying under the wheels of a tube train at Russell Square Station.'

Leaving the office as it was Spence locked the door and jumped into Hawkes car. Using the magnetic LED strobe Spence attached it to the roof. It was the middle of the rush hour, but Hawkes was a skilled unit driver and he made the short ride in minutes. He parked the car behind a fire appliance and let control know of their arrival.

'There's enough here!' remarked April, as she gathered here bag from the back seat.

'There always is for a jumper.' Spence beside the car looking around.

'See anybody you know?' April asked as she went and stood beside him.

'I'd like too. I was looking around for the figure in the stills. Very often the killer waits around at a crime scene. It gives them a buzz knowing that we're in the dark. All part of the game.'

'Some game Spence.'

'Unfortunately April, after so many years that's what this has become. Criminals commit crime and we play along, looking for clues, looking for the perpetrator. I don't suppose the victims see it quite like that, but as soon as we resolve one crime, another five takes its place.'

They stepped under the cordon that had been trailed from one side of the red tiled entrance to the far side taking the spiral staircase down. At the bottom Spence nodded at the officers guarding the entrance to the platform. He was told that fire and ambulance personnel were working under the front carriage.

'Is he still alive?' he asked.

The constable guarding shook his head. Further down the platform he asked an ambulance officer the same question.

'I'm afraid the train didn't stop in time. The front wheels did most of the damage. It severed the head and the lower halves of both legs. Anything else is lying in the pit.'

Standing beside where the train had come to a halt Spence crouched down, joined by April and Hawkes. 'Hardly a fitting way to depart this life.' he said as he followed the beam of the lights under the carriage. 'I can't see that much, do you want to get down under and have a look around for anything that might be of use, like Trent's wallet or any papers that he might have been carrying home from the office.'

April grimaced at Spence, then Hawkes. 'I get all the best jobs.'

Slipping into a protective over-suit she dropped down between the tracks and walked back to where the emergency services were doing their best to retrieve body parts and place them in a body bag. Still lying untouched in the inspection pit with his eyes wide open in both surprise and horror

Charles Trent stared back at her as she crouched down. April wondered what had gone through his mind in the split second when he realised that he was both falling and that the train was careering down the track. It was something that she would never know.

Rummaging around amongst the discarded coffee cups, fast food cartons and newspaper April found his wallet, but saw no paperwork. She slipped the wallet between the wheels of the train for Hawkes to take. Moments later she was topside back on the platform.

'Nothing else?' Spence asked.

'Just the wallet. There's a lot of people working down there and anything significant is likely to have been trampled on or kicked about.'

Pulling apart the compartments of the wallet Hawks found cash, a credit card, bank card and a well-thumbed photograph of Vivienne D'Corscy. It had been taken in the foyer of a theatre uptown. He showed it to Spence.

'So he did have an infatuation for the young lady. It's a bit late asking why.'

April looked over his shoulder at the photograph as she got out of the protective suit. 'When did the embassy say Cortelli was due back home?'

'By my reckoning sometime this evening. Dawson and Stebbings are watching the airport only I wanted to make sure that Cortelli didn't slip through the net. Although I've not met our Italian there's something about him that I don't think adds up.'

Hawkes who had been looking up and down the platform pointed out a camera that was watching them. 'That could be useful. I'll get a copy of the tape, if it's working!'

With Hawkes gone April asked Spence if she could see the photograph once again.

'She had beautiful eyes, dark like her ancestors, but beautifully endearing. I can see why she would have made any man's heart melt without trying.'

Chapter Twelve

Spence spoke with the lead detective from West End Central informing him of their interest then left. Whilst they out and about he chose to visit the house owned by Charles Trent in the trendy and expensive Islington Square. On a summer's evening with the sun on your back you could walk through the streets from the office to the square in under forty minutes. Hawkes whistled low when he saw the house.

'The literary business didn't get that affected by the last recession!'

'Jealousy will get you noticed Tom.' He looked back and smiled at April in the rear view mirror.

Inserting the key in the lock April turned the latch and opened the door to the house. It was strange, but the air seemed excessively still inside as though accepting that its owner would never tread the parquet floor ever again. On either side of the hallway the walls were lined with framed posters from numerous west shows. She slipped the keys back into her shoulder bag.

'You'd have made a good pick-pocket.'

'Probably, but I'd rather have been a scientist. I like delving into the unknown!'

Hawkes watched as they smiled at one another, wondering just how much she had already delved into his private life. Spence rarely talked about his life beyond the force, other than the times he spent with Ted, not even his plans for retirement were general knowledge.

Standing on the bottom step of the stairs, he looked. 'I'll take the upstairs.' Spence nodded.

'Im not expecting us to find much Tom, but you never know. Trent was a strange kettle of fish and I'm still not sure about the façade that masked his life!'

On the landing leading to the bedrooms and shared bathroom Hawkes found a framed photograph portraying D'Corscy and Trent standing behind an author at a book launch. Looking closer he saw the figure of a man standing in the background, he was wearing a wide rimmed dark hat. Hawkes removed the photograph and left the frame hanging on the picture pin. A short time later he joined them in a large Victorian kitchen.

'Find anything?' Spence asked. Thomas Hawkes handed over the photograph. He pointed to the figure in the background.

'If that's Mortimer Valdis, then it's conceivable that he went along to any book venues attended by D'Corscy and Trent.'

April and Spence studied the image. Whoever had produced the photograph had faded the figures standing around them. 'That's a nuisance,' April said 'we could have matched a face to a name.'

Spence flick over and looked at the back. The image had been produced by Gilbert Photography and had a batch number. 'It's worth seeing if Gilbert is still operating. They might have the images on file and be able to reverse the fading.' They found nothing else of interest so decided to call it a day, with April vowing to come back the next day with her team and examine the contents of Trent's home in greater detail.

Back at the police station Hawkes made strong black coffee whilst April ran off another copy of the manuscript. Somewhere in one of the chapters Spence had surmised that one of them would find a reference to the demise of Charles Trent and ending up under a London tube train. Pulling a chair up to his desk April sat herself down.

'Valdis appears to have been operating for some time in London and yet nobody has ever pulled together any link. Doesn't that seem a little odd?' Hawkes and Spence both agreed. Swinging his chair around so that he could see bother faces, he replied.

'That's because he's shrewd. His modus operandi is never the same, well not that we've established as yet. Valdis varies his attacks without pattern, day, time and location. It's like he is able to fine balance both crime and execution, realising that experience will help fuel his book. Without any sign of remorse what he writes compels his need to hurt!'

'Aren't you giving him a little too much credit guv'nor, Valdis is no different to any other serial killer?'

Spence shrugged his shoulders. 'Maybe Tom, but I've a feeling that if we pull intelligence with other divisions and look at their cold-case files, we would struggle to find a recurring series of unexplained deaths. Valdis fits the category of a madman, but if he has been active in and around London for a number of years then he's done so quite successfully.'

Thomas Hawkes grinned back. 'Maybe he's a retired copper turned author and the lure of the pension wasn't enough!'

Spence nodded attentively at both sets of eyes looking at him. 'That's been known before Tom. Coppers around the world are not immune from turning to crime. There could be no excuse!'

'So do we start looking at all deaths where the victim had a link with books only that could be some list Spence, librarians, literary agents, book shops, publishers, the list could go on. If Valdis is warped and driven to murdering anyone connected with his path of revenge, we could very easily miss something ourselves.'

'No... let's concentrate on literary agents for the moment. We'll expand the parameters later if we need too.'

They were interrupted by a call from control to inform Spence that Dawson and Stebbings were on their way back from the airport accompanied by Roberto Cortelli.

'I bet that took him by surprise!' said Hawkes as he finished his coffee which had gone cold.

'Going by what Dawson told control, Cortelli didn't seem that surprised!'

April looked at them both, the realisation flashing through her mind. *'Bianchi.'*

'It figures in the equation quite nicely!' replied Spence.

'There are a lot of egos at stake here.' April added as she turned to see who had knocked on the office door. Moments later Hawkes pulled then door to be confronted by a pretty young blonde female officer who handed over an envelope. They exchanged pleasantries before the door was closed once again. 'That was Sharon Trevelyan wasn't it?'

Hawkes grinned, his eyes lighting up. 'Yes, she just transferred in on group one. I asked if she'd collect the security footage covering the platform and foyer.'

April shot a look at Spence. 'And of course, she said gladly.'

Spence palmed his upturned hands outward as though affairs of the heart we're not his concern.

'He has that effect upon some of the women around here!'

Hawkes slipped the disc into the machine and pressed *play*. Instantly several images filled the screen, one being Charles Trent. He looked relaxed as he walked down the platform choosing a suitable place to stand. Not far behind they saw the familiar black hat of the suspect.

'He might vary his modus operandi, but he wears the same outfit.'

As the seconds rolled on by they watched as the train lights appeared coming around the bend of the tunnel approach and as it entered the station Charles Trent lean forward to pick a carriage. Standing alongside him Spence felt April tense as the balled fist reached forward and pushed Trent onto the track. Momentarily the face beneath the hat turned towards the camera as though knowing that they would be watching later that evening. Chilvray was however shrewd. His look at the camera wasn't high enough to capture a full facial recognition.

Hawkes paused the recording, hit control print on the keyboard and ordered several copies.

'Same as the image passing by the petrol station.' He handed a copy to each of them.

Spence rubbed the show of stubble on his chin as he stared at the printout. 'Our priority now should be to find the widow of Pritchard Davis. In the likelihood that she was involved in the publication of *Retribution of the Angst* she could be next on the list of Valdis's victim's.'

April shook her head. 'He knew that we'd review the disc. He's taunting us!'

They watched the end of the recording, but the killer was smart enough not to look up, not until he was clear of the station entrance. Spence asked Hawkes to sweet talk Trevelyan into obtaining every inch of security footage that she could throughout her night shift. He would speak with the duty sergeant and inspector. 'Butter her up Tom by promising a meal in return. I'll cover any costs from petty cash!'

Seeing the back of Hawkes disappear through the door April rounded on Spence. *'I can see you as being a real mystery on Valentine's Day!'*

Walking down the corridor Thomas Hawkes had yet to establish if Sharon Trevelyan was attached, she was really pretty, but professional. The proposal of a meal in return for the favour did however pose a problem in that he had promised to meet up with Stephanie Garland and do the same.

'So if we share another meal, will that come from petty cash as well?'

113

'I thought you said that you'd cook the next at home!'

April wanted to kiss him there and then, but the office was overlooked by the yard out back and the living quarters. She held herself in check hoping that an opportunity would arise sometime soon. 'It'll only be Spaghetti Bolognese, nothing too elaborate.'

'Sounds divine. I'll bring the wine!'

The phone on his desk interrupted any further plans, when Spence replaced the receiver, he looked serious.

'Apparently Cortelli's getting anxious downstairs in the custody suite. I think it's time that Hawkes and myself headed down that way. Why don't you head off home and we'll catch up in the morning after you've been back to Trent's house.'

'Okay, but try not to make it a long chat Spence, you're looking tired!'

'I'll just have a chat about his involvement with D'Corscy and if needs be sow the seed of doubt. We can always invite him back for another discussion another day.'

Standing in the open door of his office April turned. 'Thanks Spence.'

'What for?' he asked.

'For making me feel wanted, we'll take it up over dinner!' with that she shut the door and headed back to the lab to collect her things. Sitting behind his desk Spence allowed himself a few moments to himself, making space in his life for April. Something inside him was stirring, something that had lay dormant for longer than he cared to remember.

Sitting in the car behind the steering wheel April had inserted the keys into the ignition, but not stirred the engine into life. She sat thinking about the man two floors above. It was a long time since any man had held her, touched her, let alone kissed her. Holding onto the steering wheel she gripped the leather bound circle of metal willing her luck to change. She was still staring straight ahead when somebody tapped on the window. April jumped with surprise, glad to see who was standing outside. *'Christ Sharon, you sent a shiver of alarm down my spine!'*

'I'm sorry, but you looked lost as though something bad had just descended upon your existence.'

April shook her head emphatically. 'Just thinking about men, or one in particular. I suppose that's what we do best.'

The young female officer smiled. 'I know what you mean. DC Hawkes has just promised me a meal out if I scout around for some security footage!'

April laughed. 'That's the dilemma we women have Sharon. We're never sure if we're being used or whether they are genuinely interested. I'd like to think that they are attracted for the right reasons.' She fired up the engine and said goodnight to Trevelyan driving up the electronic gate waiting for it to open. Moments later Sharon Trevelyan drove out the yard, but turned in the opposite direction, neither woman noticing the man who stepped out from the shadows.

Watching the car lights disappear at the end of the street Jack Chilvray turned his attention to the man standing at the window on the first floor. The fluorescent glare from the light in the office shielded much of the view outside and even when Chilvray walked away from where he had

115

been observing, he went unnoticed. Jack waved at the detective in charge of the investigation, but the gesture went undetected.

On the way home April received a text from Spence *'Nine pm post-mortem for Trent. Can we do dinner around seven tomorrow evening?'*

April waited until she was inside her flat before she sent a reply. Whatever she and Sharon Trevelyan thought about men, one thing was certain and that was that they always prioritised over other considerations when it came to feeding their stomachs.

Chapter Thirteen

Cortelli was tanned, casually dressed, but smart although frustratingly apprehensive when Spence and Hawkes took over from Dawson and Stebbings. Sitting in the middle of the table was a single, half consumed cup of cold coffee.

'Just how long am I going to be here?' he asked, clearly agitated at having been kept waiting for over an hour without much conversation from the two men who had met him at the airport?

'Hopefully, not much longer.' Spence replied as he sat opposite.

'And why am I under arrest?'

'You're not. You were met at the airport for your own protection Mr Cortelli.' The Italians expression to one of surprise.

'My protection, why... I do not consider myself to be in danger?'

Was it an act for the police, Spence couldn't be sure. In the seat, sat alongside Spence, Thomas Hawkes rolled his shoulders.

'What exactly was your relationship with Vivienne D'Corscy?'

Roberto Cortelli looked from one man to another, the obvious thoughts flashing back and forth inside his head. 'We were friends, we went to see shows and for meals together, that is not a crime... *No?*'

'And...?' Spence asked, expecting more.

'Sometimes I stay over with Vivvy, but nothing else. Things… well they had become somewhat tense in our friendship. It's been three, perhaps four months since I have seen her.' It wasn't the impression that Spence had got from Franco Bianchi.

'Before you returned to England, was you contacted by a member of your embassy?'

'Yes, but only to tell me of the tragic news regarding poor Vivienne.'

Spence could sense that Cortelli's answers were getting Hawkes agitated. 'You don't seem that over-wrought or distressed to hear that she's dead? He pressed.

'Of course I am sad. Vivienne and I…' he paused 'well we were friends. It hurts when you lose someone close.' Hawkes wasn't convinced. Cortelli's replies seemed well rehearsed.

'Have you ever heard of Mortimer Valdis?' he asked.

Cortelli shook his head 'Who is he, an opera singer?' he replied.

Hawkes edged his seat closer to the desk, coming closer to Cortelli. 'You of course know of Charles Trent?'

'Yes. He was with me and Vivienne sometimes to see a show. Interesting man, although difficult to like. I think you English term men like him… an oddball.'

'Eccentric.' Spence corrected. 'Charles Trent was killed today. He was pushed under a tube train earlier this evening. *Murdered.*'

Roberto Cortelli was visibly startled by the news. The trip this time to Italy had been short, but he had not expected to hear about either being murdered.

'You said that I was in danger. Does the killer know me?'

Hawkes sensed a change of attitude. 'Quite possibly. Maybe if you told us everything, we could help.' Spence wanted to smile, but he didn't instead he just stared directly at the interpreter.

Roberto Cortelli realised that the police had no intention of letting him go until he did co-operate. He sipped the cold mug of coffee, knowing that he was trapped.

'Before I left, I went to see Vivvy, Vivienne. We argued because I had accused her of being involved with Trent. He was a funny man, always touching her, putting his around her waist. I thought he was gay the way he spoke and acted, but Vivienne told me that he was once married. I didn't see that was relevant. On one occasion I had returned from Rome unannounced and found Charles Trent coming out of her bathroom in his dressing gown. I became angry and accused her of sleeping with him. She denied the accusation saying that Charles Trent had felt unwell upon leaving the theatre and that she had offered him her settee for the night wanting to make sure that he wasn't alone.

'The argument before I left London this last time was bad. I said that if she loved me she would sleep with me every night, but she told me that it wasn't what she wanted from our relationship. I felt offended. I am Italian and so is she. It's what we do the best... we argue, fight then we make love. That evening however she threw me out. In the street below I stood there watching until her bedroom light went before I left. That night I kissed the air vowing never to see her again.'

Cortelli realised to what he had implied, he quickly held up his hands in his defence. 'What I meant Mr Spence is that I was angry, I was hurt, but in time I would forgive. I would never have hurt Vivienne, not ever. It was hard however, knowing that she was friends with Charles Trent. It was like he was laughing at me!'

'And when you outside looking back up at her bedroom, was there anybody else around that could verify that statement?'

Cortelli frowned and nodded. 'Why yes, but how did you know! There was a man and he walked towards me. He stopped and stood beside me looking up at the bedroom where her shadow was dancing across the ceiling.' As if re-enacting the moment Cortelli looked up at the ceiling of the interview room. 'Thinking out loud, I crossed myself then asked *'how many men does the whore know?'* after which I said goodnight to the man and stormed off walking home.'

'The man, can you describe him?' Hawkes asked.

'It was dark outside and the nearest streetlight is a good fifty feet away. I remember was that he was wearing a long black leather coat, a nice coat and a hat.'

Spence hung his head low and sighed. *'Anything about the man's face, the colour of his eyes, facial hair, his teeth or jewellery that you noticed?'*

Cortelli shrugged. 'It was dark Inspector. I was so angry at Vivienne, I didn't really take any notice. I didn't even stop to think why he had

120

walked up to me and stood there staring up at her bedroom. I was so angry I couldn't have cared less that night.'

Taking the stills from an envelope Hawkes slid them into view so that cortelli could see the images. 'Is this the man who stood beside you?'

Cortelli nodded. 'Yes, that's him!'

Next from the same envelope Hawkes took out a black and white photograph of Vivienne D'Corscy as she had been found in her flat. Cortelli swallowed hard and tried to look away, but Hawkes thrust the image under his nose.

'Oh Mother of Mary, what have they done to my beautiful Vivienne. She has become a monster!'

Spence took the forensic photograph from Hawkes as though studying the contents. 'Not Miss D'Corscy, Mr Cortelli, but the man who savagely tortured and executed her. He is the monster!' Spence banged his fist down on the table. 'Now think... was there anything about the man that you saw outside of her flat, anything that could help us catch him?'

Cortelli took another brief look and then pushed away the photograph of the man on the platform. 'If I could remember anything I would tell you, honest I would, but it was dark and I was angry. I didn't really look at him!'

'Did he say anything to you?'

'Only that whores cost men more than what they were worth.'

Spence pushed several more photographs under Cortelli's nose. They were taken under the tube train where Charles Trent had been decapitated and lost both legs. Cortelli looked at what was left of the man with whom he had despised so vehemently.

'The man when he spoke he had a northern accent. I know these things because I am an interpreter and languages is my profession. That is all he said and then I walked away.'

'Can you tell me what *'ricordare a casa'* means?'

'Why, remember home. All Italians know this. Vivienne had a ring with the inscription.'

Spence unfurled the fingers of his hand revealing a badly dented and scratched ring. Vivienne D'Corscy's ring.

'That's the one!' Cortelli looked at it as though it would suddenly burst into flames. 'Her father gave it to Vivienne before she left to come to England.'

'Did you go to any book events with Miss D'Corscy?'

'Yes, some.'

Hawkes pushed the image of Mortimer Valdis in front of Cortelli once again. 'And was this man ever there?'

Roberto Cortelli shook his head. 'Many people go to such places and always there is noise and free wine. It is a busy place. I don't remember ever seeing him at any.'

'Do you know where this event took place?'

Cortelli studied the photograph, then flicked the tips of his fingers together. 'Yes. It was last spring at a small bookshop between Haverstock Hill and Hampstead. Not a big place, but served good wine. I was never in any of the photographs.'

Spence lent forward. 'One last question Mr Cortelli and then you're free to go. Was it Mr Bianchi from the embassy in London who made contact with you in Rome?'

Cortelli hesitated for a moment, but decided it would be unwise to fool with the two men sitting opposite him. Each had proved that they meant business. It would be much easier to face Bianchi's wrath than theirs.

'Yes. He came to my hotel in Rome and he warned me that the police in London would want to talk to me. He advised me not to involve the embassy in any such enquiry and that it would be detrimental to my career prospects if I did.'

'Did you consider that as a threat against your welfare?'

Cortelli looked into the beaker where the last dregs of his coffee had formed a circular pattern. *'When Vivienne came to Britain she found that she had a problem with her visa and work permit. Franco Bianchi sorted it for her, but he asked favours in return for what he had done. I was in the next office one afternoon when I overheard Bianchi and another embassy aide talking about the D'Corscy family. There has long been bad blood between Vivienne's father, Ernesto and Franco Bianchi.*

'Historically Ernesto who went to school with Bianchi's elder brother had reputedly bullied the older boy for a good many years. At that time, as

123

they do now, the D'Corscy family had wealth and respect throughout the region whereas the Bianchi brothers came from a poor family. Franco, Stefano and their parents struggled to survive and to make matters worse when Stefano left school the only employment was on the D'Corscy estate.

'Franco staunchly believes that his brother's death on the wine producing estate was partly due to the poor working conditions under which he was made to work. You see Stefano was responsible for making sure that the pesticides used to prevent the vines from being attacked by pests, was himself affected by the deadly mix. Over time it corroded his lungs and sucked the life from his body and Stefano died a horrible death. From that day Franco vowed revenge. When poor Vivienne arrived Franco saw a way to destroy Ernesto D'Corscy. Deflowering his only daughter was in his eyes the sweetest retribution.'

Much to his surprise Spence released Cortelli. The Italian thought that the police would protect him and put him up in a safe house until the killer was caught, but instead to his dismay he was shown the door of the station and told not to wander far as he might be needed again for further questioning.

*****

But a stone's throw from where Cortelli had been released Jack Chilvray sat entrenched at his writing desk clutching a glass of white wine. He observed the frantic fluttering dance of a single moth under the outside light, wondering why the beautifully marked insects were relentless in their nightly transverse orientation, welcoming bright illumination as though it were a god to which they were a slave. Swilling the wine around inside his mouth he felt that there was no end to moth's plight, nor his own, not until his latest book was complete.

Tapping the screen into life then scrolling down through the list of evening arrivals he let the cursor rest on flight RA 8576 from Rome, noting that it had arrived on time. He smiled to himself finishing off the remainder of the wine.

'Welcome home my friend. We really should meet up soon only I feel that I owe you a favour in honour of sweet Vivienne.'

Chapter Fourteen

Hawkes had watched Cortelli walk down the front steps of the station and disappear from sight. He turned as a car went by, uninterested contemplating the events of the day, another busy day. Bit by bit the hazy jigsaw was beginning to take shape, but there were still a number of missing pieces.

'Nothing ever seems straight forward in this job sometimes.' Spence looked across to where Thomas Hawkes was sat on the edge of his desk looking at the photographs that April had produced. 'This investigation is like these images black and white with nothing in the middle!'

'That's the frustrating part Tom, always has been.' Spence sat back in his chair and kicked off his shoes before resting them on the desktop.

'Should we put a tail on Cortelli, it might help?'

Spence shook his head. 'No. We've only limited manpower and we've already got Trevelyan over at Russell Square. I dare not approach the section sergeant again and as for any more of his troops.' Beyond the reflection of the window he watched the lights of the houses, flats and streets flicker, thinking about April.

'How did it go with Trevelyan, you never did say?'

'We have a date sometime next week.' Spence grinned. It reminded him of the old days, when a favour for a favour was the norm and life was much simpler. He was still absently watching the lights when he thought out loud.

'I'd expect Cortelli to scurry back home where his first call will be to Franco Bianchi. They've got something going between them and I can't quite figure what. In a couple of days' time we'll invite Cortelli back in for another little chat. Adding the pressure is bound to make him crack.'

'And Valdis… it's certainly looking like his motive is murder!'

Spence dropped his feet back down to the floor. 'It rules out coincidence. D'Corscy was tortured, mutilated and murdered, then Trent met with an unfortunate death under a train, helped along by a strong arm. What we need to establish is what each did to warrant their death.'

'And Bianchi's involvement, blackmailing Vivienne D'Corscy for sex. It's a bit heavy just to get back at the father.'

'That's probably all it does take Tom. Bianchi had a motive, spurred on by his late brother's demise. Bianchi had probably been harbouring his grudge for a number of years watching D'Corscy and the development of his daughter. When she came to England seeking work he must have felt like a poker player, holding all the trump cards. Manipulation is a powerful tool in the hands of the wrong man. We on the other hand just pick up garbage, produce them before the court and move on. It's why I like the dogs to playing cards.'

In the silence the hand on the dial of the clock moved forward landing on midnight. Spence slipped both feet back into his shoes and stood pushing the chair back.

'Come on Tom, we've another day ahead tomorrow. Somewhere out there the answers are just begging to be found.'

'Yeah, I suppose so.'

Spence switched off the office light and pulled the door shut. 'Make sure you give Trevelyan a call before you Tom. I just want to be reassured that she's okay. I don't want her bumping into Valdis.'

Sitting in his car with the engine ticking over, he watched as Hawkes ended the conversation sitting in his own vehicle, when he gave the thumbs up, it was time to head off home. Spence rarely used the car and most days it sat within the safety of the station carpark, but tonight he could not be bothered to walk the short distance home. He waved as Thomas Hawkes moved towards the gate before joining the traffic going past.

Hawkes was a damn good detective, cutting the mustard better than any young protégé that he'd had before. The one advantage that Hawkes had over most others in the station was his looks, rugged, but discerningly charming, especially when he smiled. Spence engaged gear and moved forward feeling his aching limbs rebel against the pedals.

When he got home he placed his keys, wallet and ID on the side, wondering whether it was too late to call April. She would want to know about Cortelli of that he was certain. Activating her number he waited for her to answer.

*****

Waiting patiently knowing that their quarry was inside the two men had kept to the shadows, parked out of sight of the patrols who had come and gone without paying any attention to the blue coloured car entrenched between a commercial van and a small goods lorry. Having maintained a safe distance back from Gatwick where they had witnessed Cortelli being picked up by a couple of detectives they had followed their car back to the station.

'He's been in there a long time.' Remarked the passenger, becoming restless of the wait.

'Relax, it shouldn't be for much longer. They've got nothing on him. He'll appear any minute now!'

The passenger eased himself back into the leather upholstery, the waiting was always the bit that he hated the most. Matteo liked applying muscle, feeling the adrenalin run through his veins as he carried out what he was paid to do.'

'Okay, but I'm getting hungry. It's been a long time since we ate.'

The driver tapped Matteo's shoulder when Cortelli suddenly appeared.

'See... did I not say, that the weasel would appear very soon.' Matteo righted himself in the seat and cracked his knuckles.

Standing at the head of the stone steps leading down to the pavement Roberto looked both ways as though expecting someone. Taking the packet of Italian cigarettes from his pocket he lit one. Extending the handle of the case he hoisted it clear of the steps descending to the even surface below. A short distance away a car started up.

'He looks nervous…' Matteo observed as he rubbed his palms together 'I'm going to enjoy this, that smarmy bastard was always looking down his nose at me whenever we passed in the corridor.'

The driver checked the review mirror then pulled away from the kerbside. 'Men like Cortelli are like rabbits Matteo. Give them a shadow and they'll hide behind it as though it were a mountain, but catch in the illumination of a cars lights and they have nowhere to run. *Here we go!*'

Cortelli didn't look back nor up feeling the stare of the detective who was watching. He kept to an even pace as he passed the houses beyond the police station wanting to give the impression that he didn't have a care in the world. With just five metres to go to the turn he could go left and increase his pace. From the darkened interior of the car the occupants saw him take the turn then disappear.

'Don't lose him,' cried Matteo as the driver engaged second gear.

'He'll not get far, it's a long street down to the main road and our rabbit is not as fit as he believes himself to be!'

Turning at the junction the driver increased speed as Matteo saw Cortelli look round.

'He's seen us!'

The driver patted the passenger's forearm. 'No… for all he knows we're just another car leaving the station. *Get ready, we're almost upon him!*'

Cortelli sensed that he was in danger, guessed that the car was coming for him. He started to run, but the case was heavy and slowed him down as it bounced about over the uneven surface of the pavement slabs. Hearing the engine of the car increase in revs he knew that it was close. Cortelli let go of the case handle not caring as to where or how it landed, self-preservation now his only priority. His legs propelled him forward in a sprint.

Suddenly at a break between the parked cars he saw the darkened shape of the passenger jump from the car's interior. The interpreter recognised the man immediately, the huge unnerving grin on the face of the man mountain growing in stature as Matteo stood up, flexing his muscles.

'You've nowhere to run little rabbit, come quietly and it will be less painful for you!'

Cortelli tried to side-step the advancing man, but a clenched fist, expertly aimed caught him in the side and immediately expelled the air from his right lung. Cortelli sensed his doom.

'Please Matteo, I didn't say anything that I shouldn't have!'

The big Italian grinned as he hit his quarry again across the side of the head. Cortelli immediately slumped against the brick wall of the house where the car had come to a halt.

'I never mentioned anything about what you said inside the station, but you will and soon!'

Grabbing the collar of his jacket Cortelli was propelled over to the rear door of the car where he was forced to get inside with Matteo sitting alongside. A light in the house came on, but by the time that occupant came to the window the car was already several vehicles down the road and going too fast to be recognised.

'What was it?' asked the husband as he yawned and lay his head back down on the pillow, adjusting the duvet on his side.

'Nothing, just bloody kids again out joy-riding and waking everybody up in the process.'

The husband patted the top of the duvet. 'Come on, get back in, I've kept the bed warm!'

Scattered across the pavement where the case had landed heavily against a brick wall the contents of the case has spilled forth, including clothes, a pair of shoes, toiletries and a travel wallet.

Doubled up and hurting on the back seat of the car Roberto Cortelli could only wonder what lie ahead. Menacingly Matteo sat beside him grinning like a Cheshire cat that had licked the cream, yet knew that another tub was waiting back at their destination.

'I will pay you both handsomely if you let me out at the next corner. I'll disappear and never return to England, I promise!' Cortelli's voice was breaking as he pleaded with his captors. In the rear view mirror he saw the driver's eyes smile back.

'You don't have enough money to pay us both Roberto and Matteo doesn't like being denied his only pleasure.' To make sure that Cortelli understood the huge Italian cracked his knuckles together.

Blending in with the night-time traffic in the city Cortelli felt the warm trickle of urine wet his trousers. On either side late night revellers shouted and laughed as they sped past. He thought about trying to attract their attention, but Matteo wasn't a man that you pissed off nor tested.

Soon both pedestrians and traffic dwindled and became less as the driver manoeuvred between parked cars then slowed. Cortelli noticed that even the street lights beyond the car windows were not as bright as he had remembered. As the electric gate to the carpark swung back the car gently rolled down the short ramp to the underground facility beneath the pavement level where it was much darker than above ground.

Standing on the far side like a silhouetted manikin a man was waiting illuminated by a low wattage bulb overhead. He could just make out the makes face. Roberto Cortelli heard the electric gate swung back into place, recognising that his last hope of escape had just gone begging. When the car stopped not far from the open doorway Matteo lent across coming in very close. *'I'm hungry, so say what you have to say, tell the fucking truth and don't piss him off. If you do, you will suffer and remember I need to eat and soon!'*

The car door was suddenly pulled open and Roberto Cortelli was dragged from the interior by another two men whom he hadn't seen waiting, once again a fist exploded into his side. He fell forward unable to resist, knowing that a rib was fractured.

'Take him to the wine cellar.' The voice was familiar, self-assured and confident. Cortelli looked up, but he saw no compassion in the man's eyes that had given the order. Dragged along by the soles of his feet he roughly manhandled along an unfamiliar corridor then unceremoniously thrust into a waiting chair where his wrists were bound to the wooden arms.

Chapter Fifteen

Roberto Cortelli nervously looked around the stone brick cellar where the walls were lined with dusty racks full of champagne and wine. Directly above him was sited a single light bulb giving off just enough light for him to make out the men standing nearby. Dressed predominantly in black they looked threatening, but most intimidating of them all was Matteo. Still cracking his knuckles he was hungrier than before.

'You want me to soften him up a bit more?' he asked.

A man stepped forward and Cortelli recognised Bianchi once again. The ambassador's aide held up a hand. 'Not yet Matteo, lets' see what he has to say first.'

Cortelli tried to avoid the glare of the light as he raised his head to look at Bianchi. 'What is this Franco, I thought that we were friends?' Bianchi laughed as he walked round the chair to the amusement of the other men who were laughing as well.

'An amusing assumption Roberto, but friendship demands loyalty. What I see sitting before me is anything but trustworthy. I thought that I made it quite clear when we entered into our little arrangement that we would always be up front with one another!'

Cortelli kept his focus on Matteo more than any of the others. It was the big man that he feared the most, even above Franco Bianchi. 'Have I not always done as you instructed Franco?' The doubt showing in his expression as Bianchi continued to circle the solitary chair.

'I thought that was the case until you met up with Chiara Ricci on your last trip. A little bird tells me that you wanted to start a side line of your own, cut the profit margin and put your additional funds towards your retirement fund.'

Cortelli looked anxiously worried. Despite the chill in the air, beads of perspiration were beginning to form around his hairline. Standing behind the chair Bianchi grabbed Roberto Cortelli's chin and yanked it up hard thrusting the skull back so the full glare of the light exploded into each eyeball. The pain emanating from his cracked rib shot up through the nerve cortex to the brain causing him to yell out. Cortelli tried to shake away the hand holding his chin, but Bianchi was stronger than he had imagined.

'She lies Franco. She was just a girl that I picked up in Rome and shared some time with. It was nothing special, but she's obviously got the wrong impression of my visit.'

Matteo suddenly stepped forward and punched Cortelli hard in the solar plexus. He immediately lurched forward sensing that it had been the wrong answer. Bianchi grabbed the top of his hair and pulled Cortelli's head back up once again. 'Chiara Ricci is my niece and my sister's daughter is loyal to her family. She never lies and especially not to her favourite uncle!' He let the head fall back down again on the chest, causing the injured man to cry out.

'It wasn't meant to be much Franco, two maybe three percent at the most, just enough to supplement my salary and build a small nest egg for when I retired. The price of wine fluctuates all the time on the market so I didn't think that you would notice.'

With a nod of his head Matteo punched the interpreter once again, only this time across the jaw. Cortelli's head went to the right and he thought the blow would break his neck. His head was still ringing when Bianchi slapped his cheek.

'Concentrate Roberto, you can't go to sleep just yet. Two detectives met you at the airport and took you back to the station. It was a long visit seeing that you were not under arrest. What was it that they wanted with you?'

Cortelli shook his head clear and adjusted his vision. He felt the trickle of blood at the side of his mouth and his teeth on one side felt loose. 'Only to show me some upsetting photographs of Vivienne.' He didn't mention Charles Trent surmising Bianchi would not have been interested, nor known about him.

Franco Bianchi came around front again and stood directly in front of Matteo. It was a good sign and offered protection from another beating.

'Sources tell me that Mr Trent lost both feet and his head under the wheels of the tube train. A quick end to a problem by all accounts. He must have seriously pissed off somebody don't you think Roberto!' In the shadows the sniggers were just audible.

Cortelli nodded. 'I know, the police showed me photographs of him too!'

'It's very distressing and perhaps coincidental how two people that you knew rather well should both die in tragic and how shall we say,

137

disturbing circumstances. Do you think Roberto it was something to do with loyalty?'

Cortelli tried to focus his reply on Franco, but he could see Matteo swaying from side to side behind the embassy aide, wanting to get to him.

'I had not involvement in their deaths, both set of circumstances occurred whilst I was either out of the country or on my way back. The police know this.'

Bianchi came in close with Matteo not far behind. 'And what else do they know. You were there a long time just to look at some Polaroid's?'

'Nothing Franco, I swear it. The just going over old ground asking the same questions about me and Vivienne. It was like they were lost for clues as to the motive of her death.'

Roberto Cortelli saw Bianchi's eyes rise as he looked at a man standing at the back of the cellar, so far hidden in the shadows that he was not visible. Moments later he looked back at the man tied to the chair.

'I had her apartment tapped sometime back as I wanted to hear what you had to say to her. Some of the conversations between you were interesting, some less so. In a way her death has come at the right time. I am now able to exact my revenge upon Ernesto D'Corscy.'

Roberto Cortelli looked through the man who was his boss. Alongside his fear sat doubt. Did Bianchi arrange to have Vivienne D'Corscy killed so that she would never talk about the blackmail, her submission to his demands and her father's shame. Looking around the room at Matteo and the other faces that were barely visible, it didn't seem that inconceivable.

'Matteo tells me that you looked nervous when you stepped out onto the steps of the police station as though you were expecting to see somebody waiting for you. Was you?'

Cortelli shook his head. 'No… no, I was just tense. That was the first time that I have ever been inside a police station. It was an experience that I wanted to forget. Standing up there I didn't know what to expect.'

'Did you mention anything to them about my helping Miss D'Corscy with her work visa?'

'Cortelli paused for a moment so that he could think straight. 'Only that you helped, nothing else.'

'So now they know that I have been acquainted with her. You have placed me in a very awkward position Roberto, a situation whereby now I will be questioned once again by the police. This will not please the ambassador.' Bianchi straightened up and stretched back his shoulders. 'It's been a long day and it's now into the early hours of the next day. My Maria will wonder what is keeping me so long at work.'

Franco Bianchi paced back and forth as he thought through the problem. Roberto Cortelli had influenced so many arrangements that he had put in place, arrangements that had taken years to set up. He wondered how he could resolve matters quietly, quickly, but not lose face. He looked hard at the man sitting in the chair. There was no telling what he had told the police.

'Like you, I am a roman catholic and although confessional absolves us of our sins, there are some that extend beyond the walls of the Vatican.

Some sins need to be addressed closer to home. The embassy is a mere diplomatic representation of a country in another's country. The ambassador is a figurehead who hosts messages on behalf of his or her head of state. I pull the strings for our ambassador here in London Roberto. He trusts me because I have earned his confidence. Your involvement with Miss D'Corscy and Mr Trent has tainted our good name and shown you to be a disloyal subject of Italy. Mussolini suffered from a delusional psychosis that ended with him being strung up. Maybe by trying to involve me in a police investigation you thought that your paltry two, perhaps three percent could be much more. The problem that I have here, which is keeping me from my bed, is what to do with you!'

'Be merciful Franco, please and remember that we are friends. I will pay you back anything that I have taken and with interest. I will leave England and never return. As the lord is our Saviour, I swear it!'

Franco Bianchi fisted the air in triumph. At last he had the answer. 'Exodus…' Roberto 'Thou should not take the name of the Lord they god in vain'. Are you that naïve that you do you not understand the power that I wield within these walls?' Bianchi spread his arms wide. 'The Pope runs the Vatican, but I am the master of this piece of Italy here in England.'

Cortelli could only lower his head in shame as he begged forgiveness, but it was beyond that time. Not even the church could save him now. From his back pocket Franco Bianchi took a crumpled letter.

'You tried to destroy me whilst you were in Rome. You sent my wife a letter telling her all about my involvement with the wine importation and Vivienne D'Corscy. You foolishly believed that by the time you had

140

returned from your latest trip that she would have read the letter, started divorce proceedings against me and then disgraced me with the ambassador, knowing that I would be deported back to Italy.' Bianchi waved the envelope under Cortelli's nose. 'As luck would have it, I had forgotten something the day that I met the postman coming up the drive. My wife comes from Naples, not Rome. In fact she doesn't know anybody in Rome. Thinking it suspicious that she should be receiving correspondence from the capital I opened the letter. It was fortunate that I did.'

Whilst another held Cortelli by the shoulders Matteo rained down punches indiscriminately. When Bianchi stopped the onslaught, he continued.

'My wife enjoys her life here and she likes London very much. It would have been a tragedy to have been involved in divorce proceedings. You see Maria also knows too much and regrettable accidents are an everyday occurrence is such a busy city, accidents such as the one that befell Mr Trent. You have become a serious liability that I can no longer afford to have around.'

Before Roberto Cortelli had time to open his mouth and defend himself Matteo had his strong hands around the interpreter's neck squeezing the life from his body. When his head fell forward like that of a rag doll Bianchi checked to see that he was dead.

Heading towards the door of the cellar and home Franco Bianchi gave instruction for the body to be tossed into the Thames at high tide and weighed down sufficiently where the strong undercurrents would carry him out to sea. Beyond the estuary the fish, crabs and other marine life would do their bit to pick his flesh clean of his bones. In time Roberto Cortelli would be completely forgotten.

*****

In Hetherington Terrace where Cortelli had frantically discarded his suitcase it was found by a wandering vagrant out early rummaging through residential waste bins. Making sure that he wasn't seen the man gathered together the expensive looking clothes, shoes and travel wallet, clipping shut the lock.

It was a good find and he could sell the good quality contents to people that he knew down the market trading them for ready cash that would keep him watered and fed for a month, maybe more. When he examined the contents of the wallet his find would be even better, finding Cortelli's money, passport and a key to his home.

Chapter Sixteen

April awoke with a start, the bad dream coming at her like a blazing chariot down a long dark narrow alley. Sitting bolt upright in bed she felt the trickle of perspiration run down the notch in her neck, slipping eventually between the crease of her cleavage. The dream had been realistic and not just a nightmare. Depressing the button on top of the alarm clock she swung herself around and dropped her legs over the side of the bed. Nightmares were nothing new, but none had been this bad, not for a long time.

Turning the tap in the shower she let it run until it was warm enough to step under, wanting, no needing to wash away all thoughts of Barry from her body and mind. Towelling herself down after she checked herself in the mirror making sure that where he had hit her didn't show. *'Don't be fucking stupid,'* she was annoyed with herself for checking, *'it was a bad dream, nothing else!'*

When she was done she took one last look only this time turning left then right. She slapped the flesh of her posterior before lifting each breast. 'Not bad girl, considering!'

Adding a splash of perfume behind the ears and under the jaw line she hoped that it wouldn't go unnoticed by Spence and secondly act as a barrier to the overpowering air of formaldehyde. His late night call had been brief, but she was glad that he called.

Standing between Spence and Hawkes she couldn't be sure which appreciated her perfume the most. As they watched Susan Weekes push the cadaver to one side, she called them over as her assistant held the body in place on the examination table. 'You might want to see this...' she pointed to the area where Charles Trent had been stabbed in the back with the fist and pushed.

'We all know that after death coagulation begins to take place finding the lowest point of gravity and that the process of hypostasis, where the blood turns blue, it happens somewhere around ten hours later.' Using her free hand she placed it at the point where Chilvray had pushed Trent onto the track. 'That's where the coagulation is darkest!' they lowered the body once again.

'Having seen the platform security recording and calculated the angle that Charles Trent was leaning to view the oncoming train, it would have taken a strong man to push him over the edge.' She focused her interest specifically on Spence. 'The deceased weighed in at just over a hundred and fourteen kilogrammes. Eighteen stone to us old timers.'

'And the height?'

'A little under six feet, by a few centimetres. Trent was a little overweight, much of that however was down to bone structure and muscle, not fat. Our killer knew what he was doing and at which point to strike.'

'Similar to that of a hammer fist used in martial arts or perhaps the army?' Hawkes asked.

'Yes detective. A powerful forward thrust delivered with quick and intense force. On any other person it would have shattered the smaller bones in the body, but the deceased at some stage of his life had looked after himself and built up his muscle structure.' Spence looked at the naked body on the table, it didn't seem feasible that Trent was a keep-fit fanatic, but then everybody had a past and time alone saw to it that things changed. On the table nearest the deceased and staring their way was his head, as once attached to his body.

'He looked shocked.' April suddenly declared remembering her first sighting of the senior editor. Spence walked around all four sides of the examination table.

'I'd be bloody shocked seeing the train heading down the track and with my head in the way!' Hawkes averted his eyes elsewhere stifling a laugh. Only Weekes caught him smiling.

She rounded on him, her eyes burning through his 'What I was referring too was that Charles Trent didn't expect to be murdered. He lived a simple life, loved books, the theatre and attended author signings. Nothing complicated until he took a dive onto the tracks.'

Spence looked puzzled. 'And your point is?'

'That there's every possibility that the book submitted by Mortimer Valdis, Death Belies the Innocent might not have been the only submission. Trent has been at the agency a long time, long before D'Corscy. There's every possibility that he came across other work by Valdis, a manuscript that was never entered into the records. We have to explore every likelihood!'

Spence frowned and nodded, April was right, every possibility had to be investigated. He smiled at April then looked at Weekes. 'Was Trent a homosexual?'

'If we can continue, we might find out.' Weekes went through the familiar sequence performed at every autopsy confirming that Charles Trent had never had intimate relations with a man.

'Not that it is of significant importance to the investigation Inspector, but the deceased had a malignant growth on the right lower lobe of his lung. Without preventative treatment he would probably have been dead within six to nine months.'

They took themselves to Ted's café where they each ordered a substantial breakfast not knowing how the day was going to pan out. Sitting on the chair alongside Spence April could feel the energy flowing through his body to hers. When Hawkes excused himself to go the washroom April took full advantage of the moment to have Spence alone.

'I had a real bad dream last night. They don't happen often, but it's not something that I neither control nor invite. The thing is Spence on the way over to the coroners I was analysing aspects of the nightmare. In it, Barry was a young DC in the division. It was a short time after I had completed my own training that I accompanied Barry to a domestic burglary.

'Walking around the place that had been burgled I suddenly realised that it was Vivienne D'Corscy's flat. The décor was slightly different, but not the layout. Back then the block was called Pembroke Mansions and Vivienne D'Corscy wasn't the occupant.'

When Hawkes returned she continued having told Spence the reason for the nightmare. Hawkes sensed that he had missed something.

'Nothing that can't be put right by me,' Spence replied, he felt April's hand rest on his upper leg. 'April seems to think that Waterfall Heights needs another visit. It was called something else around ten to fifteen years ago, maybe jogging memories will help turn up something that we've overlooked.'

Hawkes shrugged his shoulders. 'I'm not sure. They seemed a disinterested lot when I called.'

'Alright, you pay Hamptons another visit. Finding plod on their doorstep once again won't go down well, but at least they'll get the message that we're serious about this investigation. By now they'll have been told about the accident involving Charles Trent. April and myself will take Waterfall Heights.'

Rising from the table Ted held up the tin. 'Soon...' he muttered and Spence smiled. It was a night to look forward too.

'Something I don't know about?' April asked.

'Only that you have another admirer. Ted couldn't take his eyes off you, he must have caught a whiff of the perfume that you're wearing today. It's something you don't forget!'

'So you did notice. And there was I thinking that it had been a waste of a good scent.' She knew that he'd noticed in the examination room, but it was nice to be told.

Spence however was out of practice with courtship and he proved it. 'Anything was better than that bloody awful smell. I never get used to formaldehyde and I don't know how Weekes puts up with it, day in, day out.'

April looked hurt, like she had been slapped across the face, he realised his mistake and made amends. 'Sorry that came out all wrong. What I meant was it's nice on you and I'm glad you did wear it today because going to the coroners all the more easier!'

April exhaled, it was better than nothing and he had tried to put things right. On the way over to Waterfall Heights, she asked about the talk with Cortelli.

'You didn't go into a lot of detail very early this morning when you called?'

'There wasn't much to tell. Bianchi had an involvement with D'Corscy sorting out a permit problem, but wanted sexual favours in return. It appears that there's a grudge between Bianchi and her father, something going back as far as work and school days. I got the impression that Cortelli is involved in something else, unrelated maybe to the D'Corscy case, but maybe involving Bianchi, although he wouldn't say. He seems in awe of the man, scared even.'

For the next five to ten minutes April was quiet, unusually quiet.

'Are you alright?' he asked. 'Is it because I didn't mention the perfume sooner?'

April grinned. 'Forget the perfume, I'm fine. Hearing about another female being manipulated, abused in that fashion, stirs emotions inside that make me angry. Barry did similar and I hated him for it. I hated him for lots of other reasons as well, but control is a domineering, dangerous tool.' She parked the car and switched off the engine. 'I trust you though Spence. You wouldn't have got the invite to dinner tonight unless I felt completely safe.'

Spence seemed somewhat distracted by his thoughts. 'The frailty of human emotion is fine line April balancing precariously between good and bad. Down the centuries women have been getting the raw end of male dominance, brutality and abuse, albeit physical or mental. Men, including myself find a way to hide their shame.'

April turned in her seat to face him. 'If you're referring to Siobhan, then I would probably say that her frailty was almost certainly of her own making. Sometimes Spence a relationship is just too fragile to survive. You certainly don't strike me as the *bastard* type. Barry was that and ten times over. On reflection, I should have been a much stronger person and fought back, finding something heavy that I could hold and whack him with it... *fucking* hard!'

Spence smiled, April very rarely swore and the only time that she had been known to use profanities was when she was recalling a bad memory, generally about her ex-husband. He just smiled believing it better to remain silent. Spence knew of and about Barry Moyne, but without first-hand knowledge it was inappropriate to judge.

'So where do we start?' she asked.

Spence was glad to change the subject. 'By calling on immediate neighbours, they're generally good for gossip and the like.' He looked up

149

at the flat belonging to Elsie Bracknell who had reported the strange dripping from her ceiling. 'We'll knock on all the doors except the flat below D'Corscy's.'

*****

Taking the lift the one floor Andrea found herself looking across at the handsome young detective wondering if he was attached. He was about seven maybe eight years older than her, but she liked her boyfriends to be older, more mature. Having been called down to reception by an agency temp she had decided to take the lift where she could be alone with him. Her hopes however were dashed the moment that the lift doors slid to one side and she saw Stephanie Garland look up and smile. She got up from her desk and approached.

'Word was that you'd be back sometime soon!'

Hawkes perceived that she didn't seem overly distressed by the news of Charles Trent's death. 'What's the mood in the office?' he asked as he looked around.

'People are naturally concerned. One death in the office is expected from time to time, but two and close together is unnerving. Was Charles Trent's an accident or was he murdered?'

Hawkes was cautious wanting to see what other people had to say before he released any particulars. 'We're not sure, it's one of the reasons that I've come back this morning.'

Stephanie Garland understood. She suggested that they get a cup of coffee in the kitchenette down the corridor where it was easier to talk. Hawkes followed.

'I read the manuscript, written by Mortimer Valdis. I found it disturbing in places and graphic. Had I not been in the profession I might have said that the reader expected more from the book.'

'In what way?'

'Writers have dreams, aspirations to become a name, have their work scripted for film or plays. Valdis writes without passion, but a need.' She paused. 'As though he executes every chapter with precise actions. Premeditated and with nothing left to chance.'

Garland was thinking along the lines of Spence, Hawkes and Geddings. She was intuitive and realistic.

'Trent's death is being treated as highly suspicious. Despite a packed platform there are no witnesses who saw what actually happened, just him falling. What was the opinion of Charles Trent throughout the office?' Hawkes could almost read the thoughts going through her head just by looking at the lines that had creased her forehead.

'On a personal level I could never really make him out. He was eccentric, but we all knew that. As a young man I believe that he had joined the foreign legion running away from something, only nobody knew quite what. Returning to England he devoted the rest of his life to books, the theatre and by all accounts Vivienne D'Corscy.'

Hawkes listened, the legion would explain where Trent had honed his body to the peak of fitness.

'Do you think that they were lovers?'

She shrugged her shoulder raising both palms. 'I wasn't here, so I can't rightly say.'

'How did he make you feel,' this time he paused 'when you were close, passing on the stairs, in the corridor or the lift?'

The lines on her forehead creased deeper. 'Creepy. I was never comfortable in his company. There was something about Charles Trent that made my skin crawl. It made me shudder to think of him touching me!'

'Was that the same for any of the other women in the office?'

'Some, but I can't speak for them all.'

'What about the men?'

She smirked. 'Some thought that he was queer, the older ones, well they reserved judgement.'

'Any you, what did you think?'

'No. I don't think he was, but there again I never invited an opportunity to establish either way.' Stephanie Garland handed over his coffee. 'Did you know that he was claustrophobic and that he had a fear of confined spaces? He made me go down to the archive store in our basement the other day because it was one place that he couldn't go himself.'

Hawkes sipped the coffee, it was good. 'And yet he elected to take the tube the day that he died, that's interesting!' He liked being in her company, being near her. She was easy to converse with and attractive.

'I know you wasn't here then, but did any of the others discuss another man as being associated with D'Corscy or Trent, an Italian by any chance?'

She nodded. 'Yes. When we were told about his death, there were a number of hypotheses bouncing around the office about who could be responsible, if it was an accident. An Italian was mentioned!'

'Did Charles ever come to work wearing a full length leather trench coat and wide brimmed hat?'

She looked at him, her eyes lighting up.

'What like Clint Eastwood?' she laughed, she had a nice laugh. 'In the summer the only hat that Trent would sport would be a white panama. I doubt he had a leather coat. He mostly wore suede or corduroy. As I said he was eccentric.'

'How long have you been involved with the literary world?'

'Six, coming up to seven years December with two agencies. Why do ask?'

'During that time, have you ever heard of a literary agent being dismissed in London?'

'You mean somebody like Mortimer Valdis?' she was astute and on his wavelength. 'Generally this is a pretty stable career. You go to university, attain a degree then apply your skills base with an agency that thinks you can benefit their expectations. Unless you cock up big time, nobody ever

153

gets fired. Our job is to filter the pile of rubbish that lands on our desks. Occasionally a rising star emerges from the slush and sludge, but it's rare. I not heard of anybody being dismissed nor had I heard of Mortimer Valdis, until recent events.'

'He had a book published by Pritchard Davis. Have you heard of them?'

'Yes, we did send them some work a couple of years back, but old man Davis died his wife sold up, heading back west of the country where the climate suited her better.'

'West, any idea where west?'

'*Devon or Cornwall*. She had family there.' Stephanie Garland racked her memory cells recalling what she had heard. 'If my memory serves me well, I think she lives with her sister and together they run an amusement arcade.' She flicked her fingertips together. 'Along the Torquay seafront.'

Hawkes washed his mug under the tap. When he turned to face her again, she was close.

'*Are we still going out for a meal?*'

'Sure, but can I get back to you as to when. This investigation is playing havoc with my free-time and I've not been that long working with my guv'nor.'

Stephanie Garland smiled, although she didn't feel particularly encouraged. Getting dates had always been her biggest downfall. So that he couldn't find any excuse not to call she took him back to her desk where she gave him another business card, writing her private number on the back. She watched him take the stairs down wondering if he would ever ring.

Chapter Seventeen

Waterfall Heights was divided into two blocks with separate entrances. Spence elected to take the block west to Vivienne D'Corscy's apartment. On the first floor opposite number seventeen the door was opened by a middle-aged woman still wearing a dressing gown and nightdress. April produced her ID explaining the reason for interrupting the resident's morning. She was invited in, offered refreshing which she declined. Instead April was happy to sit at the breakfast bar whilst the occupant fussed around organising her kitchen.

The flat was tastefully decorated unlike that of her neighbour, the walls festooned with posters and photographs, many from the bygone era of early theatre productions. Sitting herself opposite April the woman settled at last.

'Forgive my passion and indulgence,' she explained as she swept her right arm around the four walls the drape of her arms spreading like the wings of a dove taking to flight. 'Life tends to pass by so quickly these days and often memories are all that we have.'

'You're an actress?' April deduced.

'The one and only Annabelle Du Renard.' The woman jumped from her stall and curtsied as though she had just completed a performance. 'I've been researching my family tree, but with little success. Rumour has it that descendants had French nobility running through their veins.'

'It's a name that I would not forget.'

Du Renard smiled in response. 'You are very kind.' She looked at the poster nearest to where they sat. 'There were some days when young men would wait at the back door, asking that they could take me to dinner. Nowadays, I tend to use another exit letting younger actresses be tempted by the propositions.'

'Your name appears in nearly all the posters!'

'And yet here I still live in Waterfall Heights, virtually forgotten and without an agent calling.' Annabelle Du Renard painted a bleak picture of a struggling overlooked starlet, where time had ravaged her looks and skin.

'Anyway enough of my sentimental ramblings,' she addressed 'you've come about that poor young thing that lived in the flat opposite.' Du Renard shook her head as though her death had affected her only. 'What an awful affair, the circumstances make me shudder just to think of what she endured!'

'My colleague and myself have decided to come visiting once again, believing somebody might have remembered something that could help, anything, however insignificant it might seem!'

Annabelle Du Renard spread her wings once again. 'I was on stage that night my darling, rehearsing for the forthcoming production of the *King and I* at the palladium no less.' She let the tips of her fingers brush lightly through her greying roots. 'Of course it's a part that won't be featured on the billboard, but it will help pay for my mid-afternoon aperitif.' She looked at the bottle on the shelf and offered April a snifter. 'It's a teeny bit early, but warms the heart!'

157

April smiled. 'It's just a bit too early. Is there anything that you can tell me about Vivienne D'Corscy, visitors, callers who came with a purpose, private or commercial?'

Annabelle Du Renard feigned an indifference to the question. 'Even late at Night!' she fanned her face 'a young man, tanned occasionally left in the middle of the night. I know because I met him returning from the last performance. He seemed charming, although eager to be leaving. I thought that strange. She was such a beautiful young woman, always so polite, but private. A literary agent I believe. It's what we found as a common bond.'

'Was there any other men, an older man?'

She rubbed her forehead. 'Silly me... of course Charles Trent. An avid follower of the arts and the theatre.' She looked at the posters beside the door. 'He always appeared at a new production, enthusiastically praising my performance.'

'Did you ever see him leaving late, in the early hours of the morning?'

Annabelle Du Renard seemed hurt by the suggestion. 'Why No... Charles was a gentleman. He made it very clear that he was very fond of Miss D'Corscy, but to suggest that he took advantage of the young woman is in bad taste.' April apologised.

'You asked about callers. There was a man once. A strangely dressed man and believe me I see plenty. Long coat and wide brimmed hat. A phantom of the night. He was standing outside on the drive, just staring up at the upper floors. At first I thought he might be lost, but the closer I got to where he was standing the hairs on the back of my neck became more pronounced. I rushed inside the lobby as quickly as I could and closed my door on his memory. When I looked out of my living room window he had gone. For some weird reason that memory has haunted me often. Is that significant?'

April smiled. 'It might be. Waterfall Heights, it's not always been called that?'

'No. Previously it was called Pembroke Mansions. It was a little inconvenient, even annoying when they changed the name, but the previous owner had sold and moved back to his native Wales. We were offered the opportunity to buy our flats at greatly reduced market prices, providing we agreed to the name change. I never did find out why it was significant, but of course I agreed. At least I now have a permanent roof over my head.'

'Have you ever heard of Mortimer Valdis?'

Annabelle Du Renard shook her head from side to side. 'It sounds theatrical, is he an actor?'

'No. Valdis is an author.'

As if a light had suddenly been switched on, she remembered. 'That awful book. When the previous owner of number seventeen moved away she gave me a box of books. It was amongst the collection. I only started to read it once. It was chilling. It made me feel just when I had seen the coated stranger outside looking up at our flats.'

April was eager to push on, knowing that she was getting somewhere. *'Retribution of the Angst'* she prompted 'that was the title.'

Du Renard nodded not wanting to repeat the title. 'When I got to know Vivienne better and learnt that she was associated with books, the arts, I gave her the book. To tell the truth I was well rid of the awful thing.'

'Why didn't you just throw it away?'

Du Renard shrugged her shoulders. 'I don't know. It was as though the book was possessed by evil. As long as I didn't go anywhere near it, I was safe!'

'Before she left did the previous owner say where she acquired the book?'

'No, she just handed over the box, said that it had been good having me as a neighbour then left.'

'What was her name?'

'Rachel Roberts. She went north, up to the Midlands I think.'

April made it her mission to take one last look at the photographs and posters on the walls of the kitchen before leaving, she needed to find Spence. As soon as the door was closed shut Annabelle Du Renard went to the shelf and lifted down the bottle, ignoring the clock on the wall. Memories always made her drink.

April found Spence waiting outside. 'Any luck?' he asked.

'You?' she asked.

'Waste of time. Must be the way I look!'

She smiled. 'Maybe, I should have joined the force and become a detective instead.' She looked up at the flat above and saw a face fade from view.

'That good,' he responded, looking up and wondering what she had been looking at.

'I met an actress, nobody that you would know Spence, but she told me things that are interesting, things that will help.' She took one last look above, but Annabelle Du Renard was nowhere to be seen. 'Now, if you had knocked on her door, she would have found your face extremely interesting. A blend of Gary Grant and George Clooney rolled into one.'

'That bad eh!'

She laughed. 'Now find me somewhere to be alone with you and that does a decent sandwich and I'll tell you why I should have been a detective.'

Chapter Eighteen

Jack Chilvray ran the cursor over the screen until it landed on the web report concerning the suspicious death of a man on the underground at Russell Square. He read down the few lines digesting the facts where it mentioned that the dead man, a senior editor of the Hampton literary agency had died almost immediately at the scene. Jack laughed. 'I'd say he died almost instantly, the moment the *fucking* train rolled over his neck!'

The report was accompanied by an archived photograph of the platform taken some years when the station was about to undergo a refurbishment. He continued to scroll through various internet sites until he found a foreign report where a still of the platform, just before the train arrived showed Jack standing at the back, moments before he moved forward. He lightly touched the screen. Next to the security still was an edited summary:

'Although British Transport Police are investigating this tragic incident and working in conjunction with Scotland Yard, authorities are satisfied that at this juncture of the proceedings, no suspicious circumstances are being considered in connection with the man's death.'

He ticked off another name from his list, so far there were three ticks, but there were others to come. On the wall of the room that he used solely for his planning command, he reviewed the many cuttings that he had taken from various national newspapers. Along with maps, train time-tables and photographs Chilvray had his victims' names boldly printed on card. Polaroid images were dotted here and there, surveillance photographs where the subjects had been innocently oblivious of his presence. He focused on one face in particular. The problem that faced him now, was what she would tell the police about the night that she had seen him standing outside the flats.

Taking his thoughts to the bathroom he showered staying under the stream of water for a very long time, but some problems you could not wash away. Back in the room where he did his planning a spider walked across the wall spinning a long length of yarn across the exhibits. It stopped to look at the name on one of the boards and then the next beside it. Annabelle Du Renard and April Geddings meant nothing to the arachnid so it moved on.

Chapter Nineteen

Leaving instructions with Dawson and Stebbings to locate and talk to cortelli once again and with April busy with a spate of overnight burglaries, Spence and Hawkes decided to travel south to Torquay having phoned ahead and been given the address of the amusement arcade by the local constabulary. They caught the five past eight from Paddington, making reservations with the buffet car manager for the three and three quarter hour journey down south west.

At Torquay where the climate was different and the sun warmer a railway porter gave them directions to the harbour where he knew of the arcade. They walked to the harbour rather than catch a cab.

'I'm not sure that I could be a detective here,' said Hawkes as he acknowledged a girl loading the front counter of a bakers shop 'it'd be too quiet!'

Spence scoffed. 'I think you'll find Tom that crime is crime wherever you work. A lot of our villains have spread themselves around the country, taking refuge in places where they believe the local constabulary won't pay them as much interest as they would get in the Met. Problem is crime is ingrained into their DNA and they see places like Torquay as easy pickings. If anything, I'd say Devon Police could be just as busy, only without the troops.'

Nestled amongst a stretch of fast food outlets, souvenir shops and estate agents they saw *Aunty Amy's Amusements.*

Spence liked a flutter where the odds were good, but the days of the penny arcades as far as he was concerned had, had their day. Outside the front façade was lit by row upon row of bright coloured lights. 'The old Soho on a good night!' he remarked.

Ostensibly out of place in their suits they approached the change kiosk where an elderly woman was knitting and at the same time reading a magazine. The only other occupants were a young family on holiday playing the machines.

'Security doesn't seem to be a priority!' remarked Hawkes as he smiled and produced his warrant card introducing Spence and himself.

'The criminals probably collect more on the social that we do in a day young man. Never seen the need for any of those expensive security systems. We've got one that covers the booth, but nothing else.'

Jean Davis sniffed as she looked them up and down, rolling the bulk of her tongue over her teeth.

'You young man look too handsome to be a policeman!' she didn't make any comment with regards to Spence.

'We've specifically come here today in connection with a murder enquiry, is your sister about?'

'Amy, why yes she's in the back room, but what how can she be connected with any murder, since moving down to Torquay, she's never been back to London?'

Hawkes smiled. 'Then you're Jean Davis!'

'I am young man.'

After being briefly told in what connection they needed to talk to her, she pressed a hidden button beneath the counter, moments later a woman of same stature, age and suspicion appeared weaving a course between the gambling machines to where they stood.

'You're either customs and excise or the police!'

'They're from London Amy, they need to talk to me about something important, could you watch the booth whilst we go out back.'

Switching on the kettle she settled them in the best seats that the room could provide whilst she busied herself making herself and her visitors a coffee. 'It's a long journey from London, did you come by car?'

'No, we took the train.' Replied Hawkes.

Jean Davis appeared to recall her own journey as she stirred in the sugar. 'It seemed never-ending when I took that last journey. I wondered if I was doing the right thing, leaving my Pritchard back in London. It was as though I was deserting him!'

'It's about the publishing business that we're here Mrs Davis.'

She gave them their coffee's and took a seat opposite. 'We did everything above board inspector I assure you. Pritchard was a very religious man and he would have no shady dealing and the like.'

Spence didn't comment 'We came to speak with you because we want to ask about a book. Do you remember an author who went by the name Mortimer Valdis?'

Initially Jean Davis shook her head. 'We had the business for a good many years inspector and we dealt with a lot of customers.'

Hawkes took the copy *Retribution of the Angst* from an envelope that he had been carrying and showed it to her. The head shaking changed to a nod. She handed the copy back to Hawkes as though not wanting to keep it any longer than necessary

'Pritchard was reluctant to take this order, but the customer was insistent that we print the book. I recall him paying above our normal rate to get it made into a hardback.'

'Do you have any idea how many copies were printed?'

'No. Pritchard dealt with order and the man. I made sure that I wasn't around whenever he came in. There was something peculiar about his manner and the way that he looked at me that made me shiver.'

'What happened to the ledgers, where you recorded orders, payments and other details?'

'When I sold the business I gave them all to the new owner. It was highly unlikely, but an old customer could come calling again one day!'

'And the person who bought the business, do you remember their name?'

'Why yes. A nice man, Richard Ellis. He had a son at college at the time, but keen to join his father. I was pleased that he took over the place, he had ambition and ideas that were much needed. London sometimes moves faster than you can keep pace. Pritchard would have been pleased too.'

'I know you said, you kept out of the way, but can you describe the man who made your skin crawl. It could help.'

She promptly closed her eyes and they weren't sure if it was to place a blanket over the memory or to keep what she did see in her mind and not let him out. She spoke with her eyes shut. 'He was tall, but then most men are over me. Clean shaven with dark coloured hair, cut short. His eyes were haunting, black like pearls. When he looked at you, it was as though he wanted to penetrate deep into the recesses of your mind. I couldn't stand being around him. He always wore a long black coat and hat. During one visit, he reached forward to examine the progress that Pritchard was making with the publication, it was then that I noticed a tattoo on his wrist. It was difficult to make out, as it looked as though it had been there for some time, but the design looked distinctly military, an insignia.' She opened her eyes wanting to make sure that they were still with her. Both noticed the shiver pass through her frail body.

'I only saw him the twice, his presence frightened me. I argued with Pritchard that he should cancel the order, but my husband was a man of faith and honour, he believed in giving the customer what they wanted.

'Anything else?' Spence prompted.

'No inspector. That was enough I assure you. I didn't like the man. If a devil does walk amongst us, then he would certainly fit the bill.' She suddenly held up a forefinger, remembering one last detail. 'He had an accent, not strong, but as though he was from Yorkshire or around that way!'

'You've done well Mrs Davis, thank you!'

'He's killed people hasn't he?' Despite her frailty and her years, there was a steely look of hate in her eyes.

'We think he has. Have you mentioned any of this to Amy?'

'Good Lord No, never inspector. My sister is all bravado on top surface, but beneath that rugged exterior she is as soft as lamb's wool. Torquay is as about exciting as she could take, London and the pace would kill her for sure. If I had told her about Mortimer Valdis she would have nightmares.'

Hawkes finished his coffee and put the mug down on the side. 'Did you ever come into contact with a man named Charles Trent or a Rachel Roberts?'

Jean Davis nodded. 'Yes, many times. Hampton's were a client of ours and we did a lot of work for them. Nice couple, always polite, but never rushed for an order. Charles knew that I had a liking for the theatre so we would spend time talking over a show etcetera. Is he part of your enquiry?'

'In a way.'

She smiled. 'Please be so kind as to pass on my regards if you see him inspector. Such a nice man, a real gentleman!' Spence agreed that he would.

Sitting on the harbour wall Hawkes looked out at the boats that were bobbing about on the water. Spence sensed that there was something ailing him.

'Say what you're thinking Tom.'

'I was just thinking guv'nor, hoping that Jean Davis isn't on any hit-list of old, past acquaintances.'

Chapter Twenty

Had anyone questioned why a chief inspector accompanied by a detective had travelled all the way down to Devon and back just to hear the thoughts of an old woman, Spence would have told them to mind their own business and be done with it. He had wanted to see Jean Davis, hear what she had to say and be there when she said it. Snippets, however small gradually coloured the picture.

Somewhere outside of Paddington the train came to a halt with the guard announcing a delay due to technical problems. When they did get back to the office the cleaners were already busy hoovering the carpets. On his desk Spence found a note from Stebbings and Dawson.

'Knocked on the doors of employer, friends and known haunts, but no sign of Cortelli. The embassy staff were apprehensive about giving any answers, when asked about his whereabouts. Dobson Wallace Removals came up with an address for Rachel Roberts – 98 Glenister Road, Dudley.'

Spence handed the note to Hawkes.

'It looks like our linguist friend has decided to do a runner!'

Spence however wasn't convinced by the argument. 'I'm not so sure. Cortelli's no fool. He'd stand out in a crowd like a skittle in a bowling alley. He has a cast-iron alibi for both D'Corscy and Trent, but something else has got him running scared. It's our job to find out what!'

With the echo of a knock on the door still sounding April walked in. She was pleased to see them both. 'Good day by the seaside?' she asked.

'The sticks of rock were overpriced and out of date, so we decided to treat you to supper instead!' immediately her smile gained impetuous. She handed over an envelope. Inside was more stills.

'At least we can recognise the bone structure of the nose, mouth and chin. It's more than what we had before.'

Hawkes turned the image in the light. *'There was film recently about a tracker. He looks like the actor, Ray Winstone.'*

Spence looked at April and smiled. 'Well that makes life easier. We'll pay Mr Winstone a visit later, drag him down the cells and ask what books he's written.'

Hawkes put down the image on the desk, unruffled by the remark. 'I'd like a picture showing his eyes. I want to see if they really that dark!' Spence smiled again, he liked Hawkes tenacity.

'Have either of you thought about using a profile artist. They can work miracles from sometimes very little. We can enhance the image using 3D profile and they can work out the measurements. Anything between seventy and ninety two percent is pretty accurate.'

Spence nodded, he liked the idea. 'Do you know a good profiler?' She did. He looked at his watch, it had been a long day travelling, but not wasted. 'Come on let's get something to eat.' Hawkes said that he'd pass on the invite as he had prior arrangements, only he didn't reveal who with. Agreeing to follow up with Ellis & Son in the morning, he would report back any findings when April and Spence returned from their trip to Dudley in the West Midlands.

'The publisher shouldn't take long, so I'll root around Cortelli's flat after. There's bound to be something there of interest.' He said his goodbyes, then left.

'So who's the lucky girl?' April asked.

'I don't know, although I've a feeling that it could be Sharon Trevelyan. She sent him a text on the journey down to Devon.' April grinned, it sounded romantic. Spence locked the office door and slipped the keys in his jacket pocket. 'Although, if I know Tom, like I do now, Trevelyan will probably end up having a doner-kebab and chips back at his place!'

April nudged his arm playfully 'there's nothing wrong with a bit of spontaneity every so often. A girl likes the element of surprise!'

They were just going out the back door of the station when a duty sergeant caught up with them. He directed his message to April.

'I heard that you'd paid a west end actress a visit yesterday, it wasn't by any chance Annabelle Du Renard?'

'Yes, why Bob?'

'Control has just received a call to say that there's been an accident and she's in the Accident and Emergency Department at University College Hospital.'

'What kind of accident?' asked Spence.

'Something to do with a gantry support coming down on her head.'

April drove to UCH where they found Du Renard had been transferred to Intensive Care. Standing beside the bed the middle-aged thespian was wired up to drips and monitors, recording her heart rate, blood pressure and brain activity.

'Is she likely to survive?' April whispered to the nurse nearby who was marking up the monitor chart.

'At present that's difficult to say. Whatever landed on her head, did so with a fair amount of force. The patient has a massive internal bleed in and around the brain. The on-call neurosurgeon is on his way now to determine whether she should go down to theatre.'

Stroking her hand carefully avoiding the many wires and tubes hooked up to Annabelle's wrist April thought she looked extremely peaceful as she slept. Except for the rhythmic gargle of the tube going down her airway and the bleeping from the monitor the room was peaceful. April looked around to where Spence was standing nearby. 'Coincidence seems to be common place all of a sudden.'

He didn't get time to reply as the door to the room opened and in walked a tall woman in theatre scrubs accompanied by a male doctor and staff nurse. Spence produced his warrant and stood back as the neurosurgeon examined Annabelle Du Renard. When it was done and the staff nurse left to make other arrangements April was first to speak.

'Will she make it through the night doctor?'

The tall woman paused, looked back down at the sleeping woman and shook her head.

'She has a severe cerebral bleed, the nurse had gone to arrange additional scans, but until we see what is going on deep inside, opening her up to release the pressure could be dangerous. Do you know if she drinks?'

'Yes, aperitifs I believe, although I doubt she had consumed much today if she was working at the theatre when this happened.'

The neurosurgeon nodded. 'Why are you both here?'

'The lady had helped with a recent murder enquiry. We were disturbed to hear of her accident and rushed here to see if we could help.'

The doctor stared at Spence gauging to what depth of help he could offer. 'If we don't stop the bleeding she will die. If however, we do operate in time then there is every possibility that she will have post-op trauma. A subarachnoid haemorrhage injury is very serious inspector. She could suffer any manner of difficulties, including a stroke.'

April took up stroking Annabelle's hand once again. 'And the alcohol?'

'That will not help either way!'

'We've not been to the theatre, do you know what hit her?' Spence sensed the neurosurgeon was becoming agitated.

'Some sort of scaffolding pole, now I really must be elsewhere!' she headed towards the door.

'So an accident!'

The neurosurgeon didn't look back, but he heard her reply. 'That is for you to determine detective!'

As the staff nurse and a porter prepared Annabelle for transportation down to Radiotherapy April held her hand until asked to let go. They watched as the bed as wheeled out of the room. 'You know Spence, she was a harmless soul. All she ever wanted to be was happy and have her audience notice her on the stage.'

In the corridor leading from the ward they heard a sudden commotion of voices and machines. Spence and April ran to see what was occurring. In the middle of the corridor they found Annabelle Du Renard still lying on the bed, but her nightdress had been ripped open. As a doctor rubbed together the paddles, the nurse turned the dial to increase the joules surging through each pad.

'Stand clear!'

The command was repeated several times until the doctor called a halt to the process. The time of death was recorded and the defibrillator turned off. In the lonely corridor of the hospital Annabelle Du Renard had an audience, not the kind that would fully appreciate her talents, but certainly the most attentive. As she was wheeled back into the side room to have tubes, wires and pads removed April found a space where she was able to bend over and kiss the dead woman's forehead.

'Goodnight Annabelle, go break a leg in heaven where the stage curtain never falls and you have the biggest audience!'

Standing outside where she had left the car April suddenly had a thought. 'How did Bob Perkins know about Annabelle Du Renard?'

'Control took a call from DI Knightly at West End Central. Amongst Du Renard's personal effects was your contact card. It pays to leave those cards!' he looked at his watch. They had lost all track of time and three hours had elapsed in the hospital. 'It's late, but still time to get something to eat?'

April suddenly put her arms around his back and pulled him in real close. She kissed him for what seemed ages, not wanting to let go. When she did let go, Spence exhaled.

'I needed that Spence more than any food. Maybe we can pick up one of those fast-food all-nighters that you and Hawkes seemed to survive upon, en-route to the theatre. I'd like to have a root around before anything gets trampled over.'

She depressed the button on her key-fob and immediately the electronic locks unlocked themselves. 'Promise me that when we're done at the theatre you'll come back to my place, I don't want to be alone tonight.'

The remainder of the evening rehearsal had been cancelled and the cast sent home following the accident. Walking into the foyer they were met by the theatre manager and a stagehand.

'Albert Bartholomew, at one time an aspiring actor, but sadly now just a lowly manager.' April thought his act had been well rehearsed. 'I was telephoned to say that you might be coming, so I held Karl back, just in case!'

'Can we take a look at the area where the accident took place?' Albert Bartholomew was happy for Karl to take them through to the auditorium, taking the opportunity to disappear upstairs where he had his office.

'Is he always like that?' asked April.

'More or less. Old Bart as we call him spends more time in his office than in and around the stage. Rumour had it that another actor was jealous of his intentions towards a fellow thespian. Threats were made and suddenly Old Bart gave up acting as a career.'

'Do you know who?' asked Spence.

The stagehand looked at Spence shrugging his shoulders. 'Na... I don't get involved with poofter quarrels. They should and cuss one another, then minutes later it's all kisses and cuddles until the next time. It's a wonder Old Bart ain't caught a rear-end dose the amount of queers that he's been through!'

A sudden thought flashed through Spence's mind. 'Do you know if he knew a man called Charles Trent?'

The stagehand shook his head.

'Mortimer Valdis?' it was a long shot, but worth trying.

'Na... them names don't mean nothing to me. They're just faces that go up to Old Bart's office chief inspector. I ain't particularly good with names.'

'And was Mr Bartholomew in the office when the accident occurred?'

'I suppose so, although I can't rightly say. I was down under checking the lift mechanism when I heard the scream then the thud on the stage floor. I ran back up, only when I got to where Miss Du Renard had been hurt, some of the others were already by her side.'

Climbing the wooden steps at the side of the stage April took her camera from her bag. She immediately captured all the angles, heights and the trap door, although it had not been involved. Good practice had trained her that it was better not to leave anything to chance.

Karl stood directly under where the gantry pole had slipped away. He smiled as she snapped him, asking the stagehand to point to which clamp had caused the problem. Lying to the side of the stage where it had rolled the blood stained metre length of coated cylindrical steel had come to rest against the curtain.

'Who maintains the props?' April asked as Spence walked around below.

'Myself and Arnold. Arnie's older than me and has been here almost as long as Old Bart, but tonight is Arnie's night off. Rehearsals only call for one stagehand to be present, cut-backs and all that bollocks!'

April tried not to laugh. She liked Karl, he was rough around the edges, but no fool. 'How often is the catwalk checked?' She continued taking photographs.

'Thoroughly, the beginning of every show and at the end. When there no show just rehearsals, end of every month. It was checked last week and everything was tight as a squirrels arse.' When she wasn't looking he took a look at April's. She was fit for her age.

'What's your thoughts Karl and how did the pole come loose from the gantry?' down under the gantry Spence was listening. He'd seen Karl notice April's rear.

'Some thing or somebody must have tampered with the equipment. Arnie and me, we take a pride in what we do. We leave everything clean and safe, rehearsal or show, whatever the occasion. Them gantry clamps just don't come lose by themselves.'

Spence called up from down below. 'Who else would have reason to go up there?'

Karl looked over the top support. 'A lighting technician, a sound recordist, both need to check the equipment on a regular basis. On some shows there can be as many as three, maybe four men up here at any one time. Some women as well, if a designer wants a sneak peek at her backdrop.

This gantry could stand up to a hurricane and not topple over or come apart.'

Spence saw Karl look towards the rear auditorium doors, he spun around on his heels and did the same, only there was nobody there. 'You expecting someone?' he asked.

'Yeah... those nosey buggers from Health and Safety, Old Bart thought it best to bring them in sooner rather than later. Despite how strict we are with ourselves and our procedures, those book bashers always find something wrong!'

'Book bashers, why that Karl?'

Karl looked at the woman standing beside him. In the stage lighting she looked ten years younger. 'Always bleedin' quoting from this regulation, or that procedure. Buggers have always got an answer for everything. You can never trip up a book bashers cos' they know the stuff inside out. I reckon their old woman must be getting it elsewhere when they take them to bed. *'Have you done a risk assessment first my dear, only sex can be hazardous?'*

Even Spence couldn't stop himself from laughing and April thought Karl was wasted as a stagehand. With her camera armed ready both she and Karl knelt down and checked the clamp, she told him not to touch it, although it was likely that his prints were all over it through previous maintenance. She was still snapping away when Karl located something that had become wedged between the catwalk board and the steel. He pulled it out and gave it to April. It was a coat button.

'Actors don't come up, so it can't be a costume button!'

'And it wasn't there before tonight?'

Karl looked up and down the length of the catwalk. 'No, honest Miss. I've got eyes like a hawk. I'd notice if something was out of place.'

Leaving April to the mercy of Karl hoping that he would show her all the other salient parts of the stage he took himself off to the manager's office where he found Albert Bartholomew sleeping cradling an empty bottle of whiskey. Pulling the manager back against the rest of his chair, he opened the window wide inviting in the cool night breeze. Moments later Albert started to come too. He apologised.

'I'm sorry...' his voice was slightly slurred and his eyes were having difficulty focusing. 'It's been a difficult day and I often get the feeling that I am being punished as though I were the lead in a Greek tragedy.' He dropped the empty bottle into the waste-bin beside the desk. Shivering not once, but twice he got up to close the window, shutting out the noise of the traffic going by. From a small tin on the desk he offered Spence a mint before popping one into his own mouth. 'Are you satisfied that it was an accident chief inspector?' he rolled the mint around in his mouth then crunched down hard.

'It's a bit early to make any rash judgements,' Spence replied. He waited for the crunching to stop before continuing. I'm convinced Karl didn't have anything to do with what happened here this evening.' That seemed to please Bartholomew.

'He's a good lad and shaping up well.'

Spence asked about Annabelle Du Renard's state of mind when she had arrived at the theatre that evening for rehearsal, but all that Albert could say was that she was no different to any other night, always jovial and smiling from the moment she arrived, until it was time to go home.

'Have you been to the hospital?' Albert asked.

Spence nodded. 'Unfortunately, she died soon after we arrived. She went peacefully in her sleep.' Part of it was a lie, but Spence decided no good would come from telling the truth. He asked about Charles Trent and Mortimer Valdis. Bartholomew knew of the senior editor, but not the latter. He left the office giving the theatre manager time to get over the shock. Walking back down to the foyer he met up with April just as two members of the health and safety executive walked in through the doors. Spence directed them to the first floor. The night had just worse for Albert Bartholomew.

April waited until the coast was clear before she pulled the button from her pocket. Through the clear plastic Spence examined the item contained within the evidence bag. 'I found it wedged in between the flooring and kickboard. It's made of leather Spence.'

'From a long leather trench coat!' he responded enthusiastically.

April slipped the bag back into her pocket. 'I would stake my pension on that Valdis was here earlier!'

Chapter Twenty Two

April was awake long before Spence. She lay in the crook of his arm watching his chest rise then fall, glad to see that he was resting and peacefully. Their love making had initially been frantic, calming the second time around and Spence was nothing like her ex-husband, not that she was making comparisons. Easing gently away from him and the bed she slipped into his shirt and padded through to the kitchen returning minutes later with two coffees. The aroma of the coffee made his nostrils twitch.

'Good morning!' she said as she kissed him, running the tip of her tongue between his lips. Spence responded by pulling her into him and not letting go.

'Hi… what time is it?'

'Just gone twenty to seven, time enough for coffee, a shower and maybe toast!

Reaching for a coffee mug he handed it to April, then reached across for his own. 'It's been so long since I have had coffee made for me that I can't rightly remember just how long?'

April eyed him suspiciously. 'I'd ask about the sex, but I'm not sure that I really want to know the answer!'

Spence grinned. 'There's been nobody else since Siobhan.'

'Well none of your technique had gone rusty.' She slipped back under the cover running her legs down the side of his. Moments later she took his mug and put it down on the side, pulled his shirt over the top of her head and lay back down naked.

'We can always grab something to eat on the way into work!'

*****

Knocking on the door of Ellis & Son printers, Thomas Hawkes was greeted by a young man, a couple of years younger than himself. Offering his hand he introduced himself as Louie Ellis. Before Hawkes could pass comment Louie explained that his father was a big fan of Satchmo and Jazz.

'At least you smile about yours, my claim to fame is that in fifteen fifty five I was burnt at the stake as an English Protestant martyr!'

Louie took him through the front of the shop to the workshop out back where the bulk of their profession was conducted. He introduced Hawkes to the father, Richard Ellis.

'We don't normally get calls from the police, but Louie and I got in extra early this morning to go through some of the old records. I have to say that it's the first time that I've actually looked at the ledgers. Pritchard Davis was a meticulous man and it seems that he recorded everything.'

Richard Ellis pulled over an old green leather ledger with a gilt edging. It looked like gold, but was only flaked to resemble gold. Pulling open the page where they had placed a marker, Hawkes put down his mobile on the rolling bench.

Louie Ellis put his finger on the entry that they had found earlier. *Mortimer Valdis 'Retribution of the Angst' first print October 2007. No agent. The contact address was given as 158 Kenton Park Mews, East Dulwich. There was no recorded telephone number.*

'It's a pity about the contact number?'

Ellis senior nodded. 'I thought that. I can only assume that Valdis checked with Pritchard Davis on a regular basis and together they made any necessary amendment changes.'

Tracing across the entry Hawkes noted the initials of the printer, finding the ink used, font and type face. Cash had been paid on the second day of November the same year. It made sense as to why they could find no banking transaction records.

'We did search around for a receipt pad down in the cellar, but there were none detective. Jean Davis probably destroyed any records she believed irrelevant.'

Hawkes smiled. 'No worries. The address compensates for anything lost.' He picked up his mobile and photographed the page. When he was back outside in the street he called Spence.

'Don't go alone Tom,' warned Spence 'I'll find Dawson and Stebbings, the fresh air will do them good. I'll also get in touch with control and have a firearms unit deployed as back up in case Valdis kicks up rough!' Spence cancelled the call telling Hawkes to be careful. He was in two minds to get April to turn the car around and head back to London, but they were only a few miles shy of the Birmingham intersection.

186

April depressed the indicator taking the slip road slowing as the road veered sharply left around a sweeping bend. 'It sounds like Tom has come up trumps this morning.'

Spence turned away from the view outside. 'If he arrests Valdis, he'll leave him in the cell until we get back. It'll give Valdis time to reflect and maybe rattle his nerves!'

April wasn't so sure. 'The way that he executes his victim's Spence, I'm not swayed that Valdis has any feelings.'

He looked at her thinking she was probably right.

'Sometimes you're wasted in forensics!'

She didn't look up as the traffic was getting thicker near the junctions. 'Thanks, but I'm happy doing what I do Spence.' She darted into an open space, jumping ahead of two other cars. 'I feel I make a difference, without much effort, whereas you have to dig away sometimes for months before you get a result. You have to prove intent. I just have to prove that they were present at the scene.'

Twenty minutes catching mostly green lights April got them to Dudley. Parts of the town were underdeveloped as though taking a step back in time, whereas what was left had been residentially designed by a firm of architects, adopting modern practice, brick, timber and lots of glass. Spence studied the meandering line of rooftops that curved and dropped sharply without rhyme or reason.

'They must have employed the same architects from London looking at this place.' He shook his head at the inept space given over to living. 'I must be getting old, I much prefer traditional like old Charlie boy.'

April laughed. 'I wouldn't have taken you for a royalist.'

'We serve queen and country, so it only seems right to adopt some royal values. When I do eventually retire I see myself living like Charles, with a secluded little place with lots of open space and a big walled garden. Somewhere where I can lose myself amongst the geraniums, rhododendrons and roses. On alternative Saturdays I'd dig over the vegetable patch and watch the buggers grow in the warmth of the sun!'

'The good life' it sounds idyllic!'

They stopped at a newsagents so that Spence could ask the last directions to Glenister Road. The owner, an Asian with a brummie accent came out front and gestured with both hands where to turn left and right. Moments later he got back in the car.

'That looked easy.' April said with a smirk.

'*Going after Jack the Ripper would have been easier.*' He re-belted. 'Head for the next set of lights and take a right.'

Rounding the corner they asked a postman who gave pretty much the same directions as the shopkeeper. Minutes later April pulled up outside number ninety eight. Panning her hand across the width of the screen, she proved the difference. 'There you go Spence, traditional.'

Walking up the garden path they were aware that the curtain in the ground level bay window had moved. Spence had his fingertip almost on the bell when a young girl's face appeared around the opening in the door. She had screwed up nose and big brown eyes which were attentively eyeing the callers up and down. A hand belonging to her mother held her daughter in check.

Spence produced his warrant and showed it to the mother. 'Are you Rachel Roberts?' he lowered the warrant so that the little girl could look too.

'No, my names Brenda... Brenda Taylor and this is my daughter Tracey.' At the mention of her name the little girl stabbed her sternum with her fist, not wishing to be left out of the conversation.

'Does a Rachel Roberts live with you?' April asked, but the young mother looked puzzled.

'Did she ever live here?' Spence asked, wondering if they had called at the right number.

'Before me and my husband moved in and had little Tracey, the tenant before us was a young woman, around my age I think.' She pointed across the street. 'The old lady over there will probably be able to tell you more. She's occupied the house since the end of the last war. Snouty old bat, always watching out of the window!'

They apologised for interrupting her morning crossing the road. An elderly lady with a wooden walking stick answered the door. Coming up the hallway behind her was a ginger cat, it stroked its way between her legs

189

then to April amusements between Spence. The occupant shushed the cat back inside and ushered her callers inside.

'Sissy don't go out nowadays, too many of them dangerous mopeds and noisy motorbikes up and down the road at night to let her out. Are you from the council?' she asked, closing the door.

Spence introduced himself then April and asked if they could go somewhere where they could talk. Sitting in her parlour Sissy continued to take great delight in showing Spence her attentions. Leaning in close April whispered in his ear. 'Don't worry, I've a stiff brush in the boot that'll remove any unwanted hairs!'

'I saw you over the road,' said the old woman, clearing the wax from her ears 'young couple and a toddler, a girl, not been there long. Occasionally, the little girl waves at me from the window, but with my arthritic hip I find it difficult to get up sometimes, so she must think me rude by not responding.'

'Did you know the young woman that lived there before them?' Spence asked.

'You need to speak up young man, it's alright for you youngsters, you've got all your faculties, whereas I lost mine a way back when my Cyril was alive. Comes of living alone and talking to yourself.' introducing additional air into the ear cavity with her palm where she had picked the wax, the elderly woman asked him to repeat the question. 'Sometimes, I think I'm going mad!'

Spence looked at April, but she had her head down low trying to stifle a snigger. He smiled at Elsie Tufnell through clenched teeth. 'This is going to be good.' He muttered.

'What can you tell us about the young woman that occupied the house opposite, where the little girl lives now?' April asked the question, adding extra volume to her voice.

'She wears some very revealing clothes, especially in the summer. It's no wonder they had a baby so soon!'

April flashed a look Spence's way preventing him from making comment. 'Have you lived here long?'

'Ever since I married Cyril's. This was his too, till he passed away.'

'So did you know of the young lady that lived there who went by the name of Rachel Roberts?'

The old woman seemed to shrink as though something sad had passed through her entire body. 'Nice girl. Did my hair on a Saturday morning. Always talking about books, but never seemed interested in men. I never asked, but I sometimes wondered if she was one of those lesbians, you know, them women that don't like men going near them!'

Spence sat back and made himself comfortable, letting April take the lead. Bit by bit she was getting there.

'But she doesn't live there anymore, do you know where she went?' April enquired.

The lines around Elsie Tufnell's eyes appeared to darken. She suddenly sat herself up in the chair and filled her lungs with oxygen. 'Rachel was killed soon after moving up here from London. She'd been here about eighteen months when one night she paid a visit to the pub with some work colleagues. On the way home she was involved in one of those horrible crashes where the car comes up onto the pavement, only it don't stop. Poor Rachel didn't stand a chance.'

Spence sat forward towards Elsie Tufnell. *'Rachel Roberts was involved in a hit-and-run.'*

Elsie Tufnell who signs of tears welling in the corner of her eyes, nodded. 'The bastard never stopped to see if Rachel needed help. The police that came the next day said that poor Rachel had lay badly injured for almost an hour before she was found. I reckon that by the time that an ambulance took her to hospital her injuries were too far gone to save her.' She sniffed and wiped away the tears with an embroidered lace hanky. 'I was a nurse so I know that her injuries must have been bad. They never caught the driver and of course there were no witnesses. The young family that live in the house over the road don't know that they took over the place from a dead woman.'

'Do you know what happened to Rachel's belonging, her personal stuff?' April asked.

'Her father came down one Saturday with a removal lorry and he and a couple of men, younger men, probably her brothers or relatives helped clear the house. She never did tell me where her parents lived. Other than cutting my hair and constantly talking about books, she kept her life very private.'

'Did she ever mention an author named Mortimer Valdis?'

Elsie Tufnell wiped her eyes dry once again and looked directly at Spence. 'No. Rachel would talk to me about books that I liked, Mills and Boon. I like romances and adventures by the seaside. Reading helps take me back to the days of my youth when Cyril and I would go out for long bike rides and lay in the hay!'

It was obvious that Cyril had taken charge of her thoughts and that they'd get nothing else out of Elsie Tufnell. They thanked her and left her rolling in the hay with her late husband. In the car outside Spence took a call from Thomas Hawkes.

'Hi, tell me that you've got good news!'

The call was brief and April couldn't hear what was being said. Before ending the call Spence told Hawkes that they were already on their way back. 'The news was that good?' she asked, inserting the key into the ignition.

'Not exactly. The address that Hawkes obtained from the printers turned out to an extension of the East Dulwich hospital. We have both hit a dead end. Mortimer Valdis, wherever the bastard is right now, he must be rolling in the aisles, laughing at our efforts to find him.'

Chapter Twenty Three

Spence was quiet throughout the journey back to London, not moody just thinking hard. Once or twice she checked with him to see that he was alright, but other than that she concentrated on her driving, giving him the mental space that he needed. What had started out really good that morning had slowly faded as the day went on and along with it the possibility that it would be repeated again later that night. Nearing the outskirts of London Spence suddenly reappeared from his ruminations.

'Maybe we've channelled all of our energy into the wrong person. Perhaps even chasing the wrong shadow!'

Checking the road ahead, April glanced to her side. 'What do you mean?'

'The three of us have focused all our efforts upon Mortimer Valdis, a man that we know nothing about, the writer of a couple of books and somebody who could be totally innocent. We agree that he writes graphic tales of horror and that what he writes seems to parallel certain murders that have taken place. Is it however, pure coincidence or conjecture. The real killer could be walking around at this very moment, mocking our ineptitude.'

April came to a halt at a red light. 'No. I think that you've been on the right track from the word go Spence. You said you had a hunch at Waterfall Heights, when you pulled the book from the bookcase. Of all the detectives I know, your hunches always seem to culminate in results.'

Spence smiled, liking her optimism. For the past two and a half hours he had been mulling over the facts that they knew, restaging the murders, the accidents and trying to fill in the blanks. As with all investigations key influences were ostensibly missing.

'I'll get my team to take another look at known offenders, sometimes a fresh set of eyes can see what we can't,' he paused 'if however, Valdis is the right man then we need to step up our efforts. Valdis has been one step ahead of us and I wonder how?'

They pulled into the back yard of the station catching sight of Hawkes, Dobson and Stebbings escorting a prisoner in though the cage leading to the back door of the custody suite. Spence was out of the car in an instant.

'Who's that?' he asked.

'One Ralph McTavish, explained Hawkes 'we caught him rifling through Cortelli's flat when we arrived. So far he's not told us anything other than his name and that he lives rough on the streets.'

Spence stood in front of the prisoner and checked the profile. McTavish neither matched the stills from the security camera nor did he look like a writer, not that Spence knew what a writer looked like.

'Get him booked into custody Tom, then come up to the office. I want a word before we interview this bugger!' Spence had started to walk back over to where April was waiting, when he turned 'No sign Cortelli I suppose?' Thomas Hawkes shook his head.

Twenty minutes later Hawkes joined Spence, who was alone. 'I heard about Annabelle Du Renard. Either we've hit a batch of coincidental deaths or people are running into a lot of bad luck lately!'

Spence had drawn a circle on a blank sheet and added four names with Valdis in the centre, on the outer edge were D'Corscy, Trent and Roberts, each linked with a running line to the name Hampton's. Annabelle Du Renard sat on the page alone. Spence tapped her name with the tip of his finger.

'Her connection was that she lived in the flat opposite D'Corscy.'

'Was it an accident?' Hawkes asked.

'April doesn't think so and I spoke to Health and Safety on the way up to Dudley this morning. They've made a judgement call suggesting that the clamp holding the pole in place could have worked itself loose with the weight and movement of people walking up and down the catwalk, but I'm more inclined to favour April's verdict that it was undone mechanically rather than by chance.' He told Hawkes about the costume button that April had found.

'The killers?'

'She's checking on it now.' He stopped pacing and sat down having stretched his legs. 'If Valdis is our chief suspect Tom, we need to be thinking like him. The only motive we have so far is revenge, why, we'll know when we nab him and he talks. What we need to second guess is his next move.'

Standing before the mood board Hawkes drew a vertical line down between the names, photographs, evidence references, dates and times. Spence watched.

'If his motive is revenge, then I'd look the connection!'

'Go on...' said Spence recognising what he was doing.

'When I get the chance I play football at the weekend. I'm competitive and hate losing. Valdis might feel the same about his books. Rejection hurts. D'Corscy read his manuscript she put it to lone side, denying him the opportunity to see it published on the bookshelves. That immediately puts her in the frame. Trent being her superior might have also had a hand in the rejection and together they went to the theatre and book launches, only not Valdis's. For all we know he might have been there, but merely observing.

'What we don't know is how Rachel Roberts had been involved. She knew about the book that she gave Annabelle Du Renard, but possibly not about his other book. Whatever, the involvement it's highly likely that Valdis was the cause of her death.' His finger landed on Du Renard where he had added her name earlier that morning. 'April said that Du Renard saw a strange man lurking around outside of the mansion block. She was probably in the wrong place at the wrong time. It could be as simple as that!' Hawkes acknowledged April as she took a seat.

'Like any good writer, he thinks through his plot. Every word used in every line, sentence and paragraph has impact. Valdis operates like he is the book. Like grammar corrections, it's imperative not to leave clues at the crime scene.'

Hawkes paused expecting comments, but when there were none, he continued.

'He writes, cataloguing his work and like a diary it begins to build a broader picture of him as a person. I'm not expert, but I'm sure a criminal profiler would analyse his writings and tell us exactly the type of person that we're looking for. I was thinking about the investigation today and came to the conclusion that the recent spate of deaths are not uncommon to Valdis. Unless driven by circumstance criminals work their way up the progression line, experimenting and getting better, their methods becoming more inventive, more elaborate. Valdis has reached the top, but it seems that one death can never emulate another, each has to be different to maintain the interest factor!'

For the first time since early that morning Spence grinned and raised his eyebrows towards April.

'Now you know why I fought so hard to have Tom as part of my team. He was originally destined for West End Central until I pulled some strings and called upon some forgotten favours.' He focused his attention back on Hawkes once again.

'So we've no way of knowing what his next move will be?'

Hawkes pursed his lips together and shook his head. 'I don't think that he's finished with Hamptons' guv'nor, but guessing his next move, would be like picking the winner of the next Grand National.'

April jumped in quick before Spence went silent on her again. 'I sent a friend in the fashion industry an image of the button and she confirms that it likely comes from a commercial produced product rather than costume clothing. Theatres tend to use cloth rather than leather as it helps keep down cost!'

Hawkes made a note of it on the mood board against Du Renard. At the end of the board where there was space he added two other names. Ralph McTavish and Roberto Cortelli.

'We've no body yet?' Spence queried against Cortelli.

'I know guv'nor, but when booked McTavish into custody, he had Cortelli's passport on him!'

Spence rubbed together his palms, he was set for McTavish. 'Right lets' get downstairs and deal with our friend before custody make him too comfortable!'

Spence sent Hawkes ahead to make the necessary preparations, giving him a few moments alone with April. He apologised for the journey back, but she dismissed the apology telling him that it wasn't necessary.

'Will I see you later?' he asked.

'Will you want dinner?'

'I could bring it in with me, depending how long this takes.'

Checking that the corridor as clear, she pushed him back inside the office and kissed him, the first since early that morning. 'Chinese is always good, whatever the time!'

To begin the interview Spence laid down Cortelli's passport, evident through the clear sealed bag. When Ralph McTavish looked he immediately shook his head.

'Breaking and entering is serious, but stealing a person's passport that doubles the possibilities of extra jail time. At best you're looking at three to five years to begin with and we've not discussed any other aspects that we'd like to put to you!'

Ralph McTavish swallowed hard. In reality the prospect of three hots meals every day and a warm bed to sleep upon didn't sound that bad. He been done time before, but that was a long time ago and served in a military jail, not like the nice cosy prisons that they had on the outside. He sniffed and looked directly back at Spence, then Hawkes, contemplating his reply. Winter was coming and he didn't fancy another five months of hardship on the streets.

'I found it just around the corner from the nick, honest!'

Having been cooped up in a car for almost seven hours Spence was in no mood for games. He pushed himself forward on the chair, placing his hand over the mic of the tape recorder.

'We can sit here and play silly *fucking* games all night long or DC Hawkes and I can go home and you spend a night in a comfortable warm cell with the prospect of a cooked breakfast in the morning. Now what is it to be... piss me about and we have the cooked breakfast or you get a mug of cold tea and a couple rounds of dry cold toast. It's make up your mind time McTavish.' He removed his hand.

'It's the truth I tell you. I found a suitcase on the pavement just around the corner from the police station. It was open and I had to pick up the clothes. Inside I found a travel wallet and the passport was concealed down a side pocket. There was also some foreign looking money, Euros and some documents that looked official. Later that morning I sold the clothes, the case, the travel wallet and the money to a bloke that I know for fifty pounds. I kept back the passport cos' I know that it's worth more than fifty quid to the right person.'

'At what time did you find the case and belongings?' asked Hawkes.

'I dunno mister, it must have been about three in the morning. Some pissheads disturbed my sleep down by the pizza parlour on their way home from a binge uptown. I usually doss down around the back of the premises where the vents keep me warm. If I'm lucky they toss out a duff pizza that got burnt all around the edges. I ain't fussed as long as it still tastes okay!'

'This dealer, does he have a name.'

'Eddie Salmon. Others know him as 'the fish'. Spence glanced at Hakes, he knew the man.

'And how did you get into the flat?

'Inside the wallet was a key. I had the address so I thought I'd give it a go before the man got back from work. Nice place, flash area.'

'Was there anything else in the suitcase... anything that you're not telling me about?' asked Spence.

Ralph McTavish shook his head avidly.

'No trinkets or presents, a bottle of perfume, maybe cigarettes?'

'Nothing, just clothes and that travel wallet. What time do they serve breakfast?'

'Seven.' Replied Spence. 'Who else knows about you going to the flat?'

'Nobody. I might not look the part these days, but I once wore a uniform. I had pride, but society can be mighty cruel when it wants.' To demonstrate that he wasn't lying, he sat up straight and pulled together the lapels of his overcoat. 'Nowadays though a child will passes me by with disdain in their eyes. That can hurt the most. I had me a family once, but when they heard that I had got banged up for hitting an officer, they took the opportunity to move on.'

'How long did they give you?'

'Five years and a discharge at the end of it!' MacTavish looked hard at Spence as though selling his soul to the man opposite. 'I am telling you the truth mister. I ain't lying. Finding that case was like a lifeline!'

Thinking about April and dinner, Spence told Hawkes to close down the interview and place McTavish back in the cell until he made a decision about the man's future. Waiting for Hawkes to come back to the office, he thought about Siobhan.

'You're going to let him go guv'nor, why?' asked Thomas Hawkes 'we caught him red-handed!'

'Did he break anything at Cortelli's place?'

'No. it was like he said, he used the key to open the door.'

'Well then he deserves a break Tom. Every so often we can all *fuck* up in life and when we do life has a nasty habit of putting us down in the gutter. Believe me it's a bloody hard struggle getting back up that ladder to where others will accept you. Finding your self-respect however is the hardest battle that you have to overcome. One thing we know now and that is that Cortelli hasn't left the country. MacTavish is just an old seadog down on his luck, let's cut him some slack. Tell Bob Perkins from me, that he can accommodate McTavish for the night and let him have his cooked breakfast. Bob can boot him out around eight.' Spence couldn't help but, laugh. *'That should please one of them, but not the other!'*

Hawkes pulled shut the door of the office leaving Spence to cross through Ralph McTavish's name on the white board, eliminating at least one suspect. Descending the stairs down to custody he could only but, admire his boss. At times Spence could be deep and silent, but his heart was in the right place. It wasn't the first time that the detective chief inspector had let somebody off the hook lightly.

Switching off the office light Spence sent a text. *Collecting Chinese.*

Chapter Twenty Four

Only April went to the autopsy of Annabelle Du Renard and from the local enquiries made in the immediate area, sadly it appeared that the middle-aged thespian had very few friends outside of the theatre despite the numerous photographs that adorned her kitchen wall. Public adoration would only give back so much, cutting any ties of friendship, unless an advantage could be gained.

April looked at the lonely figure of the actress lying on the examination table sensing the sadness that Du Renard had endured throughout her life. Spence had warned her only the week before about getting emotionally attached, but lying there with her eyes closed just waiting for the angels to descend and collect her soul before the autopsy began April felt duty bound to attend, knowing that Annabelle would have wanted a friend to be there until the very end.

Oddly and inexplicably the examination room was much colder than most days as though the angels weren't the only unseen visitors and even Susan Weekes made comment as to how chilly the ambiance in the room had seemed.

'It's rare that we have any central heating on and especially in this room, but I asked Jasmin to turn it on today.'

April smiled and coughed the smell of the formaldehyde hitting the back of her throat.

'The atmosphere,' she looked around 'it appears charged!'

Weekes looked up from the electronic scales, making sure that the calibration was correct.

'I noticed that too. I'm not given to anything unconnected to science, but I'd say that we were not alone!'

Prior to April arriving the mortuary assistant had shaved Annabelle's head, her long waves and curls gone and placed in a bag ready for disposal.

Susan Weekes completed her cursory checks, recording the findings before reaching for the small circular saw. She powered up the cutter and made a cylindrical cut around the top of the head just shy of two centimetres above the eyes and ears. Lifting away the scalp Annabelle took on a very different look. April watched expecting to see a sac of unused tears where the aging actress had come to accept her final moments alive.

Photographing the damage made by the falling pole the pathologist measured the damaged tissue. Amongst the parenchyma the blood was richly dark around the injury.

'I concur with the hospital neurologist in that the deceased died as a result of a massive brain bleed, resulting in a subarachnoid haemorrhage. Not a nice way to die.' Weekes looked up. 'Has Health and Safety proved negligence?'

'They're still undecided because of lack of evidence. Ask me and I'd stretch out my neck and say that it wasn't an accident.'

Weekes didn't reply, but instead she nodded her agreement.

'How the investigation going?' she asked

'Slow. Every time Spence and Hawkes chase down a lead, it hits a brick wall. So far, we have two indisputable murders, two suspicious accidents resulting in death and a missing person. If it wasn't so serious some warped mind would manufacture a Christmas board game and make a fortune from other people's misfortune.'

'It's a good name,' said Weekes as she probed deeper.

'What is?'

'Misfortune!'

Weekes finished with the head examination and turned her attention to the normal procedures, measuring and weighing the vital organs. April stood back. She wanted to hold Annabelle's hand and tell her that it would all be over soon, but Weekes was taking her time, making sure that nothing was missed.

'Did the deceased have any relatives, next-of-kin?'

'None that we could find. I made a call to the theatre where she worked last and then to Equity before I came here. They've agreed to split the cost of her funeral. At least she gets a send-off that she deserves. Where Weekes had cut away the scalp the facial muscles on either cheek had gone taut, Annabelle Du Renard looked as though she was smiling.

*****

A couple of miles from the autopsy Spence took Hawkes along on the return visit to the Italian Embassy in Mayfair, wanting his belligerent and confrontational approach to be recognised by the embassy staff, especially Franco Bianchi. Spence wanted another go at the official over the missing interpreter, Cortelli.

'You think Bianchi knows what was discussed in the interview room?' Hawkes asked as he pulled the car into Grosvenor Square.

'He knows,' said Spence 'people like Bianchi don't rise to a position without treading on a few toes along the way. Generally they've eyes and ears everywhere.'

'Does that include, making someone disappear!'

Spence chuckled 'You've a suspicious mind Tom, but the idea had crossed my mind as well.' Spence pointed to where they should park the car. He watched the CCTV monitor above the door swivel in their direction. He made Hawkes aware of the camera.

'Smile nicely Tom and don't be over aggressive. Some of our top brass have Roman Catholic blood running through their veins and you never know with the buggers upstairs how well they're connected. The Masons might well have pull some strings for their promotion, but you've a promising career ahead of you, only your will come through grit and determination; and hard work!'

Hawkes grinned nicely. 'I did a check with Cortelli's bank account, there has been no transactions since his return from Rome, although I have to say it was a very healthy balance and unless he came from good stock and a well-heeled family, he had another side line somewhere!'

Spence looked up at the camera, but didn't smile. 'You'd think a man coming back from his holiday would want some ready cash.'

As the time before the door opened at the rear of the embassy and an official stood and awaited their approach. Spence noticed that it wasn't Bianchi. The Italian official introduced himself as Luca Tabbianchi, an assistant to Bianchi.

'Mr Bianchi regrets that he could not make himself available for your visit Mr Spence, he sends his apologies, but I am here to facilitate your enquiries in any way that I possibly can.'

They followed Tabbianchi into the building. Inside Hawkes noticed that wherever they went they were under the scrutiny of a camera.

'We didn't come to see Mr Bianchi,' Hawkes begun, but we were hoping to catch up with Mr Cortelli. He's been helping with our investigation, only as we seemed to be getting somewhere, he ups sticks and disappears, strange that!'

Tabbianchi seemed somewhat perplexed to have heard the name Cortelli. He turned his back on the nearest camera. 'We have not seen Roberto since his return from Rome. He called in the next morning to say that he felt unwell, I suspect something that ate on the journey back. We was going to leave it until later and it there had been no word from him, we was going to call you chief inspector.'

Spence raised his eyebrows, but made no comment, letting Hawkes continue. 'Before he went to Rome, did Mr Cortelli have any pre-arranged appointments that he hasn't attended?'

Tabbianchi took his time in answering. 'Roberto worked primarily outside of our walls. He would receive a call from our administrative office and be assigned a task, normally at a London hospital, a police station or occasionally a hotel, anywhere where an Italian national was having language difficulties. Very rarely did Roberto come to the embassy, unless it was deemed necessary. Roberto was paid as a consultant, paid by the hourly rate. He was not officially on our list of staff here at the embassy.' What Tabbianchi had described didn't quite match what Cortelli had said when taking to Hawkes and Spence.

'He must have mentioned Vivienne D'Corscy?'

The question was direct and delivered expecting an answer. Tabbianchi's expression suggested that he had not been expecting these questions. 'If my memory serves me well detective, she was a friend of Roberto. She had a slight problem with a visa permit, but Mr Bianchi made some calls and sorted the problem.' He held up his palms to suggest that it was no big issue. 'A trifling matter, but our embassy aide allayed her distress!'

Spence jumped in quickly. 'So I heard.' He punctuated with a pause. 'Have you ever heard of a Mortimer Valdis?'

Tabbianchi responded immediately. 'No, I am not familiar with the name chief inspector. General enquires are dealt with on a daily basis by our administrative office. He does not sound Italian.'

Spence stared directly at Tabbianchi. 'I'm not familiar with all Italian surnames, it was just worth a try.'

Tabbianchi however came back with his own retort. 'However, the name Valdis I do know. As a young scholar I studied European History. Valdis is old Nordic and means *'the dead'.'*

Spence and Hawkes passed one another a look of recognition. Valdis was a pseudonym, why hadn't they considered that. It was a clever move and would account for why there was no public records held by Inland Revenue, customs and excise, passport control, television licencing or DVLA. Mortimer Valdis only ever existed on the front cover of a book.

Spence handed over his contact details to Tabbianchi and thanked him for his help. Before exiting the building he turned one last time and smiled up at the camera knowing that Bianchi would be watching.

Franco Bianchi watched the two men get back in the car and drive away. There was something about the senior detective that he despised. Making sure that the embassy was once again secure Bianchi called Tabbianchi into his office.

'Next time Luca keep looking at the camera where I can see what you are saying. It is important. The older policeman is very dangerous!' He pressed a button beneath his desk and waited for the kitchen maid to appear. He ordered a fresh tray of coffee for them both. 'Did Matteo find anything at the flat?'

'No Franco,' Tabbianchi seemed to hesitate before fully replying 'Matteo said that the police had been there before he arrived. There were signs that the furniture had been dusted for fingerprints. Roberto's passport and travel documents were nowhere to be found.'

Bianchi stepped back from the window and sat behind his desk. 'We must assume that the police found the wallet. It doesn't matter as they'll not find anything incriminating inside.' He drummed his fingers along the top of the desk. 'The river, has nobody reported a body as being found?'

'No. If they did find one, Matteo is a very effective operative and identification would be extremely difficult.'

'Including the dentures?' Bianchi asked.

'He removed all identifying marks and the teeth. Not even his own mother would recognise the body!'

*****

On the journey back to the station Spence took a call from April, she sounded unhappy, agitated.

'Is there something wrong?' he asked.

'Not everything, I think that you had best get back here as soon as possible. You have a visitor waiting to see you!'

'Who?' he asked.

'My ex-husband.'

April didn't say anything else, instead she cancelled the call. Picking up the coffee she tried to stop her hands from shaking. Pressing her shoulders into the plasterwork of the station kitchen she needed support of the wall. Of all times that Barry had to show, he had arrived almost the same time that she had returned from the autopsy, breezing in to her laboratory as though nothing had ever changed, but things had. Lots had

211

changed and were finally on the up, going well with Spence. April was pessimistic that Barry would ruin everything. From the kitchen above the rear yard she watched Hawkes park the car.

Chapter Twenty Five

Spence wasn't sure what to expect as he rounded the corridor and saw Barry Moyne waiting outside of his office. He was older than when he had seen him last, not that cared about the man. Moyne was one of those men that you would meet once, instantly dislike, regrettably not forget, but avoid meeting on another occasion. Approaching the door to his office he nodded, but didn't offer his hand in any form of greeting. A short distance behind Thomas Hawkes followed up closing the door as the two older detectives took seats.

'I hear that you made detective sergeant, congratulations!' Spence was being professionally polite, nothing else.

'Thanks.' Moyne acknowledged Hawkes who had moved over to the window where he was close to Spence. 'Rumour is that you've two murders under investigation now, a young woman and her superior and possibly a couple of unexplained deaths as well on top. You've got your hands full.'

'News travels fast!' Spence replied, wondering how the information had been leaked regarding Roberts and Du Renard. It was almost certainly not from April, but more likely the brass on the floor above. 'And the reason for your visit?' Spence was blunt, not unnoticed by Hawkes.

Moyne realised that his visit wasn't going to be looked upon as social. He coughed to clear his throat. 'Sometime around midnight, maybe a little later a marked car stopped and questioned a man who they caught loitering down the service alleyway leading to the emergency staircase for Hampton's literary agency. The man who gave his name as Mortimer Valdis told the officers that he was an author and that he was around the back of the building procuring inspirational ideas for a forthcoming book of which the agency had promised to offer a contract.'

Spence looked at Hawkes. *'What a load of bollocks!*

Moyne guessed that his visit had not been in vain.

'He gave a back street hotel in Knightsbridge as his temporary place of residency, but said that his permanent address was in the south of France. By all accounts this was a working holiday.'

Spence shook his head. 'I've heard it called some things in my time, but never a working holiday!' He sucked a fragment of biscuit from between his teeth, rounding on Moyne. 'Tell me the officers that engaged in the stop, checked him out thoroughly?'

'That's the awkward bit of my visit. We had communication problems last night with some amateur ham radio enthusiast jamming our signals. They let Valdis go with a warning.'

Hawkes heard Spence muttered the word *fuck* under his breath.

'As routine I was delving through the overnight intelligence when I came upon the name Valdis, I had heard that he was wanted in connection with your investigation.'

Spence was in no mood to be civil. Valdis had been confronted by not one, but two officers and had somehow managed to slip through the net.

'And you felt compelled to come across from West End, just to tell this sergeant, couldn't you have just called?' Hawkes felt the tension cut through the air.

'I was heading this way to see an old friend so I thought that I'd first check on Hampton's then make sure that you got the information first hand. Trouble with most nicks is that messages get distorted somewhere down the line.'

Spence asked Hawkes to run an intelligence check on Tabbianchi whilst he and Moyne discussed the possibility of linking past cold cases. Hawkes left the office acknowledging the errand was a ploy for Spence to delve into the real reason for the visit.

'So lets' dispense with the niceties, what do you want with Charlotte Street?' It wasn't a question, but more a demand.

'I thought I'd in and say hello to April. We've not spoken since the divorce and I thought that she might be getting a little lonely.'

Spence eyed Barry Moyne suspiciously. He couldn't be sure how much the detective sergeant knew about his involvement with Moyne's ex-wife. Police stations were never the best place to keep anything secret. He did his best to protect her.

'April was attending a post-mortem earlier, I'm not sure if she's around.'

'Oh she's in, I saw her watching when I came in the back door.'

Spence quickly pulled the conversation back around to that of Mortimer Valdis. 'The intelligence report, did it mention was Valdis was wearing?'

'Black hat and long leather coat. It gave his description as having dark eyes, slightly pale complexion with the veins showing in his cheeks.' Moyne ran the tip of his tongue over his top lip. 'Hints of him being a drinker.' He'd heard about Siobhan, knew that she was in a mental institution in Ireland. He continued with the description. 'Daytime stubble, broad shoulders and looked fit. He spoke with a slight twang, given as hailing from north of Watford at some time back!'

'That sounds like what we've gathered for Valdis. He could be involved, but we're not hedging all our bets into one basket.'

'Has an electronic photo-fit been done?'

Spence nodded. 'I'll get a copy sent over. We've not released it yet until we're sure that Valdis is our man. Show it around, just in case he is still in the area.'

'And Valdis... is that his real name?'

Spence shook his head. 'Almost certainly an alias.'

Moyne got up and made his way to the door. There was nothing else to offer on the subject. Holding the door open he has one last thing to say.

'I will just pop my head in the forensic lab and say hello, then I'll be on my way. I'll arrange for Fleming and Doyle to make contact with regards to the photo-fit.'

Barry Moyne closed the door of Spence's office slowly just so he could hear the mumbled *fuck off*. Standing in the corridor outside the office he smiled to himself. Now it was time to make April feel just as uneasy.

With Moyne out of the way Hawkes returned.

'He didn't hang around long?'

'No, the smug bastard only wanted to come and gloat.' Thomas Hawkes didn't pass comment.

'You're shrewd Tom... you're no fool. Do you know?'

'About you and April... yes, although as far as I aware nobody else does and my lips are sealed. If you're asking, I'd say why not only I like April and she's had a rough ride lately.'

Spence smiled. 'Thanks Tom.'

Hawkes went on. I heard that the flash git knocked April around when they were married. The jungle drums also tell that he can be a bit handy too with suspects. I was a surprised to hear that he had been promoted.'

Spence didn't smile. I'd heard the same, what about Tabbianchi?'

'Nothing, clean as a whistle.'

'I didn't so. He didn't seem to fit the profile of a cold blooded killer!'

Hawkes watched as Moyne walked over to a waiting car. The visit with April had been brief. He told Spence.

'Do you know how the e-fit's coming along?'

'Last time that I checked the profiler was trying several variations. It was April's idea suggesting Valdis could change his appearance to fit the crime.'

Spence seemed to be thinking. 'I wonder what he was really doing around the back of the Hampton building.'

'Looking for a way in?' Hawkes advocated.

'That was my assumption.' Spence had forgotten about Moyne. 'But what would he gain from breaking in at night.'

'Looking for a manuscript perhaps,' Hawkes evoked 'a manuscript that had been rejected.'

Spence wasn't so sure. 'Why?'

'It would have his prints on it for starters. Maybe his DNA, who knows?'

'In any event Valdis is a pseudonym, so until we get anything concrete, we're almost back at square one!'

A knock at the door had them look to see who was entering. April smiled, which Spence was not expecting. 'You both look like you've just seen a ghost!' she declared.

'Not seen one, we're chasing one. Are you okay?' he asked.

'I'm fine, ghosts don't come haunting any longer!'

'I'll go check Tabbianchi,' Hawkes said as he went to exit the room, giving April time to discuss her ex-husband and Spence the opportunity to make

sure that she was really alright. April placed her hand on his arm and stopped him leaving.

'There's no need Tom. You wouldn't be a detective if you didn't know what was going on.' She let her hand fall away and faced Spence. 'He's either brazen, bloody stupid, or downright reckless!'

'Valdis or your ex-husband?' it caused them to laugh.

'Barry Moyne is just plain stupid. No, I was referring to Mortimer Valdis. Whatever his reason for being around back of Hampton's the risk must have been worth being caught. There's something inside that he wants or was checking out.'

'Tom reckons it could be his manuscript!'

April took the seat opposite Spence. No. Something else, I think. Hampton's is like his chrysalis, where he hatched his dreams of becoming known. When his plans were thwarted, the caterpillar changed its appearance. I'm not sure how, but he wants something else from Hamptons and until he gets it, nobody is safe.'

'We can't take that to Hampton's, it will have them all running scared.'

'Shouldn't we at least warn them Spence, Valdis or whatever his name, proved how ruthless he has become in dealing with Annabelle Du Renard?'

'We could set up some of our own security measures,' Hawkes suggested. It was also a way of seeing Stephanie Garland again and apologising for not taking her out to dinner, having taken Sharon Trevelyan instead.

'Hidden cameras and motion sensors, it's an idea. April can you arrange all that?' She agreed. She was about to get up and leave, when she remembered why she had come visiting.

'The e-fit is ready, I wondered if you both wanted to have a look before we go to press.'

The profiler had taken into consideration age and skin texture, bringing into line the nose, slant of the eyes, tightness of the cheeks against bone and finally the mouth and chin. The only feature that he had not been sure about was the eyes, which were still very dark.

'Not quite Ray Winstone, said Hawkes 'probably a mix with Bob Hoskins. He still has that mean look of a wilderness hunter rather than a writer.'

Spence nodded as he studied the profile. 'We need to become the hunter and have him know that he is the prey!'

April printed off a copy each plus extras. She felt exactly the same way about Barry Moyne.

Chapter Twenty Six

Keeping clear of traffic, pedestrians and any other roving police patrols that were about Jack Chilvray returned home knowing that he had been lucky. For whatever reason the two officers had, neither had seemed interested in taking his interest around the back of the building any further. Standing at the base of the fire escape he was about to ascended the metal steps when they had caught him. Had he been on the landing above, their approach might have been different.

Pouring a generous amount into the whiskey tumbler he took it outside and sat on the top step of the stairs leading down to the garden below. Toasting the moon above the rooftops he gave thanks to providence.

With several cushions supporting his head Chilvray lay back on the wood boards looking up at the night sky, approving of the universe and the panoramic endless abundance of opportunity. Jack liked big wide open spaces, to being hemmed in. Every so often a star flickered as though it was acknowledging his watching. Other than the odd comet erupting, leaving behind a fiery tail, disappearing into the deep blue of the unknown beyond the heavens seemed to be at peace.

Despite the silence all around there was a certain disquiet brewing inside of him. Jack Chilvray was surprised that after the deaths of Rachel Roberts, D'Corscy and Trent, Hamptons had not yet got the message. Swallowing the last of the whiskey, he planned his next move. The time had come again to be sending the literary agency and the authorities another message, maybe one that would have him taken seriously.

*****

Examining the e-fit that had been faxed over to West End Central, Fleming and her partner Doyle agreed that it represented a good likeness of the man that they had stopped the night before. They were questioned as to why they had not arrested the man, but both defended their actions, advocating that he had done nothing wrong. Spence however saw it as an opportunity missed. Sitting next to him on her worn leather settee April sensed his annoyance. She moved closer making him take notice of her.

'Remember, it's easy to condemn anybody on the front line Spence and unless you were there, they acted within the parameters of their training and the law. Valdis has proved that he's willing to take risks. Whether he sees himself as invincible or not, he's bound to make a mistake sooner or later.'

April perceived that he agreed he had been harsh on the two young officers, he let the rigors of the day drain from his shoulders ebbing to his feet.

'We just need a break, something whereby we gain the upper hand. Fleming and Doyle could have given us that one advantage.' April sensed that he was down. 'This is not like you, you're always upbeat, positive. What's suddenly changed your perspective?'

'Age I suppose. I've been in this game for a long time, but suddenly the villains have the upper hand. I'm sure if its technology giving them the edge, or whether I've reached that stage where I should let detectives like Hawkes blaze the trail.'

April kissed his cheek and affectionately placed her hand on his shoulder demonstrating her support. 'Tom's enthusiastic and clever Spence, but he still has a lot to learn and only you can teach him. He admires you and respects your leadership.'

'You've not talked about the meeting with Barry Moyne, did it open old wounds?'

She stayed where she was, leaving her hand on his shoulder, hearing his heart beat beneath his chest. *'There's nothing to discuss. He put his head around the door, said hi, then fucked off. I was glad.'* April pulled herself up so she could look into his eyes. 'In a way it made me wonder what I ever saw in him. He's cold, calculating and devious. In a way, he's just like Valdis.'

She let the silence between them absorb what she had just said. 'When I'm with you Spence, I feel unbroken and alive. It's taken me a long time to feel like that!'

*****

Next morning Spence and Hawkes went back to Hamptons. This time Julie was back on reception.

'Do you want me to phone through for Stephanie Garland?' she asked, her lipstick smile as glossy and insipid as the model on the front page of the fashion magazine she was flicking through.

223

'That'd be good… thanks!'

Julie raised her eyebrows at the young detective, knowing that he had a thing for the literary agent on the floor above.

Spence turned to face the reception door leading to the street, so that what he had to ask wasn't detected by Julie. *'Didn't you have a date lined up with Miss Garland?'*

Hawkes smiled back at Julie who was on the phone and replied 'I went out with Trevelyan remember. I was supposed to call and fix a date, but I never quite got around to it!'

Spence tutted. 'First rule of any investigation Tom. Never let sentiment get in the way of an inquiry. Using people gets results.'

'Blackstones.' Hawkes enquired.

'No… Daniel Spence. Blackstones Law is alright for all the mundane stuff, but thinking outside of the box is what really matters. Blame me when you see Stephanie Garland, my hide can take it.'

Julie coughed attracting their attention. 'You know the way detective. Stephanie said to say that she'll be waiting for you on the first floor.' Hawkes chose the stairs rather than the lift.

The greeting was less cordial than previous, Stephanie Garland kept her arms folded across her chest as they approached.

'Back so soon detective and you've brought along your boss!'

Spence identified the animosity in her voice, coming to Hawkes rescue. *'Tom would have been back sooner, had I not kept him working late every night. This investigation is wreaking havoc with our social lives!'*

Garland looked first at Hawkes, then Spence, then back at Hawkes, undecided whether it was just a case of men sticking together. After a few moments of doubt she began to mellow.

'So what do we owe this honour?' there was still a hint of sarcasm, but it was fading.

'A man, purporting to be Mortimer Valdis was caught prowling around at the base of your fires escape. Regrettably because no offences had been committed he was allowed to walk away. We've come back this morning to see if you or anybody else can shed any light on why he'd be snooping around at night outside Hamptons. What have you got that he could possibly want inside?'

Garland looked around the room at her colleagues who had their noses buried in their work. If you follow me, maybe we can make some sense of his visit.' She took them to a quiet room down the corridor and away from the main work area.

'With each submission an author is invited to compile a personal profile. The details that they enter gives the agent reading the manuscript an insight into the reason why they think Hamptons could help promote their work. Mortimer Valdis would almost certainly have added his aspirations.'

'Plus a residential address?' Hawkes interrupted. Garland nodded, then continued.

'I checked the record of submission. Against the date it was received the initials CT had been recorded. A day later another set VD appeared. Charles Trent had obviously reviewed what had been sent in, but decided that it didn't warrant his attention. It was unusual for the editor to read a new submission, but there was no saying why, it could have been that he was helping out on the floor below to cover sickness or holidays.'

She offered refreshments, but both declined.

'When I pulled the manuscript from our archived records, there was no profile attached. Either Valdis didn't submit one or Trent or D'Corscy kept it.'

'Has his office been used since his death?'

'No. The directors want it changed around before anybody else occupies the space.'

In the bottom drawer of his desk they found the profile. Hawkes dropped it into an envelope so that April could examine the single sheet later.

'This could be the break that we've been waiting for Miss Garland. Thank you!'

'So does this mean that you'll be working even more hours?' she asked.

Once again Spence saved the day. 'He'll return the favour soon. I promise!'

Stephanie Garland smiled, now she felt that he couldn't back down. Hawkes looked at Garland then Spence. 'Tomorrow night?' Spence concurred. I'll make my way back down to reception, you fix the time and venue!'

Between them they fixed to have a meal then catch a show. On the way back down to reception Spence had stopped to talk with Richard Quince, wanting to capture the mood of the room after the demise of Charles Trent, but Quince was wary of talking to the police and so instead he centred his conversation around sport. Spence found himself tackling the agent for inside advice regarding the forthcoming trip to the dog track.

On the way back to the station Spence made Hawkes stop at a florist where he ordered a bunch of flowers for April. Getting back in the car he warned Hawkes not to pass comment.

Chapter Twenty Seven

Jack Chilvray had lost sleep during the night eager to get to the next phase of his plan. He had put together the various elements in his mind, times, places and buildings, all that was required was to put theory into practice. Lying awake watching the night dissolve he had decided that getting inside Hampton's wasn't entirely necessary as he stood in the window of the expensive antiquities shop examining a vase reputedly dating back to the time of the Jiajing dynasty. Striding confidently towards the façade of the shop he smiled at the shop assistant as Stephanie Garland came closer.

'It's a little beyond my price range I'm afraid, but an excellent piece all the same.' He handed the vase back to the young woman, stating that he would return soon and be interested in lesser priced artefacts.

Stepping from the safety of the shop she passed by Chilvray almost within touching distance. He caught a whiff of the fresh perfume that she had applied before leaving the office, it was heavily scented, but inviting. Letting her get ahead by at least ten strides he followed, already enjoying the game. Stephanie was in a buoyant mood, already forgetting the rigors of the day as she nodded and smiled at the newspaper vendor on the street corner, Thomas Hawkes had promised her a meal that he was sure that she would not have sampled before.

It was easy shadowing the literary agent as she weaved her way through the oncoming pedestrians keen to be home after another long day cooped up in their work places, offices, banks and shops. Many were only interested in getting to their destination rather than admiring the architecture and good weather as they rushed on by. To the majority London was an evil necessity where they could ply their trade, help pay the mortgage and ignore what the city had to offer. Chilvray preferred the lure and solitude of the big wide open spaces, but London gave him a buzz as it offered so many opportunities.

Faceless strangers passed him by some looking up at the dark shifting eyes as he viewed them each with interest. In his wide brimmed hat and long leather coat he represented a film extra for a spaghetti western, but none noticed that the lowest button was missing, not even Jack Chilvray himself was aware that it had been lost. Passing a beggar he dropped three gold coloured coins in the man's hand.

'Grab a warm drink my friend, you look like you could do with it!' Before the beggar had time to say thank you Chilvray had disappeared amongst the crowd exiting the staff entrance of an office. A short distance behind the down-on-his-luck mendicant was already at the coffee stall buying a hot drink. The owner offered a stale cake as well rather than throw it away.

Still following a healthy distance behind Chilvray guessed that her journey had purpose, only other than to observe the traffic going in either direction she had looked neither left nor right. Normally his quarry was aware of his presence, but not today. Turning left she headed down a pedestrian thoroughfare where either side of the walkway almost every commercial outlet consisted of a restaurant. When the young woman waved and turned into the entrance of a Mandarin eating house Jack

229

Chilvray darted from sight into the service alley at the side of a pizza parlour where several feral cats were already perched awaiting the evenings superfluous scraps.

Laying down the menu that he had been studying Thomas Hawkes took her coat and hung it on the coat rack near the bar. He thought that he caught a glimpse of a man in a long coat and hat, but in the blink of an eye the image was lost.

'Is something wrong?' his guest asked.

He shook his head and smiled. 'No... not really, I thought that I saw something, but it was nothing. Work can occasionally play tricks with the mind, so it's not worth worrying about. Come on lets order, I'm famished!' As the waiter pulled back her chair, he took a second look just to be sure, but it had been a hallucination, nothing else. Hawkes rubbed his eyes, invigorating additional fluid across the optical lens, revitalising the parts that had gone dry.

'You look beat, perhaps we should just have a meal and a coffee back at my place!'

'That'd be good.'

They looked up and down the menu which gave examples in both Mandarin and English. Hawkes ordered for them both as this was Garland's first time, avoiding any heavily spiced dishes. Every so often he looked up at the mirror behind where she was sitting sensing that they were being watched, but the thoroughfare outside was busy, with diners both coming and going. When the wine arrived he decided to forget about

Valdis for a few hours allowing the woman sitting opposite to detract his focus elsewhere.

Using the reflection of a blacked-out sheet of glass on an empty premises door Jack Chilvray watched as the pair talked, laughed and enjoyed their meals. Every so often he checked his watch, keeping tabs on when they were likely to finish. Taking a gamble he switched his location to a coffee house where he had a good view of the entire precinct. Placing his hat on the table top he ordered a strong Italian blend, speculating that it could be a long wait.

When they did finally emerge Stephanie Garland took the opportunity outside of the restaurant to show her gratitude. Sipping the contents of his second cup Chilvray observed the pair as they kissed then walk towards the end of the precinct arm in arm. Passing by where he was sat neither Hawkes nor Garland took any notice of the man watching. Pushing the cup to one side Jack let them get ahead before picking up his hat and exiting back out into the main road.

The pair turned east heading towards Trafalgar Square which pleased Jack. The area was large and always filled with tourists. If by any chance the detective did make a connection there were a number of options available by which to escape. In fact if he was spotted it would only add to the excitement and leave the young policeman guessing. Overhead the first stars of the night were beginning to appear.

Heading down Whitehall the task of lagging behind was all the more difficult as many of the sightseers had elected to stick around the base of the column and fountains. At one point Jack had to come alongside a horse in a sentry box to conceal himself. Hawkes could feel the small hairs on the back of his neck standing on end, but could not fathom why.

'We should have taken the tube,' exclaimed a concerned Stephanie Garland as she sensed Hawkes looking behind 'only you keep looking behind Tom!'

Pulling her down Great Scotland Yard where the old police headquarters had almost completed a major refurbishment programme turning the historic building into a hotel Hawkes justified his disquiet.

'That's odd because I sensed that I was being followed from work to the restaurant.'

They waited a good five minutes, but nobody strange appeared at the junction. Reluctantly Hawkes continued walking with Stephanie on his arm. He felt uneasy about the evening despite the wine. At one point he considered calling Spence, but decided against it. Calling his superior on a whim would not go down well.

Standing where he would not be seen Jack Chilvray had taken Northumberland Avenue second guessing the detectives objective to catch him out. Pulling himself back into the shadows beside the stone plinth he smiled. It would take more than luck to outwit Jack.

In short distance of the Imperial War Museum Hawkes and Garland turned down a side street before going into a semi-detached property. On the far corner was a public house, nothing attractive nor encouraging, but the trade was going through its own recession and landlords were struggling to make ends meet. When the lights went on in the upstairs floor Jack crossed the road holding his hat down by his side. There was no point in taking unnecessary risks and especially as he just wanted to look through some discarded household waste.

Tucked behind the front hedge he found the three multi-coloured council bins allocated to each property where minutes later he pulled from within a gardening magazine that had been distributed to hundreds of potential clients up and down the country. Typed in legible clear font were the details that he needed, *Miss Stephanie Garland, 34 Chaucer Gardens, Lambeth SE1 9DX.*

Jack placed the marketing brochure in his coat pocket and closed the lid. Upstairs the lights had not gone out. Going down the side of the converted property he checked around back getting a feel for the house and the lay of the garden. For a good ten minutes he observed the occupant of the lower flat busy herself in the rear kitchen before leaving feeling that he had enough material for his next chapter. Jack left Chaucer Gardens knowing that he would return soon.

Chapter Twenty Eight

Hawkes stayed the night with Stephanie Garland leaving very early the next morning, promising to be in touch later that day. With her lying next to him carefree and satiated he however had, had trouble sleeping as something deep within his psyche had refused to let him relax despite their coming together. She was surprised that he had been up and showered so early, but Hawkes had convinced her that there was nothing wrong before he left. Walking on the back door of the station the first person that he bumped into was Sharon Trevelyan.

'Hi...' his greeting was obviously hesitant and rushed and not lost on the pretty blonde.

'I thought that we had set some ground rules Tom, that we'd be honest with one another. This job is hard enough without introducing any other unexpected surprises!'

Hawkes did his best to hide the embarrassment of where he had just spent the night. 'I'm sorry Sharon, we've just been extra busy since our meal. Can I get back to you soon and arrange another date?' The suggestion seemed to somewhat dispel her immediate frustration as a smile began to crease across her lips. She was still unsure as to why he hadn't called, knowing that he had the evening off. Their brief exchange was fortuitously interrupted by the custody sergeant crossing from the control room to the custody suite. He acknowledged both, but had a message for Hawkes.

'Spence has been looking for you Tom. He's in the canteen.'

Hawkes took immediate advantage of the communique to get away, relieved that he wasn't going to become engaged in an awkward conversation with Trevelyan as to where he had spent the previous evening.

'I'll call you later,' he was gone before she had time to reply. In the canteen he grabbed himself a coffee and sat down opposite Spence. The obvious signs of losing a night's sleep evident under both eyes.

'Burning the candle at both ends,' Spence inquired as he grinned at his young protégé 'good night?'

Hawkes breathed in long and hard. 'It was until Valdis came haunting my thoughts. I felt him close by, almost within touching distance and yet every time I looked there was nobody there!'

'Mental and physical perception Tom. The moment that we enrol in this profession, somebody unseen implants both inside of us. I've had similar experiences. Many dismiss the sensation as imaginary, a whim that you hope will come true, but believe me, as often as not those buggers are wrong. I've learnt down the years that feelings life that are real.'

Hawkes sipped the coffee which was good and hot.

'Stephanie Garland told me that she felt somebody had followed her from the office to the restaurant.'

'Valdis needs tracking down Tom. He knows that he's been close because he's involved, but now he's getting bold, getting right under our skin. It's as though he's toying with us now, laying a trap hoping that we'll fall into it!'

'Bob Perkins said that you'd been looking for me?'

'Yes. Like you, I had a fitful sleep going over aspects of this case. Waterfall Heights was originally Pembroke Mansions, the home of Rachel Roberts before she sold it onto Vivienne D'Corscy. Nice and convenient for Valdis, keeping the sale in the family in a manner of speaking. Roberts reported a burglary which Barry Moyne investigates, also attended by April and the neighbour opposite Annabelle Du Renard is an actress working at a theatre that Charles Trent attends on a regular basis with D'Corscy. It's like a bloody merry-go-round of coincidence.'

'Starting with a book!'

Spence nodded. 'Starting with a book. It's as though Valdis planted a seed, knowing it would unleash this trail of destruction.'

'And in the meantime, he's still writing!'

'Precisely.' Spence had to talk to April to see if any prints had been recovered from the burglary at seventeen Pembroke Mansions. He put down his coffee mug and continued. 'Before you arrived, I spoke to a criminal psychologist, who told me that Valdis almost certainly suffers from a distinct narcissistic personality disorder.'

Hawkes put his mug down on the table. 'Disturbed thinking process, with impulsive action, a loner maybe, with lack of feelings as to how they treat others, exploitation to the point of inflicting pain!' Spence admired Hawkes grasp of the condition.

'In a nutshell Valdis is an attention seeker with a point to prove.'

'*Hamptons.*' Thomas Hawkes knew exactly where Valdis had set his target, he needed to contact Stephanie Garland as soon as possible. They separated so that he could make the call whilst Spence went to find April.

*****

Feeling exhausted, but joyously happy Stephanie Garland missed the call, unable to hear the ringtones over the fall of the water in the shower. She let the warm invigorating water drain down over the entire length of her body not wanting to wash away the scent of Thomas Hawkes, but accepting that it was a healthy necessity. Hawkes called Hamptons instead which was answered by Julie.

'I'll put you through detective, although I've not seen her arrive!' Tom sensed his anxiety levels increase, although many of the staff used the emergency stairs out back, where many engaged in a cigarette break. When the transfer went to ansaphone Julie came back. 'I've checked with somebody else, she's not come in yet. Can I take a message?' He asked that she call him the moment that she did arrive. Instinctively he felt the hairs on the back of his neck stand up. Finding Spence with April they perceived his apprehension.

'Everything alright?' Spence asked.

'I'm not sure, she's not arrived for work!'

Spence looked at April. It was a knowing look that suggested she might just be having a lie-in. April was more sympathetic. 'She could be on tube Tom and there's no signal deep down underground!' Hawkes smiled, although remained concerned. April continued scrolling through the screens.

'Anything?' Spence asked. April pointed to a recorded reference number.

'Prints were lifted from the scene and the reference is mine.' She wrote down the number then transferred across to another programme, where she hit the *return* key. Moments later a partial thumb and forefinger print filled the screen. April quickly read down the comments that she had added. She looked up at Spence and Hawkes. 'No match made.'

Spence sighed hard. 'Another blank, this bastard has a charmed life.' Hawkes added the details of the burglary and fingerprints to the *mood board* in their office. It might prove helpful later.

When Julie called Hawkes back around ten to say that Stephanie had failed to arrive Spence made the decision to go straight to her flat. Weaving his way through the city traffic and crossing Westminster Bridge once again Hawkes pushed hard on the accelerator. He was the first to the door of thirty four Chaucer Gardens, where he banged loudly. Around back where an external staircase led to the first floor kitchen they found the door open and the flat unoccupied. It was April who noticed the tiny traces of blood on the hallway wall.

Chapter Twenty Nine

Jack Chilvray had also been subjected to a restless night grabbing something to eat from a fast food outlet around midnight then sat watching the flat throughout the small hours from the driver's seat of his van parked in the shadows of a house opposite where the property was both empty and for sale. Early as many were just waking the young detective pulled shut the front door of the flat before walking back up the road to the main thoroughfare where he would catch a tube back to work.

Chilvray waited a good quarter of an hour to ensure the detective didn't return before making his move. Patience was an essential pastime that he had become accustomed too when spending long cold lonely nights on the North Yorkshire Moors or Brecon Beacons. Having acquired a reflective jacket from an emergency gang working on an electricity repair near to where he purchased the food Jack knocked on the front door of the flat. When he got no response he went around back and used the stairs to the first floor.

Stephanie Garland heard the knock at the kitchen door. Wrapping her wet hair in a towel and pulling the dressing gown across her underwear she prised the door back sufficient to see Jack Chilvray standing there.

'I did knock around front,' he explained, but there was no reply. We're checking properties in the immediate area for suspected electricity problems, only we've got to shut down the supply soon!'

Pulling the door open so that he could pass through Stephanie Garland thought that she had seen the man somewhere before. He offered no identification, but asked to see the meter board to which she took him into the hallway. When the opportunity presented itself Jack clamped his hand over her mouth telling her not to scream. Releasing the hold she opened her mouth to ask what he wanted, but the force of the backhanded slap cut the side of her lip. 'I said not to make a sound!'

The literary agent willed her thoughts to Thomas Hawkes begging him to return. Although she had never met Jack Chilvray she knew who he was. She swallowed the saliva in her throat and felt the dread of death creeping up her spine.

'I've got money,' she whispered, flinching in case he hit her again, but he didn't, instead he laughed.

'I'm not after your money, I came here for you Stephanie... it's you that interests me.'

She tried to force herself away from the wall where he held her, but Chilvray was strong, powerful and had some with a purpose. He pulled her into the living room where the cushions from the night before still lay about the settee.

'I watched your boyfriend leave this morning. I should think by now he's already chasing another dead-end!'

Stephanie Garland felt her eyes widen as she stared at the madman holding her hostage. 'What do you want of me?'

'Merely to co-operate, nothing overly difficult.' She was aware of a clothed hand smothering her nose and mouth as the chloroform started to take effect, within seconds her head fell forward and the lights dimmed from sight replaced by unconscious darkness.

When Stephanie Garland did wake the surroundings were very unfamiliar, lit only by the illumination from a dirty street light set high in the wall and the air about was musty as though the room had not been used for a very long time. A grey mouse watched her come round then scurry across the floor before disappearing into a hole in the wall. It was quickly followed by a large brown rat.

Stephanie tried to wriggle free, but the more she struggled the tighter her bonds gripped the skin of her wrists causing a searing pain to shoot up her arms. She had been tied to an immoveable upright beam that had been concreted into the floor and went way beyond the floor above. Using her index finger she could just about reach the plastic ties binding her arms behind the beam, they were clipped fast and only a knife or wire cutters would break them free. Endeavouring to scream to attract attention was also proving useless as Chilvray had tied a twisted piece of cloth across her mouth keeping her tongue from vibrating.

Only her feet moved freely to save her from falling, but moving about only caused the brown rat to appear and investigate. Coming closer each time, it was wary, but there would come a time when it overcome its apprehension. Stamping the ground with her bare feet Stephanie disturb dust, but it wouldn't be enough.

In another part of the building Jack Chilvray made sure that the garage door was secure and that the van had all the necessary supplies should he need to bolt the property in a hurry. It had been easy, almost too easy to get the woman out of the flat. Having reversed his van onto the drive out front the vehicle had blended into the daily routine of the residential area as just another tradesman carrying out repairs or collecting unwanted furniture. When the woman from the downstairs flat went to work Jack had managed to pass the time patiently waiting around to hear the descent of the water in the wastepipe from the top flat by watching the woman dress. He had considered paying her a visit later that evening if things didn't go to plan with Stephanie Garland.

When a light suddenly appeared at the top of the stairs leading down from the floor above Stephanie watched anxiously as her captor made his way down treading carefully each wooden steps. Chilvray descended slowly, methodically heightening her sense of dread knowing that he was coming. Going slow was all part of the game, a game that he loved. When her eyes caught sight of his they looked black, incredibly dark, as though he had borrowed them from the big brown rat. Standing before her she tried to fathom his thoughts, but her mind was without soul and salvation. He heard her mumble something, but it only amused him.

'It's a strange feeling isn't it Miss Garland being powerless,' he checked the plastic ties, but they were holding fast 'power controls the future.'

Chilvray walked around her several times touching her thigh, stroking his fingertips across the contours of her body. 'The woman that lives below you, she was more developed than you, but you are firmer.' He kissed her shoulder. She tried to pull away, but the plastic ties cut in and hurt her. He laughed.

'Had Trent and D'Corscy been courteous enough to read and understand my manuscript none of this would have been necessary.' He pulled apart her dressing gown to reveal her underwear. Licking his lips he stood back to admire her. 'I did call yesterday, but unfortunately the receptionist put my call through to your ansaphone. Don't you find that annoying when somebody cannot be bothered to talk to you!'

Stephanie tried to answer, but her tongue wouldn't, could not move. Her reply was nothing more than the noise an animal makes. Stepping forward he reach around and unclasped her brassiere yanking it from her. She felt the tears of embarrassment well in the corners of her eyes as he fondled and manhandled her breasts.

'Did the detective enjoy doing this, I can see why.' He walked around her once again, introducing intrigue into the game. Coming in close he whispered in her right ear, sniffing the scent of her washed body. *'Did he control you Miss Garland as he took your flower?'* Out of the corner of her eye Stephanie saw the rat watching. From behind the beam he ran his fingertips down the side of her thigh, then back up again until he came into contact with her knickers.

'Life is very complex and we have to consider so many things from the time we wake until sleep gives us rest. Love, loneliness, hate, joy, elation and despair. Emotions, to name just a few, but each as powerful as the other. Hamptons take none of them into consideration when they receive a new submission.' He came back around front still holding the side of her knicker elastic. 'Writers share every emotion when they write a story and they deserve so much more from a literary agency than just a brief appreciation of *'thank you, it's not quite what were are looking for, now fuck off.'*

His mood suddenly changed, Chilvray had become agitated. He tore her knickers from her body and threw them in the direction of the rat. 'When he reappears he can get accustomed to your scent as well.'

Stephanie watched the shadow where the rat had disappeared waiting to see it if came back out. Amongst the dust her discarded underwear was already sullied.

Jack Chilvray suddenly came in very close and pushed hard into her groin. She moaned as the air was expelled from her body. Licking his tongue over her body he pleasured himself until she felt his hardness. Stephanie Garland wanted to scream, but for some inexplicable reason the scream wouldn't rise in her throat.

'We would have had this pleasure last night had you not gone on a dinner date. That I had not foreseen. I had to make adjusts to my plan, something I rarely do, but there's always another way to approach a problem.' She felt his hand slide down below her abdomen.

'I can see from the look in your eyes that you know who I am. I suppose that acknowledgement should please me because in a way my name is already out there, only all the wrong reasons.' Chilvray started to unbuckle his belt and jeans.

'Let me explain, first there was Rachel Roberts, a know-it-all who pushed me aside as though I was bad air that she didn't wish to inhale. She never took my calls, avoided my visits until I found out that she had moved on. Her little ploy to be rid of me almost worked as well, but I broke into the sorting office and found the records of her redirected mail. If nothing else I am logical and resourceful.' He let his jeans fall down to his ankles. He wore no briefs. 'Waiting for her to exit the pub where she had been drinking helped as the alcohol in her body addled her reaction time. When the van hit her, she never stood a chance.' Slipping his tee-shirt over his head he let it fall on top of the jeans. 'In the end it was a quick death, perhaps too quick as I had wanted her to suffer.'

As she squirmed he pushed himself against her enjoying the resistance that she was putting up, but it only inflamed his desires. Jack Chilvray entered her body watching her eyes stare back at him with white hatred. The flames of abhorrent loathing licking at his soul. He laughed as he raped her.

'You have the same look that Vivienne D'Corscy wore the night that she died.' He pushed and grunted like a beast as he forced himself upon her licking her tears from her cheeks, the salty solution lost in a sea of despair as Chilvray continued talking.

'You are somewhat innocent in this sorry affair Stephanie, although not as innocent as you were before last night, but every virtue has a price.' When he was done with her, he bent down and collected his clothes. Releasing the turns of her mouth band, Chilvray walked towards a table which had been set against the far wall. She had not been aware that it was there.

Changing the setting on the camcorder he watched the recording, pleased with the results. He set it back to play then headed for the stairs.

'One day Miss Garland you'll be as famous as me!' Jack Chilvray laughed, the laugh of a monster. Sitting on the lower steps he slipped on his jeans before climbing to higher steps where his eyes could no longer be seen.

'I think you know what happened to dear old Charles. The quintessentially connoisseur of English literature and patron of the theatre. In my opinion a queer to boot, extravagant and eccentric, but did you know that for all his passions, he was secretly in love with Vivienne D'Corscy.' From the darkness of the staircase the voice seemed haunting as though an epigraph of a story, a horror story. Chilvray chuckled to himself.

'Poor bemused, muddled Charles he didn't whether to play with himself or offer his arse to another man. The conundrum must have sent him mad at times. Still I had to help with his destiny in the end and set him back on the right track. Now he can rest in peace without having to make any choices, providing D'Corscy doesn't turn up again!'

The rat suddenly appeared with the grey mouse hanging limply from its mouth. Stephanie sucked in what air she could, but the rat had other things on his mind. It disappeared moments later swallowed up by the darkest part of the cellar.

'You see even rats have a need to satisfy their lust!'

He came back down from the stairs to peer into the place where the rat had vanished, but in the gloom it was almost impossible to detect where it had gone. Chilvray returned to the stairs.

'You might not have heard of her, but maybe your boyfriend told you of Annabelle Du Renard. Her involvement was to look back at the shadows where I was standing watching Vivienne D'Corscy's apartment. I never did get the chance to ask whether she saw me or not that night, but it was a chance that I couldn't take.'

Chilvray suddenly stopped talking. The silence was as threatening as his presence, but at least when he was talking she had something tangible to hold onto inside her mind. After a few minutes he continued again. From the tone of his voice he sounded sincere.

'Besides the actress, you shouldn't be here, but once you go down the road of revenge, reprisal grips the soul with a cold hard hand which is very reluctant to let go. Miss Du Renard met with a fitting end and no doubt the theatre manager will honour her memory with a plaque that adoring fans will see every time they pay theatre a visit. The paradox now is what to do with you. I could leave you to the rat, but he could make a mistake and bite through your bonds.'

Unable to the upper half of his body or face Stephanie Garland was powerless to comprehend what was going to come next. Flashbacks of what she had read, of what he had written, sped through her mind leaving behind distorted images of dead bodies, torture and agonising screams. Through it all she saw the face of Thomas Hawkes, he was standing over her looking down at her naked lifeless body. It was not how it was supposed to be.

The next time that she looked up at the stairs it was empty. Scanning either side as far as she could Chilvray was nowhere to be seen. The only sound that she could hear from within was the sound of the rat cleaning its incisors.

Chapter Thirty

Spence initiated an immediate search using every available man, woman and dog unit, but come midday there was still no news nor any sightings of Stephanie Garland. She had simply vanished, disappearing without a trace or leaving behind clues, except the trickle of blood on her hallway wall.

'That bastard Valdis has her!' exclaimed Hawkes as he paced frustratingly back and forth across her living room, tapping his forehead with the heel of his palm searching for new ideas. Standing in the open doorway of the room Spence was also contemplating their next move.

'We don't know anything for sure Tom, not until we get word. You of all people should know that.'

Hawkes stopped pacing. 'If we get word guv'nor then she's already dead!'

Spence had always relied upon his experience dealing with a wide range of crimes and criminals, but Valdis was different. He was more calculating than many that he had come into contact with. What he found personally annoying was that he couldn't step in line with the killer's thoughts. Spence suggested that April look around the flat for clues, whilst he and Hawkes went searching elsewhere.

On the way back to the station Spence made another decision asking Hawkes to steer towards Ted's café, where they could think without interruption or outside influence. Hawkes looked mystified by the request.

'Occasionally I do my best thinking at the café.' Spence then added. 'I also wanted to also get away from April.'

Hawkes found a spot to park switching off the engine. 'Is everything alright, only I detected an air of discontent on the journey over to Lambeth?'

Spence scoffed. 'I'm not sure Tom. She was fine this morning and grateful for the flowers, but when she received a message from Barry Moyne asking that they meet up for a coffee, the mood instantly changed and she didn't want to discuss it. I've never let anything personal get in the way of the job before, but April has.'

Hawkes shook his head in agreement. 'We lead less complicated lives when we're not involved!' They laughed, two men on the same wavelength.

'Come on, let's do our brooding with Ted.'

The café owner brought over their order. Ted being Ted immediately picked up on their vibes. *'Blimey, you pair look like you backed the favourite and it came in last!'*

Spence smiled back at his friend. 'At times Ted, it feels like we have.' He laughed loudly heading back to the counter. 'You just pick the wrong women!'

'So what do we do next?' asked Hawkes, scooping up his drink.

'The way that I see it Tom, is that so far we've been chasing a shadow. Valdis holds all the trump cards, which is generally the way until we start putting together a picture in our favour. We both sit around and wait to see what happens or we initiate some old fashioned, tried and tested methods of policing. We start over again from the beginning. We turn over every stone of evidence that we know about and ask questions. The one thing that has been nagging at the back of my mind is how does manage to stay one step ahead.'

'He has help?'

Spence nodded. 'I told you this café helps.'

'Somebody on the inside?' Hawkes suggested.

'It's been known Tom. Leaves a nasty taste to suggest as much, but swearing an allegiance does always mean that you keep to the rules.'

Hawkes exhaled between his lips. 'That could upset quite a few people, not in the least the top floor!'

Spence lent over the table 'Fuck the top floor. They've forgotten what real policing means, only don't quote me on that!' He retrieved his mobile from his pocket which had started to buzz. It was from April. *'Hi. I'm sorry about this morning. Loads of rubbish going through my mind that I needed to be done with. I am ok now. Can we do dinner later x'* Spence shook his head in reverence of the text.

'Problems?' asked Hawkes.

'No, not now. Maybe the flowers complicated things. Men rarely get it right Tom.' They were about to get up from the table when April called.

'Where are you?' she asked, her voice calm, but full of energy.

'At Ted's doing some thinking, why?' he kept the tone of his voice low and calm to avoid any misinterpretation.

'Door to door enquiries has turned up something interesting. A neighbour reported seeing a blue van parked on the drive of number thirty four Chaucer Gardens sometime between eight and nine this morning. The informant is elderly, but she managed to get a partial index YW_ 37 _ _. It could help Spence.'

'It's a big bloody help. How comes she only got a part index?'

'Her eyesight is failing, but she remembers the letters and numbers because her sister is called Yvonne Wilson and she was born in the autumn of nineteen thirty seven.'

Spence thumbed across to Ted that they were leaving and that he would catch up with him later. Using his free hand he intimated that the odds had changed. Ted thumbed back three to one.

'Well done, we're on our way back to the office. Are you almost done?'

'I'm just going to check the drive out front then I'll be back.' April paused. 'Did you get my text about later?'

'Yes and yes to later!' he replied.

April stood on the pavement and took a photograph of the drive. Divided by a strip of grass the concrete on either side had seen better days. Spence told Hawkes about the van, it was the start that they had needed.

Scrutinising each concrete wheel bed closely April found a strand of old carpet. She dropped it into an evidence bag. It could something or nothing as all around the street there were pieces of discarded takeaway containers, aluminium cans and paper.

Chapter Thirty One

On the way back Spence checked with the detectives covering the neighbouring streets, but nobody still around had seen the literary agent. Enquiries at Hampton's had proved just as unhelpful with staff speculating her absence as picking up a bug, to an abortion. Spence kept the latter from Hawkes wanting to keep his protégé's mind on the task at hand. Driving into the yard Tom suddenly remembered his walk to the tube from her flat.

'Christ, there was a blue van parked in the road when I left this morning!'

'Don't let it eat you up Tom. There are a lot of vans parked all over London streets.' He didn't ask if he saw the occupant.

Back in the lab April confirmed that the fibre she had found was from a carpet. Examining the strand under the microscope she deduced that a possible origin was Turkey or Egypt.

An hour later the control room handed Hawkes a long printout of vehicles bearing the prefix given by the witness. The closest that DVLA could supply was a van registered in the Yorkshire area.

'It narrows down the search. It's a pity that we don't an owners details.'

'Providing it started out as blue.' April added.

Spence smiled her way. 'Think positive, it's always been blue!'

Hawkes ran his eye up and down the list. 'Unless a mobile patrol stops it soon, we could be back to square one!'

Spence looked at them both, he sensed their anxiety for Stephanie Garland. 'We have a damn good lead, albeit a partial sightings, but it's better than what we had this morning. Theories?' he asked.

'There was carpet in the van?'

'He used a carpet to get Stephanie out of the flat?' they each looked at Hawkes, it was bizarre, but feasible. Hawkes shrugged. 'We've said it before, Valdis is resourceful.'

Going back over old ground Spence injected. 'I don't recall any mention of a van in any chapters from the manuscript.' They both shook their heads to indicate that they hadn't either.

'Taking what is written, added Hawkes 'Valdis varies his methods every time. Things are not looking good for Steph!'

April surprised them both, dismissing the negativity that had crept into the room. 'No, she's alive Tom, I sense it. Don't ask how, but just call it feminine intuition.'

Spence stood up to look across the carpark, where below officers were arriving with a prisoner.

'Then we stick with what April feels... until we know otherwise.'

They spent the afternoon going through everything that they knew, previous case statements and photographs looking for something that had been missed previously. Spence was convinced that there was a hidden indicator just waiting to come to the fore. Mid-afternoon April pulled the file regarding the burglary at Pembroke Mansions reported by

Rachel Roberts. Reading through the statements she came across a blue coloured van where the prefix started with the letters *YW*. Her head dropped when she read the name of the officer who had obtained the statement. It was none other than Barry Moyne.

When April showed them both the statement Spence glanced over at Hawkes without April noticing. They didn't need to say anything, but both had the same thought going through their mind. What they were thinking neither was willing to disclosure or share with April.

*****

With trepidation Stephanie Garland watched as Mortimer Valdis descended the wooden staircase again feeling that her nakedness was a disadvantage that he would relish. She hurt internally from where he had forced himself upon her, but kind, considerate and possibly loving thoughts of Thomas Hawkes had contrived to build a mental barrier to what had taken place. The rape had been a terrifying, demoralising ordeal, but what had concerned Stephanie most was that every action had been recorded. Was still being recorded.

Chilvray didn't speak instead he went straight to the camcorder where he lay on the table a sharp looking instrument that had sharp spikes protruding from a metal claw. When he turned he apologised for the length of his absence. He looked as though he had showered and changed his clothes. He perched himself on the edge of the table top.

'I thought you'd be interested to know that I've just completed half of my latest chapter. Sometimes though the right words take longer to appear than at other times. You see I find it imperative to get my thoughts recorded as soon as possible whilst the energy is still flowing through my veins. Do you understand that Miss Garland?' Stephanie nodded. He was pleased, he smiled.

'At last, we agree.' He used the tooth of the claw to scrap the underside of a fingernail that the shower had failed to remove. 'We would have made a good team, you and I, in different circumstances.

Chilvray patted the camcorder lightly so as not to disturb the recording.

'Videography was a recent introduction and idea of mine. I wish that I had used it before as it helps with my writing. Helps show me things that I might have missed. When this is over, I'll download and use a still from the recording that is certain to attract the readers.' He grinned, licking the tip of his tongue across his top lip. 'The image of a pretty naked young damsel unable to escape with a darkened background is always an incentive to read what lies beyond the front cover.'

'Suspense, horror and sex sells books Miss Garland. Videos so I've learnt is another outlet that I hadn't thought of until recently. I feel that you understand these things, whereas Charles Trent would have struggled to have seen my viewpoint. The man was a dinosaur living in a different era.

'Depravity and reality shows is what draws in the punters. Society had changed values regardless of the consequences.' He paused for a moment to see if the expression on her face changed, but it didn't, so he continued. 'Sex and violence is a way of life. 'You, me and many others could die today, but in the grand scheme of the almighty's plan we're but, a mere drop in the ocean.' Again, Stephanie remained unmoved by his philosophical speech, even when he mentioned that she could possibly die. Every thought that she had was for the young detective.

To her surprise he suddenly walked towards her without the metal claw.

'I have a few things to arrange before I prepare dinner. Perhaps if you behave, we can be civilised and share a meal together!'

Jack Chilvray checked her bonds then left the cellar. The camcorder was still recording.

Chapter Thirty Two

On the floor above the cellar Chilvray busied himself in the kitchen pouring a red wine into a glass, before washing the chicken then adding seasoning and herbs. He chopped and prepared the veg, checking that he had all the ingredients. Fast food served a purpose, but he preferred to eat good, wholesome food and having a guest was a rare treat.

The only irritating factor was that he'd had to adapt the top of the kitchen table so that Stephanie Garland could be handcuffed by at least one wrist to prevent her escaping, otherwise everything was set down to his best plates and cutlery, each piece accounted for as he laid the table.

When he did return to the cellar with the food simmering in the oven and on the stove he took with him the carving knife. Switching off the camcorder he sliced through the plastic ties binding her wrists and warned her that if she so much as screamed or called out, he would end her life instantly. As soon as she was free of her bonds Stephanie Garland pulled together her dressing gown, wrapping it tightly across her body. Following behind he held the band of her gown as she climbed the stairs. At the table he attached her left wrist to the handcuff.

'As much as it pains me, there are certain precautions that are necessary to keep us both safe!' she didn't reply as she watched him put together the meal on two plates. Laying the food before her, he removed the band from her mouth. The look in his eyes was enough to remind her.

The food smelt good and the last meal that she had consumed had been at the mandarin restaurant with Thomas Hawkes. She waited for him to take his seat opposite before she picked up the fork. Filling her glass Chilvray raised his own in a toast, Stephanie played along, although there was nothing good about the encounter. As Chilvray ate she picked at the food looking around the room, memorising every aspect. If she did escape the kidnapping, Hawkes would need as much detail as she could provide. In the better light she memorised his face as well, down the mole on the side of his neck.

'Is the chicken to your liking?' he asked, interrupting her thoughts.

She nodded. 'It's good.' There was no thanks. 'You have a nice place.'

Chilvray looked beyond the kitchen to the through lounge. 'It serves my purpose, although I prefer the freedom of the open spaces.'

As he continued to eat her eyes were fixed on the photographs on the wall, behind where he sat.

It was a gamble to mention one in particular, but if she was going to die, it didn't matter. 'You were in the army?' she asked.

Chilvray looked up, his eyes lighting up. 'Yeah. I went to the Falkland's in eighty two. You probably recognise the beret, it's all I have left, that and some good memories. Best time of my life.'

'It must have been scary, the Falklands!'

260

Chilvray shrugged his shoulders. 'Didn't think about the danger. It was a job that needed doing. I left soon after, trouble is when you leave the regiment, you leave behind an identity. It can be hard to pick up again.'

Looking at the photograph next to it, she thought it best not to mention it. Chilvray however wasn't finished. 'My brother was in the navy at the time. He was on the Antelope when the plane crashed into the ship's mast. He was lucky that the captain abandoned ship minutes before the magazine went up.'

'I remember that, didn't a bomb land in engine room, only it didn't go off... well not until somebody tried to diffuse the detonator.' She looked up from her plate. 'Your brother was lucky!'

Chilvray smiled, until he caught her studying him. 'Remembering everything about me?' he asked. The light had gone from his eyes once again.

'No. I was just wondering where all the stories come from, only I've only been an agent for just over a year.'

Chilvray wasn't sure whether to believe her or not, but his vanity decided to give her the benefit of the doubt. 'The stories or how I get my ideas?'

'I guess they're one and the same!'

Jack Chilvray left the table and went to a bookcase the far end of the lounge, he returned with an old book, frayed around the edges, but still holding together. He put it beside her plate.

'Please be careful when you look Miss Garland, it's not exactly valuable, but holds fond memories that I'd be heartbroken to lose. She laid down her fork and picked up the book *'Tales of a Boy's Long Summer'* by Matthew Armstrong. Published by Pelican Print in Lancashire.

'I was given that book one summer holiday when I was a young boy, when the weather was particularly bad. The stories and the exploits of the characters mentioned in each of the chapters kept me enthralled for hours, probably days. By the time that I was fifteen and coming to the end of my school days I was inspired and I'd read that book several times over. I was writing two or three of my own books every couple of years. I had little interest for school other than English.' He held out his hand so that she could hand back the book. 'Rejection is a painful experience.'

He returned the book to the bookcase, sliding it into the vacant space as though it was made of the finest china.

'Writers, authors, poets and illustrators, they each have a fire within that is unquenchable. Words, stories, poems and pictures that they feel need to be shared with the public.' He picked up his wine glass. 'I have nurtured a hatred of your profession for what you do to writers. No individual should weald the power of failure upon another simply because they get out the bed the wrong side that day, or things are not going right in their own life. Writers deserve a respect for all the long hours they afford their work. Imagination is a gift, not something that is simply tossed aside.' He put down his glass. 'Tell me Miss Garland, how long do you contribute to a submission, please be honest!'

She looked at him without flinching. 'Ten minutes, maybe fifteen tops. At Hamptons we get at least five hundred, maybe more submitted in a week. It's all the time that the directors allow.'

Chilvray grinned. 'Maybe, I've been killing the wrong people. Perhaps I should have started at the top and worked my way down.' He picked up his wine once again, watching the contents course its way around the edge of the glass.

'That's not long for something that has taken months, in some cases years to prepare.'

Realising that the conversation had steered itself around and landed on unpredictable terrain Stephanie thought it best to keep agreeing. *'I suppose not!'* she apologised. He was quick to suggest that the blame didn't lie solely with her, but everybody in the business. He seemed calmer.

'When Hamptons get a copy of the recording that I've made in the cellar below, I think you'll agree, that they'll see reason in the future and offer me a contract. I think my books have originality wouldn't you say?'

Like a madman he laughed at his own witticism. He honestly believed that his material was better than anybody else. She watched as he took away then plates and laid them on the side of the drainer ready for washing. When he sat back down he arched his arms into the shape of a temple spire.

'I have a dilemma as you know. Ordinarily by now I have done with the entire chapter and you would have become history in a book. Somehow, although I'm not entirely sure how, you've managed to redress the balance of my plan and I don't break with tradition, as I consider it bad luck.'

He finished off the wine on the glass then stood behind his chair. 'When you sneak up on a foe, the trick is to be swift, act fast, but with deathly silence. Watching your downstairs neighbour dress this morning had me all fired up inside. I needed, wanted you. I didn't want Roberts or D'Corscy, but there was something about you that I had to take!

Stephanie guessed that it was Thomas Hawkes that he was referring too. Knowing that he had spent the night with her, Chilvray needed to prove that he was as good. He wasn't, would never be anywhere as good, but madmen rarely ever accepted their failures.

Making his way to the door of the kitchen he explained that he needed to use the bathroom. He warned her again that if she called out, she would die before the police could arrive at the front door.

As soon as he was out of sight she slipped a chicken bone down from the inside of her dressing gown sleeve where it had been concealed when he had gone to fetch the book. Working the end of the bone around inside of the brace lock she felt it click free releasing her hand.

On the floor above Jack Chilvray flushed the toilet. She heard him run the tap to wash his hands. Grabbing a long handled broom that was standing beside the kitchen door she headed out into the hallway. When she heard the latch of the toilet door open her heart started to race. He was on his way back down.

The madman was halfway down the descent when he saw the shaft of the broom protrude through the banister rails. He tried to side step the obstruction, but she managed to entangle his feet causing him to fall awkwardly forward. Chilvray landed heavily on the steps below hitting his head on the newel post.

For several seconds Stephanie Garland stood with the broom in her hand ready to lash out should he move, but Chilvray was unconscious. She kicked him hard in the side, just to make sure, but he didn't react. Throwing the broom aside she ran towards the front door.

In the street outside she didn't dare look back. Holding the front of her dressing gown together she made for the end of the road where she could traffic going to and fro. When she reached the main thoroughfare she ran in the path of an oncoming bus. The driver felt himself tense as he slammed on the brakes almost standing willing the vehicle to stop before he hit the woman. Stephanie banged on the door demanding that he let her in. At the back of the bus a couple who had been shopping couldn't believe what was happening.

'Drive... NOW,' she demanded 'I'll explain why in a minute.' The driver had the sense not to argue as he released the pressure on the brake and engaged gear. A mile up the road he stopped the bus as police units approached having been radioed ahead. Moments after the police arrived so did an ambulance.

When they took the call Spence, Hawkes and April ran from the office. It was unbelievable that Stephanie Garland was alive, let alone having escaped her captor. Racing through the traffic Hawkes was in no mood to stop for anyone. Sitting alongside him Spence suddenly punched a fist into his palm in triumph.

'What's wrong?' April asked sitting in the back seat.

'Wrong... nothing's wrong.' He placed his hand on Hawkes left shoulder. 'Stephanie Garland is alive and Mortimer Valdis has just made his first big mistake. Now the hunt begins!'

Reaching forward April also laid her hand on Hawkes shoulder. 'She'll be fine Tom, I said she would, remember female intuition!'

Focusing on the traffic as they approached the hospital Thomas Hawkes smiled back at April in the rear view mirror, inside though his guts were already churning wildly at what they would find.

Chapter Thirty Three

When he did come around Jack Chilvray opened his eyes wondering why he was lying at the base of the stairs. Groaning where his head hurt where it had collided with the newel post, he saw double until his vision cleared. Jack had been knocked unconscious before, but never by a woman. Pushing himself up on all fours he adjusted to his surroundings.

'The bitch!' like a wounded tiger using the bark of a nearby tree he used the banister to help right himself. With teeth clenched he vowed to kill her when he got his hands on her. As his pupils righted themselves he became aware of the additional light from the street outside. His mind registered that the front door had been opened and she was nowhere to be seen. At first he felt the raw anger tighten every sinew in his body wanting, needing to tear the life from somebody, anybody. Searching every room including the cellar his mood gradually changed to maddening annoyance, mostly aimed at his own stupidity. He should never have trusted her, women had always played him for a fool.

Ignoring the pain on the side of his head Chilvray guessed that he had five minutes tops before the police started to arrive. Rushing back up the stairs he splashed water over his face grabbing the towel taking it through to the bedroom where he pulled his rucksack from under the bed. By the time that he returned to the hallway the rucksack was stuffed with fresh clothes, toiletries and his passport. Jack took a last look at the photographs on the kitchen wall before he picked up his laptop and van keys. Using the rear garden he crossed to the garage at the back.

Stowing his rucksack in the passenger footwell he fired up the engine before throwing open the doors. If the police were already waiting outside he would run them down. It was a risk driving around during the day, but circumstances had changed his plans. Jack had never added any contingency to any of his plans being confident that they were fool proof. Pulling shut the driver's doors he engaged first gear then released the brake.

The blue van hit the service road out back of the property like a racing car leaving after a pit-stop, but to his relief he found the way unobstructed. It wasn't until he was at the end of the service road that he remembered the camcorder. He thought about going back for it, but the approach of a police siren had him focus on the road ahead instead.

At the junction he accelerated hard towards the main road, almost hitting a delivery driver on his rounds. The man raised his fist in a threatening manner, but Jack ignored him. As Jack accelerated once again the delivery driver punched in the emergency number for the police. Passing the *Duck and Drake* he nodded in homage of the fine ale that they had swerved down the years. He would miss the busty redhead that had always served him his beer with a smile. Sitting at the junction of the main road Jack pondered, left towards Dover and cross the channel to France or right to the mid-city railway station going north to visit his sister. Pushing down the indicator he turned right, it had been a while since he had seen his two nieces. A while since he had read them a bedtime story.

Leaving the area Jack passed the police car that had been rushing down the road with its siren blaring. It was now parked on the side of the road and the officer was talking to a speeding motorist.

Chapter Thirty Four

They located Stephanie Garland on a mixed medical ward in a side room, where a constable had been stationed outside to protect any unwanted visitors. Having been fast tracked through the accident and emergency department by a female doctor she had avoided all unnecessary confrontation with drunks, drug addicts and irritable time-wasters. When Hawkes opened the door and walked in followed by Spence and April she could contain her emotions no longer. As Hawkes went to comfort her, April pulled Spence back outside.

'We should give them a few private moments alone. Let Hawkes deal with this one Spence and she'll be more receptive to any questions that you might have after the initial meltdown.

'Are you okay?' Hawkes asked as he sat on the edge of the bed.

'I am now that you're here Tom.' Through the viewing panel she could see Spence and April waiting patiently.

'They can come in if you want?'

Hawkes looked and smiled, indicating that it was okay to enter. April went over to the bed and gently stroked her finger down Stephanie Garland's forehead. 'Have you been examined yet?' it needed to be asked.

'Yes and the doctor took swabs. She said that you'd probably want them for evidence.'

Spence stood in reserve at the end of the bed listening. He was surprised at how well she seemed to be coping. She suddenly looked directly at April, before telling her what the men already knew.

'He took me solely to use me, abuse and rape me. I was so scared that he would kill me if I didn't co-operate with his demands. He's a monster, a vile sick madman!'

The outburst was not unexpected. April sat down very close allowing Stephanie Garland to crash into the safety of her shoulder so that she could let the ice cold brutality of her ordeal emit forth. Spence came around the side of the bed and laid his hand on Hawkes shoulder. He didn't say anything, not that there was any comfort in anything that he could say, but he wanted Hawkes to know that eventually things would get back to normality, eventually. When she next raised her head the look in her eyes had turned to that of anger. First she looked at Thomas Hawkes, then Daniel Spence.

'You'll catch the bastard, won't you?'

Spence nodded in response. 'We got things in our favour now Miss Garland, thanks to your heroism!'

'Please call me Steph, my mother calls me Stephanie, but I much prefer the shortened version.' She had calmed, but Spence was experienced to know that anger, confusion and judgement would continue to ebb and flow, back and forth for several hours, maybe days to come, perhaps even longer than that. It was all part of the healing process.

Holding both Hawkes and April's hand, feeling their energy flow through her veins, Spence noticed the tension in her face subside. *'I need to tell you everything, before I forget!'*

'When you're ready.' He replied.

'Now's as good as later.

'He said that he was from the electricity board and needed to check my meter. He had on the clothing of a workman. Not that it would have helped, but I didn't ask to see his identification.' She pointed to her lip where it had been split. 'Valdis hit me in the hallways and told me not to call out or scream or he'd kill me there and then. I remember a sweet smelling cloth being forced against my nostrils and then nothing.

'When I did come too I was in a dirty, dusty cellar beneath a large house.' She looked at Hawkes. 'There was a big brown rat, it killed a mouse and took it back to a hole to do whatever a rat does to a mouse.'

She inhaled filling her lungs building up her reserve for the next part. 'I recognised Valdis from the photograph that you had shown me. He is evil, his eyes are full of evil, dark black immorality. Dressed in just my underwear and a dressing gown he tied me to a wooden beam where he tore away my underwear before assaulting me. Whilst he raped me Tom, I managed to blank out what was happening thinking about you!' Pulling away her hands from theirs she subconsciously smoothed the creases of her hospital gown.

'When he came back down after preparing dinner he cut my bonds and let me cover my body with the dressing gown. We went upstairs together and ate chicken. Over dinner he told me about his days in the army and when he had served in the Falklands. He has a brother in the navy.'

April saw the look of a man who had just made a successful coup standing at the side of the bed. Spence was taking everything in, sensing the missing pieces of the jigsaw were coming together.

'From the time I arrived in the cellar, until the moment that we went upstairs, Valdis recorded everything on a camcorder. He's vile, but I feel so ashamed, humiliated.' She swallowed the saliva that had gathered in her throat and looked at Hawkes. 'He said that he'd post photographs of me naked and being raped on the internet. That he'd send Hamptons images as well as a message to the others working there. I don't think I could ever go back Tom.'

Hawkes squeezed her hand for encouragement. *'We'll sort it!'* she didn't ask how.

She took a mouthful of water to refresh her mouth before going on. 'Valdis admitted doing all those horrible things to Vivienne D'Corscy, Rachel Roberts and Charles Trent,' she looked up at April before adding 'and somebody called Annabelle. He killed her just because she saw him step out of the shadows. She was innocent!'

'They all were Steph as are you,' April smiled, a knowing smile between two women 'Can you tell us anything about the place that you were held... you said that you had dinner upstairs?'

'It appeared to be a large house, nicely decorated. Some of the furniture looked foreign. On the wall behind the kitchen table were photographs.

One was of Valdis when he had been in the army. He was a paratrooper. There was another photograph alongside, it looked like Valdis was wearing a policeman's uniform!' All three looked at one another in astonishment.

'The Falklands conflict was in nineteen eighty two.' Said Hawkes. 'It should be easy going through his military records. It was definitely Valdis in the photograph?'

'I would recognise that bastard anywhere now!'

'Outside of the house, can you tell me anything about the colour door, garden, trees, plants or hedges, anything that will help us find the place, help us catch Valdis?'

Stephanie Garland understood the information that Spence wanted. She closed her eyes and retraced her tracks.

'The door was painted blue, dark blue. I ran down some stone stops, not many, I they were concrete. There was grass in the middle of the driveway.' She paused as she continued running. 'I ran down the middle of the road. I remember seeing a house to my right, it was bright, yellow maybe like a carnival float that they have at Brixton. I ran past a pub on the corner before I saw the bus. I stood in the road not caring if it stopped or not!' She opened her eyes. 'Next thing I recall is the bus being surrounded by police and an ambulance arriving.' She looked at Spence. 'Did that help?'

He smiled. *'Oh yes, you done great Steph!'*

Hawkes and Spence stepped out of the room so that they could contact the station nearest where Garland had stopped the bus. Looking back through the viewing panel they saw the two women talking.

'She'll come through this just fine Tom. She's strong willed.'

Hawkes only nodded, he didn't add any reply.

'Find out if anybody got a statement from the bus driver will you?'

Hawkes took another look through the viewing glass. Spence was probably right, Steph was strong minded.

'Running barefoot and taking into account that she's young and fit, I'd estimate that the house wasn't overly far from where she stopped the bus and somebody must know of the pub, coppers normally do. The same goes a brightly coloured house.'

'We find the house, we'll probably find a whole heap of evidence, including the photographs.' Thinking of the woman with whom he had shared her bed, he frowned, the lines exaggerating his concern. 'What steps can we take to make sure that Steph's safe. Valdis could come looking for her and the hospital would probably be his first port of call.'

'I've already thought of that Tom. I'll get a firearms unit to pick her up soon and transfer her to a safe house in Hertfordshire. Para or no para, not even our own bloody commissioner knows that the place exists.'

When Hawkes went in to explain April came out. In the privacy of the whitewashed room Stephanie Garland felt suddenly vulnerable once again.

'He did things to me Tom that repulsed me, degrading things. I couldn't fight back, I tried to get free, but I couldn't!'

He held her close allowing her to cry into his shoulder, gently and soothingly patting her back. 'Had you managed to fight back Steph, you might not be alive now. You did the right thing.'

'But… the bastard filmed it all, everything. I feel sick knowing that he could show it to the world.'

'We'll cross that bridge as and when it arises. Once we find the house, we might get lucky, who knows!'

Through her tears she looked closely into his eyes. *'Does this change anything between us?'* Inside her stomach was churning, pleading to hear the right response.

'Should it?' he replied

'No. Or least I hope not!'

'Then we're good Steph. We take everything at your pace.'

He assured that the safe house was the best option and assured her that he would visit that evening after they had made their enquiries. She was still wiping dry her eyes when April looked back in.

'I thought that we'd find her dead Spence!'

'But you was certain that she was alive?'

'I know, but on the way over to the hospital something significant changed.'

'Like what?' she was about to reply when a nurse walked down the corridor coming towards them.

Chapter Thirty Five

The nurse walked on by to the next room affording them a courtesy greeting, but no more. April waited till she had closed the door to the room before she continued.

'Valdis has created an agenda, not just to fill his new book, but in what victim's he selects. Steph had nothing to do with the original submission, but somehow he found out that she had taken over from where Vivienne D'Corscy left off. There's no telling now who he'll take next!'

'So you don't think he'll stop now that she's escaped?'

'No. If anything he's goings to be more determined to prove that he can still stay one step ahead. Revenge ended with Charles Trent. Annabelle and Steph were picked for other reasons.'

It was discerning news, although inevitable. Spence wasn't surprised. 'If this was all about revenge over one book then I would have thought that the debt had been paid. Even somebody like Valdis must realise that abducting Steph was a mistake. It's now become a controlling game!'

Spence looked through the glass. 'She was lucky. I thought we'd find her dead.'

April sucked in through her lips. 'I know that I was optimistic and saying that she was still alive, but somewhere in the back of my mind there was a nagging doubt. It's an ordeal she'll never forget Spence. One that will haunt her forever!'

Inside the room Hawkes took a call on his mobile, he called them back in when it ended.

'They've found the house, they guarding it awaiting our arrival.'

The house was exactly how Stephanie Garland had described it. A road with trees, not quite an avenue, but the tall beeches were there all the same. The properties were larger than the average house, built around the mid-twenties and each had a short drive and several stone steps leading up to the front door. The yellow house was gaudy and easy spotted as was the blue door. Looking up and down the thoroughfare the road reminded Spence of a paint catalogue.

From the outside number twenty five Rosalind Avenue looked like any other property in the road. It had been surprisingly well maintained, although there were signs of age on the chimney stack.

'It's surprising what goes on behind closed doors,' April remarked as they approach the steps.

It seemed ridiculous knocking, but Spence did, just the once before he stepped aside and let a uniformed officer break the door lock with a metal ram. Others went around back in case the writer tried to escape via the rear.

As police stormed the house calling out, Spence expected Valdis to appear, armed with a weapon, but when one of the officers was let in from the garden out back, he explained that the rear garage door was open and it was empty of any vehicles. Spence ordered that they check

279

every part of the house, including wardrobes, the loft and cupboards. He gave specific instruction not to touch the cellar.

'Why?' asked April when the group had dispersed.

'I don't want them destroying any evidence that could be down there!'

Standing in the doorway of the kitchen Hawkes asked Spence to join him. He looked around, the whole space went from back to front of the house, a through lounge, diner come kitchen. Spence saw the expression on April's face change as she looked at the photographs on the wall. She pointed to them, the colour draining from her complexion.

'I know him, I know the man in the photograph!'

'How?'

'He was... might still be a friend of my ex-husband.'

Spence removed the photograph of Chilvray wearing the police uniform.

'That looks like the Hendon training facility.'

'It is. He and Barry joined on the same intake. His name is Jack Chilvray. I met him during their training, when they'd go drinking together.' She looked closer making sure. 'It was the drink that got Chilvray booted out of the force.'

I know because I was introduced to him one evening when he and Barry were going out for a drink. Barry told me that Chilvray liked to drink. It was what got him booted out of training.'

Spence looked at Barry Moyne, then Chilvray, they looked young, but so did Spence in his training photograph.

'But if he'd been in the job, the prints that you found at Pembroke Mansions and later Waterfall Heights would have been matched in the system?'

April shrugged her shoulder, she didn't have an answer. 'Somehow they slipped through.'

'That's a big somehow!' Spence expressed.

I'll run it again, but nothing showed on prints, DNA or photograph match. It's possible that he isn't in our system.'

'How's that?' asked Hawkes.

'He got his marching orders before they were taken.'

Under his breath they heard Spence swear. He continued looking at the array of photographs on the wall, studying each one. 'Right, take the lot, we'll work through them back at the office.' It was then that something else dawned on him. 'I asked for back-up from West End Central and yet Moyne isn't here.' He asked Hawkes to check why.

Pulling April to one side where they could talk he wanted to make sure of some facts. 'Why'd he get the boot?'

'Chilvray and Barry broke into the sergeant's bar because Chilvray needed a drink. According to Barry there was nothing that Jack Chilvray couldn't do, being an ex-paratrooper he was resourceful. An hour later security found the insecurity and confronted Chilvray. Barry was in the loo having a leak when things in the bar got heated. Unfortunately the civilian guards were no match for an ex-soldier and as a result they spent several weeks in the hospital after being despatched by Chilvray.

'When Barry came back out he found Jack Chilvray pissing over the injured men and the place a mess. He said he helped Chilvray back to their dorm room and put him to bed all the worse for the drink. By the end of the next day an investigation concluded that the ex-paratrooper had alone been responsible for the break-in and the assault on security, he had his contract terminated with immediate effect and handed over to a local station to be charged with both offences. Neither of the injured guards knew about Barry being in the clubhouse and Chilvray never revealed Barry's involvement.

'Chilvray was bailed to appear before a court, but he jumped bail and there's a warrant still out for his arrest. Before we split up Barry would assure me that he had never kept in touch with Jack Chilvray although now I come to think of it, I was never that sure. Chilvray caused a few arguments amongst Barry and myself, but they were never resolved. He had been a thorn in my side and for some reason I felt that he had something over Barry for the bar incident.'

'Like the occasional favour?' Spence asked.

'Maybe. I once told Barry during an argument that he had no right to be a copper, let alone a detective and that he was a coward. I said that his conscience ruled his head. If I didn't know better Spence, I would say that Jack Chilvray controls my ex-husbands conscience.'

'That could account for a hell of a lot.' Spence concluded.

'Barry was nothing like Chilvray, Spence. Barry's a fool and he always will be, but he's not a murderer.'

'Maybe not, but he might be implicated.'

'Then why come and see you the other day?'

'That's what I've yet to determine and figure out!'

On the request of Spence she sent Barry Moyne a text message asking for his whereabouts, but received no reply. April elected to be the first down in the cellar wanting to capture everything first hand before it was disturbed, giving a good argument in return for his reluctance.

'Chilvray has been playing us Spence. He believes that he was infallible, a water-tight loose cannon who could do what he liked, when he liked. Well now's our chance to strike back. Let me gather as much as I can from down below, then come in about half an hour. I should be done by then.'

'And if the bastard is hiding down there!'

April capitulated, it was possible. 'Alright, but don't touch anything.'

With just the light from the open door at the head of the stairs they descended into the dungeon where Stephanie Garland had been held captive. The lower they went the darker the gloom forced itself upon them.

'There's no telling what went through Steph's head being held down here.' April said as she reached the bottom step.

'Sheer bloody terror I imagine.'

April switched her camera to night-mode and took several pictures to encompass the whole basement, when she gave Spence the signal he went back up and switched on the single light, there was just sufficient light to see wooden beam in the middle of the room. Lying around back of the beam April located the plastic ties that had held Steph's wrist together and to the side lying amongst the dust she saw the torn undergarments. April felt the shudder of abhorrence race through her bones knowing how the young woman must have suffered and felt knowing that the only defence and protection against her attacker seeing her naked had been savagely ripped from her body. From a darkened corner of the room she heard a familiar scratching sound. Spence picked up a broken wooden shaft that he had found, he held it across his chest.

'Don't worry if the rat appears, I'll strike first and ask questions later!'

'Ignoring the rat, this place makes my skin crawl. This is in stark difference to the rest of the house, do you think he brought anybody else down here?'

Spence looked around. 'I was just thinking the dame thought. It's too dark to collect anything positive April, we need some arc lamps to light this room.' April agreed. She bagged the plastic ties and underwear, taking in one final sweep of the cellar before going back upstairs. When she bumped into the table a small object fell over on the table top. She turned to tell Spence, but he was already by her side.

'The bastard left the camcorder behind. He must have been in a real hurry to escape in leaving this here!' April was about to slip it into an evidence

284

bag, when Spence asked her to remove the memory card and give it to him.'

'Why?' she asked.

'What we've found here. Hawkes doesn't need to know about nor see. I'll keep it somewhere safe as evidence, but hopefully it'll never see the light of day. At some point when she can take it, I'll tell Stephanie Garland that it was destroyed. It should help heal some wounds!'

In the gloom of the cellar April kissed him.

'Beneath that armour Daniel Spence you've a beating heart full of compassion. I like that!' He kissed her again, feeling her close to him. 'I like that!' he said. They heard a noise at the top of the stairs and Thomas Hawkes call out.

'You might want to see this guv'nor!'

When they went back up April had placed all what she had found in her forensic bag. Standing in the hallway Hawkes was holding up a long black leather coat, a pair of gloves and a wide brimmed hat. April immediately checked the style of the button running down the left side and found a missing space where the last should have been stitched on.

'What's that?' asked Spence, noting that Hawkes had something else in his right hand.

'It's what I thought you should see.'

They went through to the kitchen where he put down the articles of clothing. Opening up a buff coloured document wallet April put her hand immediately her mouth, swallowing the saliva from the back of her throat. Spence briefly read through what had been scrawled and documented. In bold capital letters at the head of the page was the name *APRIL ANNE GEDDINGS*. Spence flicked through ignoring that he was contaminating any evidence. Under the first sheet of paper were photographs of April at work, at home, sitting in the car, coming out of a supermarket, in the kitchen, the bedroom and even one of her in the shower. April felt the nausea rising in her throat as she excused herself and ran to the bathroom.

'He's been watching her for time!' said Hawkes.

Spence sensed the anger rising inside. Chilvray was more resourceful than what he had given him credit.

'They need to lock the door and throw away the key on this bastard Tom!'

Together they managed to flick through what was relevant before April came back down from the bathroom above.

'You okay?' asked Spence.

'Well I'm not happy...' she paused to gather her thoughts and balance her emotions *'fuck it, I am shit scared Spence... really fucking scared. Chilvray's a madman on the loose. He's been spying on me for a long time!'*

Several officer standing nearby witnessed her outburst, Spence ordered everybody outside for a break leaving just Hawkes, himself and April alone.

'I'll make immediate provisions to keep you safe!'

April smiled weakly at him, although not her eyes had a distinct look of doubt.

'Even you couldn't protect me twenty four seven Spence. It's a nice thought, but I've a job to hold down and it mean me being alone. Chilvray could take me any time he liked!'

'Let me make a call and then we'll discuss our options!'

Spence headed for the garden out back, but April let him get only a few feet away before she called after him. *'Don't even consider taking me off the case. I might be scared, but I'm not giving in, not just yet!'*

Standing by her side Hawkes put his hand on her arm. 'Spence and me, we'll catch him April, I promise.'

'I don't doubt you Tom, but he got to Steph easily.'

'Yeah, but she wasn't expecting it, you are.'

'And there's a difference?'

Thomas Hawkes liked April, he wished or maybe, perhaps hoped that when he did eventually settle down it would be with a woman like April.

'Steph's okay, but she lacks that certain something that I need. It's something that you have April.'

She looked bewildered. 'Elaborate?'

'You fight for want you want, reserve judgement, but when you find it, nothing will stop you getting it. Steph rolls over to get it. She thinks her looks alone would be enough to crush any man's resolve.'

'And what about Trevelyan back at the station?'

They saw Spence coming back up the rear staircase.

'In many ways she's like you!'

April nodded. In many ways she had felt similar when she had first met Barry Moyne, but events had moved along faster than she had wanted and she had accepted her fate without a fight. The next that she knew was that she was standing before a registrar going through the wedding ceremony.

When neither were watching a brown snout with whiskers appeared at the corner of the stairs leading down to the cellar below. Taking the opportunity to check out the rest of the house, the rat ran across the hallway and proceeded to climb the stairs to floor above. All the mice in the cellar had been caught, but the rat had heard others scurrying around at night. Like the recent owner of the house, the rat was a skilled operative in the art of killing.

Chapter Thirty Six

Barry Moyne was almost three quarters of the way up the tree, when he heard the doorbell echo from the front of the house through the hall and kitchen to the garden out back. Resting precariously at the top of the ladder he could just see down the side alley to the gate. He called out and suggested that visitor come around back, hoping it wasn't another student selling Greenpeace packages or wanting to save a third world nation from the brink of annihilation. When he saw Jack Chilvray push the gate shut, he was both surprised and apprehensive.

'What this...' announced Chilvray as he approached, 'you decided that the house isn't big enough, so you're gonna build a tree house?'

Moyne laughed. 'No. I've been meaning to prune back these top branches since the end of last year, but there's always something else on the agenda that takes precedence.' Barry noticed that his long established friend had his rucksack with him, although there was no sign of the van. 'You planning on camping out at the weekend?' he asked.

Chilvray spread his hands and arms wide. 'The city is good and it serves my purpose, but every so often you know I have to get away and have big wide open spaces Barry. London can become claustrophobic at times!'

Moyne tied a loop around the end of the hand saw attaching it to the nearest branch then started to descend the ladder. 'Steady the ladder for me will you Jack. You know I've never been good with heights.' Reaching midway the ladder whipped in and out under his weight. From below Jack

Chilvray watched with a wry grin. He braced the lower steps with his right foot, keeping balance with the left.

'I would have thought that on a detective's salary, you would easily have afforded a gardener to do this!'

Taking each rung with care Barry Moyne was glad to reach the last step. 'You know me, save a buck wherever I can, only it all adds up and bolsters the retirement fund. Only a few more years to go before I hit the sunny climes of Spain.'

Stepping aside Chilvray feigned interest. 'Has it really been that long?' he asked. 'It only seems like yesterday that we were both at Hendon.'

'Nineteen years this November.' He stepped down onto the grass, relieved to be back on terra firma. Moyne arched his back and stretched his shoulder muscles hard. 'Arthritis has decided to kick-in so it's another good argument to head away to Spain when I'm done.'

Chilvray shook his head playing along. 'Time flies and so do the years. My old bones are unforgiving of the times I spent in the Falklands, Wales and the rain forest.'

Barry Moyne didn't like being reminded of their time at Hendon, but he knew that Chilvray would get it into the conversation at some point. It was like a thorn in his side. The last time that he had seen Jack Chilvray had been after his trip to Dudley. Jack never did say why he had gone there and Moyne hadn't pressed the point.

'Heard from the wife?' Chilvray asked.

'Saw her the other day at work. There's a rumour going around that she's got herself shacked up with a chief inspector. I went over with the intention of saying hello and gives my blessing, but he snubbed me!'

'She was bit of alright from what I remember, good looker and had nice body etcetera!'

Barry Moyne looked over, it wasn't wise to bite-back at Jack. His emotions could go either way and Barry had seen some of Jack's handy work. 'If you say so Jack although it's been so long since we shared a bed I can't really remember. I suppose shagging that blonde straight out of training school didn't help calm stormy waters.'

Jack Chilvray slapped his friends back. 'Shagging anything young is a memorable experience. I had me one only earlier, trouble is it leaves me parched and I've got a throat like the inside of a camels arse on a blistering hot day, any chance of a cuppa?'

Barry Moyne invited Chilvray over to the patio offering him the best chair whilst he went and put on the kettle. Watching from the kitchen he knew that Jack was wanted by the police, but also acknowledged that if he so much as picked up the receiver Jack would be upon him before he ended the call. Five minutes later he returned with a tray, two mugs, a teapot and a plate of biscuits. The afternoon sun was warming to the face, although bright on the eyes. It was an advantage that Barry could watch Jack and not have his own expression analysed.

'I see you left the saw up the top, you not finished?' asked Chilvray.

'No... I left the most stubborn branch until last.'

'I'll give you hand after we've had our tea and cleared this plate.' Moyne didn't reply.

So where you heading?' he asked nodding at the rucksack down by Chilvray's side.

'I'm not sure. You know me Barry. I follow my feet and I'm happy to land anywhere. I've been busy lately and run out of ideas for my latest book so I need a fresh approach. Recent chapters have either dried up or buried themselves deep underground.'

'You're still burning the midnight oil writing then?'

Chilvray grinned. 'Yeah, on and off. It's a dog eat dog world though Barry. Agents and Publishers don't want just a pint of your blood, sweat and tears, they want the *fucking* bucket load as well.'

Sensing that Jack was in a good mood he pushed his luck to see if it got any reaction. 'Did you hear about that agents in the city, Hampton's I think, if my memory serves me right. Had a real bad run of luck. One of their literary agents was murdered not long back and then to top it off their senior editor jumps in front of a tube train.'

The expression on Jack Chilvray's face didn't flinch an inch. He took another biscuit, dunked in his tea the replied. 'No, I didn't know about that. I tend not to follow the news much these days only it all seem so depressing, terrorist attacks, teenagers on the rampage and old ladies getting done over for their pension. *Fuck* the worlds going mad Barry. To tell the truth when I've got my head down and on the job, I'm only focused on one thing. I can't say that I'm sorry to hear about the agent and the editor though, they're a mercenary band of people and some will say that justice is served.' He poured himself another mug from the teapot. 'Is April still busy with scenes of crime?'

'She took promotion, she's the head of the divisional forensic department. Like a dog with a bone, she never knows when to put it down.'

Jack Chilvray smiled behind the cover of his mug. When he got hold of April Geddings, it was exactly what he intended giving her.

'And what about you?' he asked 'how's work?'

Barry Moyne knew he'd get around to work sooner or later. 'You know Jack, up and down. The city's changing, becoming over populated, very cosmopolitan and times change. I tend to duck and dive and keep out of trouble. I'm a DS now so I let those below me take the strain and risk life and limb.'

Chilvray feigned a whistle of surprise. 'A detective sergeant, well done!' He picked up the plate and offered the last biscuit to Barry Moyne, who politely refused patting his stomach. 'Gotta watch the waistline!'

'Come away with me this weekend Barry,' he asked 'we could take in the Brecon Beacons and sample some of the night life in the evenings. I hear that those Welsh women are practically begging for it!'

Moyne's mind raced ahead thinking of an excuse.

'Sorry mate, any other time I would jump at the chance, but I'm due in later today, something to do with a task force being put together to catch some loony bastard who has kidnapped a young woman.' The moment that the excuse left his lips Barry Moyne realised that it was a mistake. Again though Jack Chilvray didn't flinch. 'I have some leave due soon. What about taking a trip out then?'

'Sounds good. Pity about now though, it would have been like old times.' Jack Chilvray looked up at the sky and the top branches of the tall oak. 'Now, how about we finish off that bugger up there!'

Barry Moyne was almost three quarters up the ladder when Jack Chilvray asked 'Did they say whereabouts this young woman was held?'

Moyne felt his knees knock together as he climbed higher. He realised that it had been a mistake to go back up, but Jack would have never let him forget it, if he hadn't.

'Somewhere near your neck of the woods I heard, although sources can very often be wrong.' He reached out and started to undo the knot that was holding the saw in place. 'I suppose it'll give me the opportunity to see April once again only she's bound to be attached to the task force.'

'Do you still miss her?' Chilvray asked from below.

'It's funny, I didn't, but I've been thinking about her a lot since the other day when I went to visit. It would be good to see her again.'

Under his breath Chilvray muttered *'me too'* only Barry didn't catch what he had said.

'What was that?' Barry asked. Jack Chilvray smiled as he looked up the length of the ladder, he cleared his throat of leftover biscuit, the replied 'I said, not before I do!'

Barry Moyne suddenly stopped untying the knot realising in that instance what Jack had meant. Forgetting his fear he began descending the ladder. Down on the ground Jack Chilvray went around back of the ladder placed his foot against the trunk knee height and pushed as hard as he could. Moments later the ladder came away from the upper branches and swung towards the house. Barry Moyne tried to reach out and grab a sturdy looking branch, but his palm snagged a broken shoot where the end had frayed. It cut into the soft tissue making him loose his grip. He fell without time to call out.

Jack Chilvray walked over to where his training school dinking partner had landed heavily. He watched as the heart beat fast inside Barry Moyne's chest, as his brain tried to evaluate the damage. Placing the heel of his walking boots on Moyne's neck Jack added his body weight and twisted the boot. The vertebrae snapped with a resounding crack, but was soon lost amongst the sounds of the birds singing nearby. To any neighbours out back it would have resembled a branch breaking.

Walking calmly back into the house, Chilvray made himself a cheese and pickle sandwich, adding some fruit for the journey ahead. He could stay longer, but there was no telling who might come calling. Pulling open the wallet that he found on the kitchen worktop he removed cash, a cash point card and warrant badge. He thought about taking the keys to the car, but it was safer travelling by train. Standing on the patio he retrieved his rucksack took one last look at his friend then walked towards the side gate tutting to himself.

'Cutting branches from tall trees can be so hazardous and especially if you've not had the training. It's amazing how many domestic fatalities occur every year climbing ladders.'

On the way to the railway station Jack considered it was best to leave going after April Geddings for a day or so, maybe longer. As part of the taskforce she would be hard to get at. Walking down towards where the road took a bend around the junction ahead he had to duck behind a hedge to avoid a car going by where the occupants looked as though they had a purpose. He watched as the vehicle stopped outside the home of Barry Moyne.

Stepping back out from the hedgerow Jack continued walking in the opposite direction. By the time that the cavalry started arriving he would already be at the ticket counter in Paddington. It was handy visiting his old friend, although he had not reckoned on him paying for his fare.

Chapter Thirty Seven

Stephanie Garland had been transferred to the secret location in Hertfordshire accompanied by Thomas Hawkes, a friendly face with whom she trusted. Spence called to enquire as to how she had settled in and was told better than Hawkes had expected. She was however still not certain about the future nor whether she wanted to remain with Hamptons.

With an ensemble of detectives, firearms officers, dog units and uniformed officers gathering together in a briefing room at New Scotland Yard the Assistant Commissioner was late in arriving having just come from a media update. He appeared agitated having answered their deluge of questions, many of which had remained unanswered because they didn't have solutions. Sitting himself down on at the front of the room he asked Daniel Spence to address the room.

Spence kept the discourse brief factoring into the communique the recent deaths, including Rachel Roberts and Annabelle Du Renard. He kept his main brief detailed to the kidnap and abuse of Stephanie Garland, omitting anything relating to the camcorder in the cellar. When he was about done he warned the many faces looking his way that any one of them could be a potential target. Jack Chilvray had proved time and time again that he was a psychotic madman who would stop at nothing to escape.

Douglas Reynolds finally rose from his seat having listened intently to every word that Daniel had said grateful for the short-lived respite before going back to his office. He reiterated the warning that Spence had issued regarding the danger stating that he didn't intend addressing the media again until the next day. Telling them that an officer had been hurt was not on the agenda.

Before leaving he turned and had a final word for the detective chief inspector. 'Keep me posted, whatever you find!' April came forward having been stood at the back. She went to his side and smiled encouragingly.

'Is Reynolds always that cordial?'

'More or less, although I wouldn't want his job. The press can sing before they get anything out of me. I still didn't see Barry Moyne amongst the crowd, did you?'

'No. Perhaps one day that bastard will take this job seriously. I did send him a text, but he's ignored that as well as your briefing.'

'Don't worry, I can catch up with him later!' April wasn't sure in what context Spence was going to catch up.

They were about to exit the briefing room when a female in a suit from West End Central entered coming directly towards April.

'Are you April Geddings?' she asked, not knowing the woman.

'Yes, why,' she paused 'who wants to know?' At the same time nodding her head towards Spence 'and this is Detective Chief Inspector Spence.' The female introduced herself.

'I'm DC Lynda Warrington. I work in the same office as your ex-husband. Is there somewhere where we can talk privately?'

April watched the last of the stragglers leave the room. 'I'm happy to discuss anything connected with DS Moyne, with the DCI present.'

Warrington acquiesced. 'I'm sorry to inform you that your ex-husband was killed in a freak accident at his home address sometime today!'

April felt the wave of shock sweep from her head to her feet. The number of times that she had wished Barry dead was countless, but her wishes had only ever been in anger. 'How?' she asked.

'He was up a ladder pruning the branches from a tall tree. It appears that he slipped as the ladder toppled.'

April looked at Spence. 'He could never stand heights!'

'Did anybody medical attend the scene?' Spence asked.

'The paramedics attended the initial call, but he was pronounced dead at the scene by an air ambulance doctor.'

'Did he land on anything other than the ground?' April had reverted back putting on her forensic head.

'Just grass. The officers first on the scene saw bruising to the side of the neck. A post-mortem will confirm cause, but at present no suspicious circumstances are suspected. Death was probably caused by a heavy landing fracturing the neck.'

Warrington excused herself stating that she would be in touch. April said that she would contact Susan Weekes direct with regards to the arrangements for the post-mortem.

'You want to attend?' asked Spence when the detective had exited the room.

'Yes. Barry was shit at heights Spence, but he was no fool. He knew enough to take a leg lock and not take chances.'

'I'll give his inspector a call when we get back and see if he knows anything else!'

April sat herself back down on the nearest chair. 'I know officers all look ahead to the day that they retire, but I never thought Barry would meet his end in circumstances so inane.' She looked up and caught the look in Spence's eye. 'What are you thinking?'

'You said Jack Chilvray was a friend. I was just surmising putting two and two together, probably coming up with five, that's all.'

April finished off his thoughts 'that Jack Chilvray paid Barry a visit!'

'Something along those lines.'

'It's odd Spence, because when Warrington told me I'd had the same thought flash through my mind.'

'Are you okay?' he asked, noting that she had got back up.

'I'm fine. I'm over the initial shock.' April stood up. 'I can honestly say that I really feel nothing inside for Barry. He hurt me on more than one occasion, so I suppose summary justice has been delivered. Out of respect for his family I'll probably go to the funeral, but I won't grieve.'

'We could we go over there if you want, I'll square it with the local station!'

'Damn it Spence I'm the ex-wife and if I can't visit the scene, who can?' She realised her outburst had been without justification, she apologised. 'Get their approval, but we should head that way regardless of what they say and a fresh pair of eyes might be handy for Susan Weekes.'

*****

April engaged the handbrake outside of her old house, where she had once lived. Nothing much had changed in the street except the odd fresh lick of paint around the eaves and front doors. 'This always used to annoy Barry, my blocking the drive. I did it just so that it did irritate him. Call it petty, but to me it was a huge victory whenever I saw his blood pressure rise.'

Spence smiled. Later when things that calmed, he would invite her to stay at his place, where she could be safe. Flowers had been a good idea, but asking her to move in, albeit temporarily was a different matter and demanded more tact.

Going down the side of the property April left the gate open and propped back. It was an old habit for when she was putting out the waste bin. Going directly to where the grass had been crushed in the fall, she knelt down to examine the density of the earth.

'What are looking for?' asked Spence.

'That's strange, there's no blood. Not even a splatter.' She looked up to where the rough-cut saw was still hanging tied to the branch. 'A fall from that height would damage soft tissue externally and almost definitely inside the head. In any event the jaw is likely to snap shut catching the tongue through bone or dentures. I would have expected to see some blood.'

The ladder had been propped against the edge of the patio, but there was evidence in the grass where it had landed. It had bounced creating a small groove. April examined where it had been resting at the base of the tree. She found a boot print where Chilvray and dug in deep with his other foot pushing against the stump to attain leverage.

'There was definitely a second person here Spence, look!'

On the patio table they noticed the two mugs and empty plate. April dropped all three items into evidence bags. *We can at least prove that Chilvray was here today.'*

She took one last look at the garden where the beds had once been lovingly tended by herself. Many were overgrown with weeds. It seemed a shame. Heading back down the side alley she kicked the gate away from its prop and heard it click shut. The end of an era had finally come. Standing beside the car she shook her head back at the house façade.

'I never did like this house. I always maintained the place had an aura that had never accepted me.' She scoffed. 'Now there's one more ghost to add to the occupancy!'

They were about to get back into the car when a neighbour rushed across from the house opposite. April remembered her, although they had rarely spoken.

'I thought I recognised you when you pulled up. I am sorry Mrs Moyne.' She looked at Spence and wondered who he was. Spence showed her his warrant rather than get into any lengthy discussion. The woman scrutinised the details and the photo.

'You look younger in the picture!'

April couldn't stop herself from laughing. 'He's very good at his job though.' Spence just grinned back at the woman.

'Did you notice anything usual...' he pointed 'with the house here today?'

'A man about your age came calling this afternoon. I thought he was one of those street traders because he had a rucksack. My Alfred used to have one similar when he was in the army. A dusty Khaki and seen better days. Handy things though because they hold a lot and useful when you go hiking or camping.'

Spence showed the neighbour the photograph of Jack Chilvray that they had taken from his kitchen. Again the woman rolled her tongue around inside her mouth and took a long look.

'He's younger too, but that was him, the caller at the door!'

Spence took her details and said that a constable would be around later to take a statement. They thanked the elderly woman then left before she invited them over for a bit of cake and a cup of tea.

'Chilvray's cleaning up loose ends.' He said as April approached the junction.

'Now we'll never what involvement or hold he had over Barry. He didn't just come visiting socially Spence, there was always an objective, besides going down the pub. I'm sure that Barry was also giving him money!'

Before they joined the main lines of traffic going in either direction Spence asked that April pull the car over.

'The call that I made earlier, back at the hospital was to my sister. I wanted her to go around to my place and make sure that it was clean and tidy.'

'Why, was it important?'

'It was if you were coming over tonight to stay!'

'I don't get my sister around when you stayover.'

'I know, but my offer is for than one night April. Chilvray was compiling a dossier on you. Stephanie Garland struck lucky. I'm not prepared to take that chance, not where you're concerned.'

April smiled then lent across and kissed him. 'I would have to call home first. I don't tend to go around with spare underwear in my forensic bag. Least way's not mine!'

Driving back to the station April occasionally gave Spence a sideways glance. He was like no other man that she had ever known. At times he could be deep in thought and others he didn't let the thinking get in the way of a decision. She saw Spence as a philosopher, intelligent yet decisive and ready to take a gamble with life, love and the dogs. Pulling into the back yard she also realised that he was right. She wasn't strong enough to tackle Jack Chilvray on her own. Chilvray had dispatched Barry with deadly ease, he would have no trouble killing her. Sliding the car into the parking bay provided for her use, she pulled the car to a halt.

'Thanks Spence, I promise that I won't get under your feet!'

'Maybe that's exactly what I want you to do.'

Chapter Thirty Eight

'Are you in the SAS?' the young woman asked, struggling to keep her focus as she reached for her glass of wine. Jack helped her guide the stem of the glass to her lips as he undid her bra strap, moments later pulling the garment away from her body.

'Not yet, I'm not!' he replied.

Megan Lewis swallowed the last of the wine, dropped the glass down the side of the bed and lay back so that the stranger she had met in the pub could remove her knickers. Running hands up and down his arms she stroked the muscles feeling the strength of his sinews tense up as he threw the article across the room. 'You're very strong, you won't hurt me... will you!'

Chilvray grinned as he took off his pants, his erection pleased to be free of the restriction. 'No, of course not, but we will have ourselves some fun.' Reaching down to the rucksack sat at the side of the bed he extracted two small coiled lengths of twine.

Megan closed her eyes nestling her head in the crease of the feather pillow lying in anticipation of what was to come next. When she felt the first loop cover her wrist, she looked back at the headboard wondering exactly what fun he intended having. *'Here what's your game?'* the words erupting from her mouth in a slurred garble. She tried pulling her hand free, but the loop held fast on the latticework. Megan hauled herself up by her elbow, but Chilvray quickly slapped her across the face knocking her back down. He didn't say anything as he placed the loop over her free hand.

'I ain't into these kind games, you let me go!'

Chilvray forced her legs apart and knelt between gorging himself on her helplessness. 'I paid for this down the pub, now you're gonna feel what it's like to sample the delights of a real soldier.' He clamped his hand over her mouth as he entered her feeling the scream pulsate through his fingers. 'I bet you've had your fair share down the years,' he said as he pumped hard, bucking her thighs into the mattress. 'All those young men coming through, doing their bit for queen and country. You girls are all the same. Drink a bloke dry of his hard earned cash, but don't want to give back in return, well tonight I'm gonna take a payback for all my comrades that went before me!

Megan tried to scream, but now the noise hurt her head. She succumbed to his assault of her, lying there taking whatever he had to give. The longer the assault lasted the more the wine in her stomach swam back and forth dulling her senses and her head felt like rubber as she tried to consciously stay awake, desperately memorising every detail of his face so that she could tell the police later when he left.

When Chilvray had finished with her he calmly tore a strip from her bed sheet and tied it across her mouth so that she could call out. He gathered together his clothes and went into the bathroom to shower. Megan wanted to cry, but she didn't have the energy. She looked down at her naked body wondering why she did what she did. Why wasn't she like her sister, sensible and unadventurous?

Through the pain, the discomfort and the haze she remembered how he had smiled at her in the pub. He was older than the men that she normally picked up, but there was a certain something about his smile that intrigued her and when he spoke he was more intelligent than many of the others. They had spent the evening drinking and he regaling his stories, exploits from the eighties and unrelated events that had been more recent. Megan had assumed that he was a black ops operative working undercover. When he had suggested going back to her place, it had seemed like a good idea.

The air that night had been fresh, coming down from the mountains and hillsides and the additional oxygen had made her wobble a few times on the way back. Chilvray had held onto her to steady her pace. The rest she wanted to forget. As she watched him dress, she wanted to know what he intended doing with her.

Picking up his rucksack Jack Chilvray hoisted it up onto his shoulder. 'I enjoyed our evening together. If I am ever this way again I will look you up!' Megan tried to lift her head, but it felt like a lead balloon as she crashed back down on the pillow. Pulling open the bedroom door he laughed before passing through and going downstairs.

Relieved that he had not accompanied the sexual assault with a beating Megan closed her eyes accepting sleep as a welcome reprieve. She would have to wait now until Jeannie came back from her visiting before she could have the bonds released. Surrendering to the misery of her stupidity she felt her mind drifting, taking her to where the sun always shone and the blue water came lapping up the beach. She wondered why her groin hurt when she sand down on the sand, but she knew that in time the ache would go. In the distance she saw Jeannie sitting far away. They had argued and Jeannie had shouted at her, telling her what a fool she was, not that she ever learnt.

Pulling open her handbag Chilvray rifled through the purse removing what little cash she had. He tossed aside the receipt where she had withdrawn fifty pound from the ATM. He stuffed the crisp new notes in his back pocket then through the purse aside heading for the kitchen. From inside the fridge he tore the breasts from a cooked chicken, helping himself to an unexpected feast. On the wall of the kitchen he studied the photo collage of two girls sitting on a beach taken when they were abroad. One was Megan and the other girl looked remarkably similar, almost certainly a sister. It was then that he remembered the photographs in his own kitchen. It was too late to doing anything about them, but sometime soon he'd return and put things right.

Setting the timer on the microwave, he placed a sealed tin inside, before opening the rings on the gas cooker. When he looked up at the bedroom from the pavement all was quiet. He pulled shut the front door and turned to climb the short gradient back to the junction. Maybe in some respects it was just as well Barry had not come with him to Wales. He wouldn't have approved of leaving the girl in the house, but then again Barry didn't approve of a lot of things that Jack had done down the years.

Taking the bend where the white painted fencing paralleled the pavement Jack Chilvray nodded at a young woman walking home alone. She smiled weakly being courteous, but it was obvious that she didn't intend encouraging the action any further. Jack smiled, she was the other girl in the photograph.

As Jeannie Lewis approached her house coming down the incline on the opposite pavement she sensed that something was wrong. The night seemed to be calling to her and yet she didn't know why.

When she suddenly stopped walking clasping a hand to her mouth she recognised why she had felt the dread going through her subconscious. The smoke coming from the back of the house was billowing up the chimney like an angry dragon, only the smoke was thick and black. When the front door and the windows exploded from their casings she screamed. Up and down the street the lights had started to go on. Jeannie Lewis preyed that her sister was still down the pub.

A couple of street away Chilvray heard the girl scream followed by the sound of the explosion as the hot combustible gases had erupted from inside the kitchen. In the distance he heard the gathering of two tones that were coming his way. Balling his fingers together to stave off the chill in the air he felt elated. Coming to Wales had always been eventful and one day soon he'd come back again. However, now it was time to head off and spend some time with his own family.

Chapter Thirty Nine

Jack Chilvray reached his sister's house around midday startling her by walking in through the rear kitchen door, where the custom was to leave open the door for visiting neighbours. Madeleine Croxton quickly towelled dry her hands then joyfully cuddled her older brother having not seen him for some time.

'Where have you been Jack, the girl's often ask about you?'

'I've been busy Maddy doing this and that. You know my life, my feet take me different places!'

She offered him a chair at the kitchen table. 'Here sit yourself down and I'll fill the kettle.'

Jack Chilvray took in the layout of the moderate kitchen space. Madeleine had never left the area, never really wanting to travel far. She had married a local man whom she had met at school, settled into marital life with harmonious ease and produced two beautiful girls. Madeleine was happy with her lot and had no desires to travel the world nor expect anything that she could not afford herself. In a way Jack envied her. He watched as she opened the cake tin cutting him a generous slice.

'How's Derek?' he asked.

'Doing well, they gave him a promotion last year, so he's unit supervisor now. Of course it adds more pressure to his daily tasks, but Derek revels in the challenge. The extra money comes in handy, especially with two growing girls. He's a good provider and a loving husband Jack, I made the right choice.'

Chilvray was pleased for his younger sister. He had chosen his path many years back, leaving full-time education without nom particular direction or any concrete ideas as to where his destiny lay ahead. Walking past the army recruitment office he had walked in, signed up for three years. Like a duck taking to water for the first time Jack had found his niche in life. The forces gave him a bed, paid his board and provided him with food, to Jack the lifestyle was idyllic. The only drawback that he detested was taking orders from snotty nosed officers who thought themselves better than him. Other than this he had little or no responsibility. Being sent to different hotspots around the globe to deal with rebel insurgents or governments in trouble suited Jack. He could get in fast, deal with the trouble makers, killing some, then leave, departing with just his footprints embedded in the mud. On the mood board surrounded by drawings and pictures of his nieces, was a photo of Jack receiving his coveted red beret. Not a day went by that Jack didn't wish he was back in the regiment.

'That's good. I am really pleased for you Maddy and how are the girls doing?'

'Fiona has learnt to ride a bike and play the recorder, whereas Alice prefers ballet and reading. They're doing well at school, but they're growing so fast Jack that sometimes I can't keep pace with them. I catch myself looking in the mirror, wondering where the years have gone. It seems only yesterday that mum was around and dad was bouncing the girls on his knee.'

Chilvray bit into the cake, it tasted good. 'Time waits for no man Maddy and change is inevitable. I miss them both too. Maybe while I'm here I'll pop up to the cemetery and pay my respects.'

'How are the books coming along, are you still writing?'

He smiled. 'I'm still burning the midnight oil searching for new subjects and ideas, only some of the characters in my stories not as receptive as I would like them to be.' He washed down the cake with a mouthful of tea. 'It's why I've not come visiting for a while, I've been on the road looking up old friends!'

'That's nice that you keep in touch only you need friends Jack.' She refilled his cup. 'The last time that you came to visit you were upset at how the literary agents were treating your submission. Has circumstances changed?'

Chilvray smiled back wryly. 'Let's say that they probably take me more seriously these days. They're a self-righteous opinionated bunch, but you know the old ways and means act Maddy, be resourceful and you'll overcome any challenge. As mum would often tell us both when we were kids *where there's a will, there's a way around every problem.*'

'Are you staying long?' she asked.

'I can hang around a couple of days, but I must be back in London as I've some unfinished business there. My latest novel is almost complete, but there's one last chapter that I need to research!'

Madeleine wiped her brow with the back of her wrist as she took the chair opposite. 'You're always rushing here and there Jack, it's a wonder that your shadow manages to keeps pace with you. What's the book about?'

He shook his head, chuckling low. 'When it's finished, I'll get a copy sent to you.'

Pouring herself a second cup she cut him another slice of cake. Since a young boy Jack had always liked his cake. Reaching over to where her cookery books were stacked, she retrieved a photo album. Turning the pages they looked at the sepia images of their parents when they had all been a whole lot younger.

'I'm not suggesting that we have ghosts, but I always feel that they're close by Jack.'

He put his arm supportively around her shoulder and pulled her into him. 'They'll always be around for you, Derek and the girls.'

'And you...' she added.

Jack scoffed. 'I'm not sure about that Maddy. I don't think that they ever got over the embarrassment of my having to leave the paras or the police training.'

'They loved you Jack, I know they did.' Madeleine pointed to a photo taken at Hendon where Jack had met Barry Moyne. 'Do you ever see your roommate, I can't quite remember his name?'

'Oddly enough we met up yesterday. I did invite him away this weekend, but he was busy at work with some big investigation!'

'That was a pity because you always did so many things together.'

Jack put the rim of the cup to his mouth as she continued turning the pages. So far he had told Madeleine no lies and not that he believed in ghosts, which he didn't, he checked out the corners of the kitchen, just in case.

Chapter Forty

Spence sat in the armchair making a few calls whist April darted here and there gathering together fresh laundered clothing, toiletries and feminine essentials that men never had to bother about. He smiled approvingly every time that she went by, not wishing to intervene or get in the way. He was still amused at her reaction, expecting a polite rebuff to his proposal, but for once the idea had not been analysed nor rejected. Standing in the doorway with an overnight bag and holding onto an average size suitcase, April indicated that she ready. 'Are you still sure about this?' she asked.

'Absolutely!' Spence picked up the suitcase, it was heavy. On the way over to his place they took in a detour to a pub to eat out as Spence explained that he didn't have enough food in until they went shopping.

'You'll be foregoing your bachelor lifestyle whilst I'm around!'

He looked at her curiously, wondering how much change was coming. Most days the canteen at work served his purpose for maintaining a diet, but he wasn't prepared to divulge all of his secrets.

'In times of emergency, Ted helps out!'

April smiled. 'He makes nice coffee, I'll give him that.'

He watched the road ahead as an oncoming vehicle looked to be nearing the middle white line. 'That was only because it was you. Most days you have to stir in the granules.'

They chose from the bar menu and took their drinks to the table. 'This is nice, where did you find this place?'

Spence loosened the knot of his tie. 'Ted and I came here after going to the dogs one night. On a Tuesday evening they do a sublime Peking duck.'

April laughed. She never thought that Spence would be a connoisseur of fine culinary dining. There were so many things that she didn't know about him, but moving in with him would resolve that. When he wasn't looking, she did. She really liked him and found his company easy to be in. With Barry out of the way, she suddenly felt free and that her life was no longer complicated.

'What do you think Chilvray will do now?' she asked.

Spence looked up over the edge of the glass. 'I would expect him to go to ground. If I was in his shoes, I would put as much distance between myself and the police. He knows by now that we turning over every stone looking.'

'You don't think that he'll strike whilst the irons hot?'

Spence heard his stomach rumble, an indication that he was ready for his food. 'Are you referring to getting rid of loose ends?'

'I suppose so, although I had been thinking along the lines of Annabelle Du Renard and Rachel Roberts. Neither saw their demise until it was too late.'

When the waitress arrived with their meals, Spence cleared a space on the table and waited for her to leave before continuing.

'Chilvray's calculated, although somewhat predictable.'

'How?'

'Talking over his exploits with Stephanie Garland he mentioned his new book. Dispatching of his victims he picks a different venue and modus operandi to suit the occasion. Nothing overly elaborate, but effective, all except Garland. When a killer suddenly fails to achieve, they start to amass doubts about their ability. They become predictable, foreseeable. I would expect him to continue making mistakes.'

'You don't think that he'll go out of his way to prove himself?'

'No. Stephanie Garland escaping will play on his mind. He doesn't just kill at random. He kills because it has purpose!'

He knew that eventually she would get around to her.

'I'm happy moving in with you Spence, although I'm not entirely over the moon about having my movements curtailed. The dossier that we found at his house was quite unexpected, in fact shocking to say the least. I feel in a way that I've been raped!'

He put his hand over hers. It felt warm and caring.

'Nobody else has seen it April, other than Tom and he'll never say anything to anyone. Tom has a lot of respect for you. When this over, we'll destroy the evidence, I promise!' She pushed her fingers through his showing him that she believed him.

'The photograph of the woman in the picture. Do you think it was a relative?'

'Almost certainly. The curve of the eye line and the bone structure in the face. It's genetic.

'Can't we just have the images put in the newspapers, surely somebody out there would make a match?'

'No. That would be my last resort. If I did that and it was a family member, we might put them in jeopardy as well. Chilvray doesn't leave loose ends. He's a pathological psychopath remember!'

April chewed on her food as nodded her agreement. 'Even if it means hurting his own flesh and blood Spence, that's desperate.'

'He has already shown us how desperate. Chilvray lives in a black and white negative existence where empathy and remorse do not exist. Deceit, cheating and lying his way to freedom, he will stop at nothing to achieve his aim. That probably includes family.'

April lent across her plate coming closer to Spence. *'Then thank fuck I'm staying with you!'*

When the ringtone of her mobile sounded in her bag, April reached in and opened up the message. She dropped the phone on the table causing Spence to look up from his food.

'It's him, I know it is...'

Spence picked up the cell phone and read the message *'we'll meet again, soon'* he saw that it had only just been sent. Running to the door of the pub he looked up and down the street outside, but the only movement came from a cat sitting in a doorway rummaging through a discarded fish and chip wrapper. Returning to the table he told her that Chilvray was nowhere near.

'It was sent from Barry's mobile. Ghosts don't text!'

Chapter Forty One

It was an enjoyable, relaxing couple of days spent with his sister's family and they were sorry when he said that he had to travel back down to London, but Jack Chilvray had thought about nothing, but April Geddings lying on his bed at night. He wondered how she felt now, having learnt about the demise of her ex-husband, was she glad or sad. Of all the times that they had met Jack felt that she had kept herself aloof.

Every so often when the house was quiet, the girls at school, Derek at work and Maddy down the shops Jack would hear the voices inside his head telling him what needed to be done. In the quiet moments he would contemplate his fate hearing the echoes of the girl's shrill laughter as they played hide and seek with their uncle. He would miss them all, but Jack knew that it was dangerous not to heed the advice that the voices gave.

On the last night before he left he drafted his last chapter, planning how he could trap April Geddings into coming to him, rather he going to her. Like a hunter setting bait for game, he had the venue, it was now just a matter of finding the right time and the opportunity. For hours Jack pondered over the problem until the moon had travelled around to the far side of the house. When he added the full stop to the last sentence, the plan was hatched. Over the years April Geddings had unwittingly been gathering evidence of his exploits, crimes as she liked to label them, but soon the time was going to come that she paid for her interference.

Closing the lid of the laptop Jack switched off the light and lay on the bed gazing up at the stars outside. Somewhere in the expanse of the universe

April Geddings destiny had long been written in the tablets of time. Somewhere, if his plan was executed right he would make sure that she met that destiny.

As the first rays of the new day hit the windows of the house Jack slipped out of the kitchen door pulling it shut very quietly. He had never been good at farewells and didn't want to see his nieces upset. He left a note on the kitchen table for his sister and her husband adding money for both the girls. As usual when he left he wrote them all a poem drawing a cartoon owl in the top right corner to symbolize the wisdom of the night, when dreams were supposed to come true.

Alice had once said that the owl was wise to hoot to let your enemy know that you were coming, so in the bottom left corner Jack sketched the small figure of a mouse.

He caught the express coach back down to London passing by several road blocks that had been erected on the opposite carriageway where the police were checking vehicles going north. Nobody had expected him to be coming back. Jack smiled whenever they saw the coach go by, none would suspect that he'd be on board.

Stepping down from the footplate at London Victoria he quickly mingled with the crowds crossing the concourse. With his rucksack slung over his back he resembled any other tourist arriving. Taking a seat inside the nearest coffee bar he ordered a tall latte and two croissants. They would keep him going until he found lodgings. From where he sat he had a good view of everything outside, surprised to see so few police walking about. One or two he could easily deal with, but more could cause him problems.

When he had finished his breakfast he read the message on his phone

'The girls were upset that you didn't say goodbye, but I told them you had been called away on another secret mission. They said to say thank you for the money and they loved the poem, owl and mouse. Thanks Jack. Don't stay away so long next time. Love Maddy xxx'

He smiled and saved the message. They were all he had and he loved them too. He didn't send any reply, but he would go visit again when it was all over.

Keeping primarily to the back streets he slipped into a two star hotel where the desk clerk looked as though booking him a room was an inconvenience. The foreigner handed over the key, but said nothing about what time the kitchen served dinner. At two star Jack guessed there'd be nothing on offer.

The room on the first floor was stark and the furniture had seen better days, but everything suited Jack. Nothing fancy, nothing that the police would come checking. Outside of the window the drop to the ground as about fifteen feet, ten maybe less if he landed on the waste bins and directly opposite the side of the hotel overlooked a fashion warehouse where the brick wall had no windows. 'At least I can't be overlooked,' he mumbled to himself.

Going out for food or refreshments the Hungarian on reception would nod at him when he left and acknowledge the same when he returned. The arrangement suited Chilvray as there was never any conversation nor questions asked.

Jack spent the Monday and Tuesday watching the back yard of the police station where he pretended to sweep the pavements and empty the lamp-post bins. He kept his head low and avoided looking up at the security cameras disappearing every so often so as not to attract unnecessary attention. He had seen her leave and return twice in the past thirty six hours, but she had always been accompanied by a male colleague. Jack noted how long she was gone for each occasion. Proper surveillance meant being patient and he had plenty of time to execute his plan.

On the third day there were no sightings of the forensic examiner and the pavements around back of the station had never looked so good. Jack realised that snatching her in broad daylight was the less attractive option. To get close he had to make some minor adjustments. It meant going back to Hamptons, but the alternative option was already buzzing through Jack's mind. Leaving the dustcart against a commercial gateway he walked off smiling to himself. Once again the voices had come through for him.

Later that evening, later than dusk he called the police emergency line and reported a disturbance at number seventy four Adolphus Tower, on the Paddington Green estate. When the first police units attended they looked up at the foreboding edifice already knowing that the service to the lift would not be available to them. A hike of seven floors would mean running the gauntlet of rubbish and gangs that controlled the tower.

Just over ninety steps to the reported incident gave Jack enough time to lever open the boot and steal a stab-proof vest. By the time that the crew realised that the call had been a hoax Jack would be long gone from the area. He gave some young boys watching nearby twenty pounds to keep their mouths shut, adding another score when they said that they'd puncture the tyres as well.

Carrying a pizza box under one arm and the vest under the other Jack nodded his greeting at Andric sitting on reception. The Hungarian waved a hand in response, but he was busy watching the dance show where the legs were smooth and long and the costumes revealing.

Chilvray tried on the vest for size. It was a little tight under the arms, but it would do for what he needed it for. He turned left and right catching himself in the reflection of the mirror, reading the words *'POLICE'* emblazoned across the back. Jack smiled, he was happy. It would fool a fool, if only for a few minutes.

He ate the pizza realising that he only needed another night in the hotel, the time had come for him to put his plan in operation. When the pizza was gone he flipped open the lid of the laptop, tapping into the search field *Article 15*. He was pleased that the search came back blank, it meant that the secret facility in Whitehall was still an unknown entity.

With the imminent threat of a terrorist attack Article 15 was a secret set of rooms on the ground floor of a building in the heart of London where Special Forces could gather, be briefed and carry out a defensive strategy, coming and going as though they never existed. Very few knew of its existence, but the web of passageways and tunnels that criss-crossed under the streets emerged only in specific locations, where members of the royal family, the prime minster and high ranking military personnel could be taken to a place of safety and out of the immediate danger zone. Jack had kept a regular eye on Article 15 and as far as he knew, it had not been used for some time. Not even the spring of two thousand and seventeen.

He waited until five thirty the next morning when Andric went to make a coffee before slipping out of the hotel again. It wasn't hard to locate and steal an unmarked commercial van hotwiring the ignition. Parking around the back of the Hamptons offices he waited until the traffic on the main thoroughfare started to increase in volume.

Somewhere around seven he saw the first lights go on, on the upper floors. Any other time he would have been tempted to go up, but today he had to keep to the plan. From his vantage point in the drivers cab he saw his quarry go past the end of the service alley heading for the front doors. Keeping a watch on the time he waited knowing that the red postal van was due. When it left to rejoin the traffic on the one way system Jack Chilvray made his move.

He waited until the receptionist was on the phone before he entered the lobby. She looked up seeing a man coming towards in black combats and a stab vest. Chilvray turned around and thumbed the name on the back. Julie nodded that she understood. She symbolised with a single finger that she would only be a moment. It was all Jack needed as he slipped around the desk and put the cloth over her mouth. Within seconds Julie was unconscious and slumped in his arms. Kicking open the emergency door at the back of the reception stairs he loaded her into the van. It had been that easy, sometimes too simple.

Chilvray pulled out into the traffic heading east towards Trafalgar Square. As he passed the post van the driver was inside talking to a pretty young reception. He turned when Jack drove by, sensing that a connection had just gone past, although he was unsure quite what.

Reversing up to the electricity cupboard door Chilvray switched off the engine and waited several minutes, observing every shadow and trick of the light. It made good sense to stay alert, just like the owl. When he was confident that he had the place to himself he exited the cab. Jack knew that the military frequently changed the code on the front doors, but that nobody ever bothered with the service cupboard. A long time ago he had found the secret entrance quite by chance. He tapped in one, nine, four and two into the keypad pulling back hard on the handle, grinning as the door swung open.

Carrying Julie Carter through the interior of the cupboard he shut the door behind him and let his eyes adjust momentarily to the gloom inside. Punching in a second code on the inner door he kicked it open, covering his mouth to the dust that had gathered on the other side of the door. He walked across to a long metal workbench where the troops would clean their weapons whilst awaiting the word to go out on the streets. Taking a length of adhesive tape he covered her mouth and fastened both wrists to the upright bench supports. The light in the room was evidentially a lot brighter, but there was no fear that anybody could see inside as the glazing had all been smoked over during the mid-eighties. Checking one more time that she was unlikely to regain consciousness he left.

Jack Chilvray drove the van down a side road where it was likely to be found very soon by the local borough enforcement officials. After giving the obstructing van a ticket, it would be another seven days before the van was removed. By then Jack intended being as far away as possible.

Applying the second code once again he pushed open the door to the inner room instantly gazed upon by the conscious receptionist. He checked the time writing something down on a notepad that he kept in his leg pocket.

'When you're on ops, it's always advisable to keep a check on progress, only complacency is what leads to failure.'

Julie watched as the man in black took items from his rucksack and checked them. She looked at his profile wondering where she had seen his face before.

Chapter Forty Two

Daniel Spence was sat at his desk busily going through the list of items that had been removed from Chilvray's house, when Thomas Hawkes walked in. He was glad that his protégé had returned as he needed helped, feeling snowed under. 'How did it go at Colchester?' he asked. Hawkes placed a fresh mug of coffee before his superior taking the seat at his desk.

'Colonel Jenks was extremely helpful. A little reticent to begin with, but I had expected that he would be. When he had all the facts he was only too pleased to assist.'

'So anything interesting?'

'Jack Chilvray made corporal, but that was as far as he went. In the time served with the paras he visited several hot-spots around the Middle East and the Congo, before coming back to England to attend Credenhill.'

Spence put down what he was holding. 'The base at Hereford where the Special Air Service do their training and selection.' Hawkes nodded only he didn't grin.

'The personnel file made interesting reading. Credenhill scored his combat and tactical knowledge high, but what had Chilvray fail the course was his attitude and lack of respect for officers.'

Spence sighed loudly *'He didn't get in?'*

'No. Everything is black and white, there's no in between. You either pass or fail. The SAS is as tough as the reputation and they do not suffer the slightest ineptitude. To be a black ops operative you have to be extremely disciplined and very self-controlled, whatever the situation. Chilvray by all accounts lacked the self-control.'

'As demonstrated when he killed Vivienne D'Corscy.' Spence interrupted, although Hawkes wasn't dissuaded from what he had to add.

'Chilvray dipped out on an abduction and interrogation exercise, conjured up by the trainers. He led a three man team into the welsh hillsides where they had to sneak up and overpower another course candidate standing guard over a jeep. The object was to blindfold the captive and take him to a place of interrogation. The record tells that Jack Chilvray was skilful at seizing the hostage, but refused to stand down when ordered to do so during the interrogation. He argued with a sergeant on the course, who thought Chilvray's action were over-zealous and bordering on the dangerous.

The training officers recognised a flaw and it concerned them. Jenks said it was apparent that Chilvray over-reacted and showed little compassion for the other candidate. It was though he himself was being controlled.'

Spence listened intently every so often jotting down a specific word, gathering together a picture of the man that they sought.

'They gave Chilvray one more chance, putting together another similar exercise and low and behold it ended in almost the same circumstances. Chilvray's file was marked 'REJECT' and 'RED MIST'.

Spence wrote psychotic against his list of words. Hawkes handed over a copy of the rejection endorsed form that had accompanied the file. In the comments section were the following remarks *'Corporal Chilvray is a good soldier, but suffers distinct pathological tendencies that have been identified when dealing with other candidates on the course. There is also an underlying problem with his respect for authority and officers. 'His lack of self-control was clearly evident on the abduction exercise with an unacceptable and unreasonable level of violence attached, enjoying the pain inflicted upon other members of the armed forces. It is recommended that his regiment colonel seeks the advice of the medical assessor to determine Corporal Chilvray's active role as a future leader of men.'*

Hawkes waited until Spence had read the recommendation before he continued. 'Before leaving Hereford he the officer-in-charge what he thought of their training and selection process. A month later Jack Chilvray handed in his papers and walked out of the base a free man and ready to take on Civvy Street.'

Spence shook his head in resignation. 'The bloody army taught him every skill that he would need on the outside and Chilvray started to show his prowess with the two security guards at Hendon.'

Hawkes swallowed the last of his coffee. 'He's a force not to be tangled with, unless you're holding a Hecker and Koch MP45.'

Spence put down his pen. 'How's Steph holding up?'

'Good. She's determined to block out the memory and medical section have sent across one of our counsellors. In time I think she'll get her life back on track. I called Hampton's on the way over and they've promised to keep her position open, although I'm not sure that she wants to go back.'

Spence finished off his coffee, which had gone cold. 'I can't blame her Tom. What about you though, how do you fit in with her plans?' He seemed hesitant in replying as though he himself had decisions to make.

'I'm undecided guv'nor. I like Steph, but I've been seen Trevelyan as well.'

Spence tried not to laugh, but he couldn't help it and it burst from his lips. 'You young people always complicate your lives.' He put down the coffee unable to suffer the last dregs. 'Take your time to work it through on your own Tom and I'm here if you ever need to talk!'

Hawkes smiled, Spence was like an older brother. 'Thanks guv'nor!' He took back the regiment report and replaced it in the file. 'How's April holding up?'

'April is April... you know. Generally she is as calm as a baby asleep, but that dossier tossed aside her resolve. She's moved in with me temporarily, where I can make sure that she's safe.' Hawkes didn't pass judgement and Spence told him about their visit to Moyne's house.

'So where is she now?'

'Would you believe me if I told you that she's taken the day off to go visit Weekes then go shopping.'

Hawkes sat at his desk going through the crimes that had happened overnight. There were the normal occurrences to fill the cells, street thefts, assaults and vehicle crime, but nothing significant to indicate that

Chilvray could be involved. Hawkes spread his search nationwide going around the major cities. 'Do you reckon Chilvray has gone abroad?' he asked.

Spence opened the drawer of his desk and pulled out a passport. 'He's have a bloody hard job without this!'

Hawkes stopped at a report of a house fire in the Hay-on-Wye region. It had occurred in a small village called Ferengaurd. Hawkes read through the report twice absorbing each detail. He called Spence over to look.

'The fire service were quickly on the scene of the tragedy where a young woman lost her life having been asphyxiated by smoke as fire engulfed the remainder of the house. Investigators at the scene believe that the woman might have left the gas and the microwave on going upstairs to the bedroom. Police however are treating the fire as suspicious.'

Hawkes checked a thought racing through his head as Spence looked up the number for the station at Hay-on-Wye. Hawkes was the first to come back with his search. 'Ferengaurd is just shy of twenty miles from the SAS base at Credenhill.' Spence wrote down the telephone number.

'I've stopped believing in coincidence Tom. There's something about this fire that has the hackles on my neck rising.' He dialled the number. When he came back off, his hackles were slightly less responsive. 'The deceased woman was found tied to the bedhead and a tin in the microwave had started the fire!'

When the mobile on the desk vibrated Spence grabbed at it reading the message that had been sent. *'Saw Susan Weekes. Barry had his neck broken, it was no accident. Been up one side and down the other in Oxford Street. Dare not check my bank balance. Visiting the Tate soon. Anything new your end?'*

As Hawkes took a report of the fire from the fax machine Spence sent back a reply *'very quiet here.'*

Standing in the doorway of the coffee shop where she intended having a midmorning break April wondered if Spence was referring to the fact that she wasn't in the office or that crime in the capital was also taking a day off as well.

From her seat beside the window she had a panoramic view of both Trafalgar Square and Henry Tate's National Art Gallery. It had been a long time since she had been inside and looked at the selection of paintings. She was excited about the coming afternoon and losing herself amongst the nation's treasures.

When a second fax arrived, it contained a statement taken from the sister of the deceased woman. Hawkes read through the content stopping at where she had given a description of a stranger seen in the vicinity moments before the fire ripped through the lower floor swallowing up her beloved sister. The description given matched that of Jack Chilvray.

Chapter Forty Three

Julie Carter watched warily her captor secure the door from the inside adding additional metal to the broad flanks to prevent it from being opened from the other side, doing the same with the internal door opposite leading through to the inner sanctum of the archive office. Jack Chilvray had learnt his lesson and was not about to lose his quarry once again. She wondered why she had been taken.

Unable to communicate Julie surveyed the room in which she was being held prisoner, it was extremely grim, unfriendly and everywhere was dust laden with cobwebs. Two windows had thick latticed bars across the outside and every pane of glass was frosted with impenetrable screening. She tried bucking her back to see if the bench would move, but it was too heavy.

Amused at how quiet she had remained Jack Chilvray moved about getting things ready sensing her eyes on his every move. With the checks made and what he needed in place he turned his focus her way.

'I know that you cover the reception at Hamptons, so it's quite possible that you've not heard of me, but my name is Jack Chilvray and my pseudonym is Mortimer Valdis.' He saw the recognition in her eyes as he mentioned the alias.

'Good, I like it when things aren't complicated. You're probably wondering why you're here… well let me explain. Quite simply you're bait to help me achieve another objective. I don't intend harming you, unless you give me reason to make me change my mind.'

Jack paced back and forth as he talked, he liked to control the situation as best he could listening the advice coming from the voices inside his head. Julie's eyes went left and right, then right and left.

'You've no doubt heard about the demise of Vivienne D'Corscy and Charles Trent, each regrettable incidents, but quite necessary to have my work taken seriously. Stephanie Garland however was meant to do what you now need to help me with, although in a moment of weakness I allowed her a little more latitude than I should have. It has cost me dearly, but soon I'll be the one in control again.'

He took the tape away covering her mouth allowing her to breathe more easily.

'I would advise from screaming or calling out. We are near to Trafalgar Square so the constant barrage of traffic noise should deafen any sudden screeching, but in the circumstances it would be more civilised it we just communicated at a more acceptable level.' Julie nodded letting him know that she understood.

'What do you want me to do?' she asked quietly.

Chilvray smiled, he liked her appreciation of the situation. 'Nothing my dear, simply nothing. All I ask is that you stay here whilst I attend to a little matter not very far away.'

He knelt down beside her and checked the pulse in her wrist, it was a beating strong, but then he expected it to be fast.

'Was it you who killed Miss D'Corscy and Charles Trent?'

He stood back up and continued walking back and forth.

'Yes. Although I have to admit Miss D'Corscy's death didn't go as planned. I had gone along to discuss my manuscript, but when she refused to give me any answers to the questions that kept going around and around in my head, I was forced to act. Events shall we say overtook the evening and she died as a consequence. Charles Trent however, was different. He was pompous and over indulgent of his own importance. He saw me as a fool and I've never taken lightly to people who look down upon from a greater height. Army officers were like that. Fresh from Sandhurst they arrived with the air of Berkshire stuck right up their arse.' He apologised for using the term, then continued. Trent had the same deportment, but he paid for his ignorance when he met the oncoming train that afternoon.'

He liked the young girl, she was co-operative and quiet, seemingly unmoved by what he had said so far. 'Tell me, did you know of an Italian that used to hang around with Miss D'Corscy.'

Julie nodded. 'Yes. Mr Cortelli.'

Chilvray liked names, they helped. 'Yes, that's him. I need to pay him a visit only I think we've met before, once outside Miss D'Corscy's flat.'

Julie crossed her legs wishing that she had worn trousers to work instead of a skirt. Chilvray laughed as he took a mobile from his back pocket and asked her to sit perfectly still. Taking a photo on the phone, he scrutinised the look on her face then saved it.

'Perfect, that was all that I required. At this rate you'll soon be free!'

Jack Chilvray attached the photo to a number in the phone and sent the image. Moments later it was received.

Going over to the window in the gallery where the signal was better April felt her teeth coming together as she answered the call. *'You bastard, you've got Barry's phone!'*

Chilvray laughed. 'Come now, is that a way to greet and old friend. Did you get the image I sent you?'

He allowed hr a moment to upload the photograph.

'Let her go, she's just a receptionist, a young girl!'

'I know April, but so far we've got along just fine and she has been very co-operative.' Jack heard the sound of muffled voices in the background. 'Where are you, it sounds public?'

'The Tate.'

'That's handy. Lots of witnesses should anything happen.'

'Why is it going to happen?' April tried to sound confident.

He laughed again. 'Let's say that it'll be a surprise!'

'Like going to see Barry. We know you killed him, we have the evidence Jack!'

'That's why we need to meet April, to go over old times and discuss certain aspects of my life. Of course how you handle this situation will determine this young lady's fate.' He looked at Julie and shook his head, indicating that it was merely an idle threat, but needed to be taken seriously at the other end of the line.

'He didn't deserve to die!'

'I lost count with the number of times that I told him not to climb heights. That was a long way up when he fell. Accidents around the home happen all the time April, surely you should know that.'

'He died because you broke his neck!'

Chilvray paused for a moment. 'I ended his life rather than have him confined to a wheel-chair for the rest of his life. I can be merciful April.'

'Like D'Corscy, Trent, Roberts and Du Renard, was that merciful?'

'Necessity.'

April had moved away from the window taking a chance that she wouldn't lose the signal, at the side of the gallery room entrance she saw an office.

'Have you hurt the young woman like you did Stephanie Garland?'

Chilvray tutted into the microphone, sensing that she was becoming angry. 'Not yet, but I can if you don't co-operate!'

Placing her police ID against the glass so that the person working on the inside could see she placed her index finger to her lips. The door opened slowly and the woman working inside remained silent. April went across to the desk phone. Letting Chilvray wait a few seconds she dialled the number. When it was answered she muted the call and told Spence not to talk, just listen.

'So what do you want me to do?'

'What happened, you went silent?' she sensed his apprehension.

'The signal Jack, just the signal. I've moved to where it's stronger.' She could him breathing down the phone.

'Alright, as you're at the Tate, we're not that far from one another. I'm going to give you instructions that you follow to the letter or else you know what will happen, is that understood?'

Listening in Spence wrote down the time and location pointing the pen nib at the pad and indicating to Hawkes to say nothing. He arrowed from the Tate to the word *firearms*. Hawkes left immediately to make the arrangements.

'I'll do whatever is necessary to secure her release Jack. Promise me though that you won't hurt her?'

'You have my word.' April knew that it counted for nothing, but stalling for time was the only advantage that she had.

'One thing that I need to know before I do anything. Why Jack, why come after me?'

'Principle's April, nothing less nor more. You have been to every crime scene that I have committed and the evidence is stacking up nicely in favour of the crown prosecution service. It was time that I turned around the advantage in my direction. By the way you looked nice when you was taking a shower!

April felt the sensation of the nausea rising up from her stomach and into her throat. 'That's my job!'

Jack Chilvray checked his watch and looked at his plan that had been hatched back in the hotel.

'Time to leave the Tate and start walking across the square towards the column.'

Hoping that Spence had heard she repeated the instruction. 'Across the square to the lions, I'm on my way!' she nodded at the woman in the office and mouthed *'thank you!'*. April left the office phone off the hook so that the woman could talk to Spence. Walking, she continued the conversation.

'Was this all worth it Jack, all for the sake of a book?'

'It's not a book April, but a way of life. We're born, we survive, we die. How we live our lives is what matters in the in-between.' He heard the sound of passing traffic and good indicator that she was on her way. 'At first it started with just my imagination, but that can only provide so much to keep a reader interested. Soon I had to influence the story with let's say more guts. I started a long way back with a tramp that would not be missed, then a pissed lout who gave me a hard time. It got easier every time and adapting a different approach made the chapters come alive!'

'And Barry, did he ever help?'

'Occasionally. He hushed up the tramp's death and covered up evidence regarding the drunken lout. Things were going alright until you turned up at the burglary at Pembroke Mansions. From then on I had to meticulously consider every step I took.'

April shook her head in recognition of Barry's adding and abetting of the crimes. She knew that her husband was weak, easily influenced, but to be complicit in acts of murder and assault, she was repulsed at his memory.

As if he had read her thoughts Chilvray laughed down the phone. 'You obviously didn't know your husband that well. Did it never occur to you how he arrived at a crime scene so fast? Barry orchestrated the occasion, he made it happen April. He owed me big time for protecting his integrity at Hendon. I made sure that he never forgot it!'

'Whatever his faults and he had many, Barry was still a good police officer.'

'Because I made him so. Look at it, that when I committed a crime, he helped put together the pieces of the jigsaw. I helped mould his career and his path into CID.'

April turned the conversation around directing it back at Chilvray. 'You said that I was close. Where are you?'

But Chilvray was no man's fool, he grinned to himself then laughed. 'Nice try, but that's not important. What is relevant however is where and when we're going to meet.' He looked back at Julie Carter. 'You see this young lady is the bargaining chip that is going to assure me success. Non-compliance means you will be very busy professionally once again. You know the script.'

The thoughts were racing through her mind. April had been dreading this moment, but now that it had arrived she felt that she was in control. She cut through the crap and went straight for the jugular.

'Before I give myself over to you, you've got to let me know that she's alive, every couple of minutes. I'm standing by the lions.' At the far side of the square she saw Spence and Hawkes arrive along with a firearms unit. There were no two tones nor blue lights. April waved, but nearby at a fountain a group of Chinese tourists waved back.

'I'll leave the mobile running so that you can see she's been unharmed.'

'When and where now Jack?'

'Cross the road and head for Charing Cross Mainline Station concourse, I'll give you exactly ten minutes.'

'That's a busy station Jack, how will I find you?'

'You won't, instead you'll come to me... now remember the clock's ticking!'

Leaving Barry Moyne's mobile recording on video mode he left atop of a chair seat before resealing Julie Carter's mouth with tape, checking her bonds. In the street outside he reached out and stretched his limbs as far as they would go, invigorating additional blood into his muscles. This was the moment that he had been waiting for all morning. Walking briskly towards Charing Cross Road he sensed that the mission was progressing well and very soon that zenith moment would be his for the taking.

Chapter Forty Four

Walking down the opposite pavement to approach Charing Cross Station April sent Spence a text to let him know her location. She was concerned that two constables standing near to the entrance would be spotted by Chilvray would might think that she had asked for them to be there. Spence replied to say that they were on their way.

April checked the video link and saw that Julie was still alive and that her clothes were still intact. There were no signs of Jack Chilvray. She wanted to triangulate the link to Spence, but her phone wouldn't make the connection.

On the way to the station Hawkes took a call from Sharon Trevelyan who told him about the missing receptionist. She was Hamptons making enquiries. He told her to stay there and that he would catch up with her later. Spence looked across.

'Is that wise?'

Hawkes shrugged. 'I know, but what do I do guv'nor. Sometimes you've got to follow your instincts rather than follow uncertainty.'

Spence made the driver of the armed response vehicle pull up short of April as she reached the station entrance ignoring the constables standing nearby.

'What's she looking for?' one asked.

'A serial killer!' replied Hawkes.

Coming towards them other armed units approached the station. Spence gave the two officers accompanying them instructions to deploy the units in and around the station where they could take advantage of the advertising screens, only not be seen.

'If Chilvray gets wind that we're on scene he might kill April and then go back for the hostage. Remember also that the man that we're after was in the paras and he's nobody's fool!'

The officers quickly worked out who would take where and made their way to their strategic positions. Spence sent Hawkes to speak to the station manager whilst he tracked April.

She saw him trailing behind some ten metres away, although there was still no sign of Jack Chilvray, April was concerned that he had seen the armed units arrive and called off their meeting, until she was alone. When he called, she jumped.

'I see you've got your boyfriend in tow. I thought that he'd appear anytime soon. You should remember April that I've done this sort of thing before!'

'You can't blame me for protecting my back Jack.'

He laughed. 'No. Good field tactics. I would have done exactly the same.' There was a pause. 'Only it won't do any good.'

April Stood beside the information board on the station concourse and signalled Spence not to approach, he saw that she was talking on the phone. As Hawkes came into sight he too understood to steer clear.

'What next?' she asked.

'I've kept my end of the bargain, you can see that the girls unharmed. Now it's your turn to be compliant. Start walking down platform one, just keep walking. I can see you coming and I'll give you further instructions as you near the end.'

Spence and Hawkes joined forces as April walked towards the platform. On high ground Spence guessed that the firearms units could also see April.

'Where are they?' he asked.

'Behind the advertising hoarding, in the station masters office and the announcers office. They have a good sight on April, although I've not spotted Chilvray so there's every possibility that they haven't either.'

'I know. The bastards concealed himself somewhere where he can watch April and us!'

'Have they got the word that they can take Chilvray out if needed?'

Spence nodded and watched April disappear behind a waiting train, he was in no mood to wait. 'Come on let's keep her in our sights, before Chilvray pops up unexpected.'

Watching the movements of the passengers already on the train April made her way along the platform wondering where Chilvray was hidden. She was tense and scared, but she knew Spence would have firearms in place.

'When are you going to let Julie Carter go?' she asked.

'As soon as you and I are clear of the station and the detectives following have stood down the firearms units. You're doing well so far April, only don't *fuck* it up!' She knew that he meant business. 'If you do, then you'll never find her, well not alive anyway. I won't kill her, but thirst and starvation would.'

April wanted to respond and tell him that he was completely insane, but she kept her emotions in check realising that it could be detrimental to Julie's health.

'I'm almost at the end. What next?'

'As the trains roll out of the station they pass an old signal box and wooden shed. Keep walking towards the shed and I'll show myself when you are close enough to take the bullet rather than me. If you make any sudden moves, I'll disappear and so will Miss Carter. Eventually, she just be food for the rats and other vermin crawling our sewers.'

'I get the picture.'

As April took the descent down from the platform Spence watched her every move. They were beyond the end of the train and still he couldn't see Chilvray. Hawkes looked back and up at the hoardings. The distance was almost five hundred metres. It would be difficult to get a good shot.

April wanted to look behind at Spence and Hawkes, but she dared not anger Chilvray, realising that Julie's life depended on her forsaking her own. The ground underfoot was difficult to walk upon without the proper footwear and the stones were unforgiving. In her ear she heard Chilvray counting down the distance to the shed. When she was almost alongside the wooden structure he appeared holding a large combat knife. He stood behind her using her as a human shield. Not far away Spence stopped Hawkes from advancing any closer, recalling that Chilvray had scored well at Credenhill for his expertise in hostage taking, it was the aftermath where he had failed to score any points.

With April hostage Spence ordered the firearms officers to stand fast. He couldn't take the risk that they miss Chilvray and hit April. Talking into their radios the unit that hadn't reached the platform were sent down to the street below the bridge.

*****

For a minute Jack watched as the police stood where they were in a stand-off position. Looking at the bank to the side, he saw that the way down was unobstructed. He had hold of April's arm and had turned her around so that she faced the police.

'Why haven't you hurt the girl?' April asked, trying to distract his attention.

'Because in a way she reminds me of my sister and she looks like her as well. That went in her favour!' He pulled April towards the stone steps that descended to the street below.

'Where are we going?'

'Somewhere where we can be alone.' Chilvray called out to the two detectives who were the closest. Noting that the black suited firearms officers had vanished. Jack knew why.

'Nobody has to die here Inspector,' he called out 'unless you want it on your conscience!'

Behind them the train rolled away from the platform and across where April and Chilvray were standing. Jack took the advantage as his opportunity to escape. He pulled April down the steps to the road below and opened the gate out onto the main thoroughfare. The traffic running alongside the embankment was busy for the time of the day.

'Walk naturally and if you try to run, I'll gut you here and now!' April did as she was told. Ahead of them the Parliament building looked a long way off. Behind her April heard the end of the train roll across the bridge. A long way behind Spence was only just able to descend the stone steps.

Chilvray and April were about to take a right turn down a side street when a voice bellowed across the busy carriageways.

'Jack... Jack Chilvray, you old scrote!' the man calling was stocky and powerfully built and around Jack's age. He was waving frantically.

Chilvray looked across at the man calling his name. When he recognised the face, he smiled back, it had been years since he had seen Jock Armstrong. Drawing back her elbow April punched it back as hard as she could into Chilvray's stomach. There was going to be only one chance to avoid the ordeal ahead and this was it. Chilvray felt the blow push the air from his lungs as he let go of her arm. April took a quick look then jumped into the lines of traffic heading east. A woman driver who was nearest the point of collision slammed on her brakes causing the rear end of the vehicle to skid. April managed to jump out of the way as Chilvray regained his breath.

Running across to the central reservation she saw Spence, Hawkes and several firearms officers running her way. She quickly looked behind and saw that Chilvray, his face flushed red with rage was already off the pavement. Coming towards her she saw a dustcart, April decided that she would rather die under the vehicle than let Jack Chilvray abuse and torture her, before he finished her off. She jumped into the path of the dustcart and closed her eyes. On the other side of the road Spence yelled for her to watch out.

In the cab of the dustcart the three council workers all stamped their feet hard on the floor of the cab, but only one connected with the brake. The driver felt the seat of his trousers leave the seat as he stood on the brake pedal turning the wheel hard to the right.

The screeching of tyres from both carriageways was the only sound that April heard as she expected the thud of metal to hit her body any moment now, but when instead she felt the side draught of the vehicle pass her by she opened her eyes, in time to see Jack Chilvray scream out and drop the knife as the front of the dustcart collided with a builders lorry coming in the opposite direction.

She put a clenched fist to her mouth as Chilvray disappeared between the two vehicles and a man on the pavement, Embankment side called out Chilvray's name in vain. When the two heavy goods vehicles collided with one pirouetting sideways Jack Chilvray knew that the end had come. He only had time to call out for his sister, but his sorrowful cry was lost in the entanglement of metal and glass as each driver brought their vehicle to a halt.

As police with machine guns surrounded the bloodied mess Spence came around back of the dustcart to comfort April who was sat on the kerbstone. She pointed as he sat alongside her taking her in his arms.

'Is he dead Spence?'

'He's dead. The nightmare is over!'

'Somehow he didn't suffer, unlike his victims.'

'Well this is one chapter that he won't finish.'

April suddenly remembered Julie Carter, but Spence didn't seem overly concerned. He checked the time on his watch.

'Around about now she should be getting an unexpected visit.'

*****

When Julie first heard the scurrying of feet she thought that they belonged to rats, knowing that old buildings often accommodated the unwanted vermin, but when the explosives blew open the door from the inner chamber and in rushed several men in combat fatigues, armed with sub machine guns she realised that somebody had heard her prayers.

'How did you know?' asked April.

'It was Hawkes, he put a call through to a Colonel Jenks of the Paratroop Regiment. He told Hawkes about Article 15. Rumour has it that there are several dotted around the city although nobody is prepared to say where or how many. When Chilvray said that you were close to where he was, Jenks banked on the location as being Whitehall. Julie Carter had to be in the same place for him to have set up the video link. If you hadn't offered yourself we might never have caught up with him.'

She looked over at the accident which had ended Jack Chilvray's life.

'I would like to say all's well, that's end well, but it seems inappropriate to the memory of those poor souls who suffered at his cruel hands.'

April peered at his side on profile, his handsome, although slightly craggy features ravaged by the sands and crimes of time, wondering how they would spend each and every long hot summer night ahead. There was however still one burning question that needed asking.

'Does this mean that I'm packing my bags once again?'

'That's entirely up to you, although if you're asking me do I want you to stay, then the answer is yes. I have a feeling that there are plenty more Jack Chilvray's out there on the streets and ultimately somebody has to look after you!'

She lay her head on his shoulder, holding onto his arm, although the moment alone was short-lived when a uniformed officer came over and asked Spence to talk with the man who had called out, giving April the opportunity to get away. April let Spence go, opting to talk with the two lorry drivers who had saved her life. They would need her testimony to help with the police accident reports. A short while later standing alongside Hawkes, April and he watched Spence talking with Jock Armstrong.

'Ironic really, that an old regiment colleague should be the one instrumental to bring about Jack Chilvray's downfall.' She turned and looked at the thoughtful young detective at her side. 'What else is odd, is how life can inevitably run the course of our destiny Tom. I like Steph, but I also like Sharon Trevelyan.' She saw him smile, only she didn't ask why.

Hawkes stood watching Spence, not knowing where his future would place him professionally, socially or emotionally, but one aspect of his life that he was certain about, was that for the present he wanted to continue working with them both.

Printed in Great Britain
by Amazon